Flying With One Wing

Robert Reese

Library Of Congress Catalog Card Number 92-73257

ISBN Number 0-9633351-2-X

Blue Pacific Press
8539 Sunset Boulevard, Suite 139
Los Angeles, California 90069
213-882-4275

9-20-92

For Stan, Kelly, Randall, Mark,
Bob, Carol, David, Tim,
Linda, Jan, Alan,
and Steven

Dear Betsy—
Hi dear. I hear your
new house is gorgeous. Send me a photo.
Have ownership — is a great hobby/obsession,
don't you think? Congratulations.
Well, here's an early copy of my first
book. I'm really pleased. I started writing it
the night I left Betty Ford — and now it's
a real book! Tell your parents & friends
to buy it. I need sales!
How good — enclosed is a photo of me
with my answer — Alan. His guest.
Send photos— Jane,
Thom

Jump

Into the sky

Over those clouds

And you'll see the moon

Even on a rainy day

-- Japanese folk saying

Chapter One

nother New Year's Eve, another crowded London nightclub,
another chemically induced haze. A mushroom cloud of murky
grey smoke obscures my view of the room. I stand in a dark
corner, smoking a hash cigarette as I watch people dance between dark
shadows and white strips of light. The smoke fills my lungs and singes my
tongue. Skull grows heavy and thoughts battle a chemically induced fog.

I drop the roach on the floor and crush it with my heel. I've been
dancing and partying here since ten. Feet are stiff and sore, head pounds.
A typical euro-techno-pop-disco tune shrieks from the souped-up sound
system. It's hard to tell if the singer is human or computer. Maybe it's
Depeche Mode or Erasure. The record is slick and very danceable, but I
need a break.

The club is located in the west end of the city. The rooms are jammed
with celebrants of numerous ages, sexes, sexual persuasions, races,
religions, and socio-economic groups. Two French guys dance together,
flashing bright smiles after drunkenly staggering into a well-dressed
Japanese couple. I dance alone or with whoever is nearby, willing, or
interested.

The sound is cranked up to an ear-splitting decibel, sending a wave
of static crashing inside the eardrums, momentarily deafening me. I cover
ears with hands to regain equilibrium. The explosion inside my head
subsides, replaced by the noisy music and a persistent ringing in the ears.

I'm thirsty and dehydrated from an hour of heavy perspiration. My
brain is sizzled from the killer hash. A black man with a braided
Rastafarian hairdo gave me the joint in the bathroom a little while ago.
He was very stoned, but handsome and charming. He complimented me
on my eyes, then presented the hash as a gift. I immediately smoked it in
one of the stalls. It was potent stuff.

My knees feel weak. The pain in the temples crescendos. Stomach
begs for food. It's been hours and hours since lunch. I forgot to eat before
leaving the hotel tonight. The time is twenty-two minutes after eleven.
Soon it'll be midnight, and the dawn of a new year.

A couple dressed entirely in black leather stomp close enough for me
to hear the steel studs and chains jangle at their wrists, ankles, waists, and
necks. Clang, clang, clang. Their hair is chopped into matching mohawks,

but colored differently. The man's is tinted blue and magenta, the girl's is purple with carroty tips. What a zoo.

They look ridiculous. I appreciate their need to rebel, but they look like jerks. How can anyone take a person with a purple mohawk seriously? Where do these people work? Certainly not at any of the department stores I've looked around since arriving a week ago.

I smile. They nod back. I light a cigarette with shaky hands and try to recall where the men's room is located. I aim myself toward the stairs. I know they lead to the bar. Progress is slow with the sea of human bodies. I walk to the bar on the landing. I purchase a vodka and grapefruit juice, then situate myself at the railing. Below is the dance floor. I'm within earshot of some upper-crust socialite types. They're dressed in tuxedos and fancy gowns. They guzzle champagne, smoke cigarettes, and try to act devastating.

My cocktail tastes excessively tart at first, but mellows as it lashes the taste buds into submission. My head feels less constricted with a few more gulps.

Guts feel hollowed, limbs thrashed. This vacation has been one long, exhausting binge. Long nights, short days, constant drugging, excessive drinking, little sleep, and a fair quantity of raunchy sex. Going on a holiday can be hard work. I haven't had the luxury of actually relaxing.

The grapefruit juice neutralizes the bitter flavor of the hash. I ask a young woman in a glittery silver dress whether she knows where the toilets are. She points toward a dark corner. I thank her and make my way to a flight of stairs that descend to the subtereanean toilets. I spill some of the drink as I navigate the poorly lit steps, turning right when I reach the bottom. The set-up is creepy. Lord knows what dangers lurk in these murky corners. The odor of urine permeates the narrow corridor. I finish the drink and drop the plastic cup on the floor.

There's dust in the air. I sneeze twice, then step toward a puddle of buttery light a few yards up. The handle on the door is slippery. I wipe both hands on my trousers as I enter the brightly lit lavatory. There are six sinks, five intact mirrors, and six stalls. The shattered sixth mirror's pieces are piled under the fourth sink. I pass three black guys crowded around the first stall. They speak in a foreign tongue, Jamaican perhaps. I enter the fifth cubicle and bolt the door behind me.

After wiping the toilet seat dry with several tissues, I sit, cross-legged, atop the bowl and extract a wad of yellow toilet paper from a pants pocket. The walls are covered with graffiti. My favorite message is written in red pen.

"Everytime I wake I'm in shock...I live in shock, " it says. Sounds a lot like me the last few months.

Unwrapping the tissue reveals the remainder of my New Year's Eve stash. There are five yellow Percodans, three white Codeine tabs, two blue Valiums, and a tiny pink pill. The painkillers are my favorite, particularly the Percodan. It's a narcotic derivative of opium and packs a powerful high. The other pills are for relaxation, backaches, and any other discomfort that might arise.

I remove three Percodans and the little pink tab, then dry swallow the lot, gagging as I force them down. The pink pill is called Ecstasy. It's certainly lived up to its name the few times I've used it.

I've been saving this hit for a special occasion. Ecstasy ignites an intense happiness and triggers a greatly enhanced sexual appetite and appreciation of sensual pleasures. Touching and kissing feels intensely euphoric with Ecstasy. It's fun. Combined with Percodan, hash, and alcohol, I should be flying high come midnight. What the hell. In less than forty-eight hours I return home to Los Angeles, so I may as well enjoy this frenetic holiday while it lasts.

Exiting the stall, I station myself at the nearest sink and wash my hands and face in the cold water, trying to avoid looking directly at my reflection for more than a second, afraid of what I may see. In my peripheral vision, I catch a glimpse of an older man cruising me from two sinks down. I study him in the mirror.

He stands six-two or so, wears a tux, no tie, a pale blue shirt unbuttoned to the middle of his hairy chest. He has a handsome profile, accentuated by dark hair, thick ponytail, stripes of grey at the temples, a prominent, romanesque nose, and emerald-green eyes. His mouth is a little small, but acceptable. I'd guess he's around forty.

Turning back to the looking glass, I confront my image. Face looks pale and slightly haggard. Shallow bags encircle both eyes, souvenirs of too many late nights and a surfeit of mind-altering chemicals.

The eyes' whites and rims are a little red, but a few splashes of cold water improve their appearance. My hair is getting too damn long, it touches the shoulders in back. I'll get it cut when I get back to L.A. I look considerably younger than thirty, but feel much older.

The time is twenty-nine minutes to midnight. I need to make a New Year's resolution. Perhaps I'll try to quit taking drugs again. After Thanksgiving, I spent two weeks without Percodan, but it was a living hell. The withdrawal aches, pains, and depressions quickly drove me back to the pills.

The first time I used Percodan was after a painful dental surgery five years ago. Soon I was buying the same pills from a pharmaceutical connection for occasional Saturday night blowouts and special occasions.

Later, I developed a bad back and started seeing a doctor for treatment. The doctor gave me Codeine initially, but I quickly needed something stronger to control the painful spasms. He suggested Percodan. My back kept hurting, the prescriptions kept flowing. Job stress and personal problems led me into using the drugs to escape emotional discomfort as well as physical pain. The back pains worsened with time, causing a dramatic increase in my intake of the medication. Finally, I quit working and withdrew into my home and narcotics.

I became an opiate junkie. My days and nights revolve around maintaining a pain-free existence. I watch television, read hundreds of books, see movies, garden, party. I'm nearly always high. I've been addicted to Percodan for over three years now.

At first, I enjoyed unemployment and a vacation from ambition, money, schedules, and feelings. If I didn't like something, I'd swallow a few pills to improve my mental or emotional outlook. I've grown tired of depending on pills to make me happy and safe. I feel more agitated and depressed as time goes on. I've lost respect for myself. The pills rule my life and moods. I'm sick of it.

I know that one day I'll kick the pills, I'm sure of it. I've grown tired of their transitory charms. Feeding a daily habit is costly. It's time to experience life and feelings without mood-altering drugs.

The john reeks of sweet-smelling reefer. Drying my face with paper towels, I notice the tuxed guy staring. I gaze back at him in the mirror. We make direct eye contact, then I drop the towels in the trash and march out of the toilet, driven by a desire to escape from myself and my problems through vigorous dance.

Back upstairs, I pound the floor near two women decked out in elegant evening gowns and high heels. The tall one is wrapped inside a form-fitting gold lamé frock. She barely moves to the music, performing a rigid twist in her mummified shell.

A strange man nods at me. He looks vaguely familiar, but it's difficult to tell in the dark. His date is a petite woman in her twenties. There's a sense of drama about her. Short brown hair is swept across the left side of her head, revealing a single spiral earring dangling on the right. It's encrusted with shimmering rhinestones and cascades from earlobe to shoulder.

Her leather miniskirt and leopard-print blouse accent long legs and a slender neck. Her eyes are liquidy and inviting. Her luscious lips are painted pink. Silver bracelets hang from both wrists. All in all, she's dazzling. She's dazzling.

He's the man who cruised me in the john. I spin in a tight circle and edge closer. He smiles and winks. I grin with half my mouth and bounce to the rhythm of the music. The medication has greatly relieved my headache and provided a needed infusion of energy. Eyes feel unnaturally wide. Earthquakes of drug-induced happiness tickle my insides and ripple into the brain. The Percodan have kicked in. The Ecstasy will take a little longer.

I notice a person curled into a fetal ball on the floor near the wall. Looks like a girl. She must be really smashed. I whirl around, effortlessly gliding to the insistent beat. Legs feel lighter and lighter. I feel graceful and sexy. The man from the toilet is dancing at my left elbow. His ponytail swings wildly. I'd like to grab hold and pull him near, get a closer look at the goods.

The girl sways and looks up into the balcony. Dozens of people peer over the side at the dancers. The music builds, led by a dueling guitar and bass. The male vocalist wails the words, his voice filled with angst.

"IIIII....don't need to sell my soulll..he's already in me...I want to be adored...I want to be adored..."

I ease into a warm, friendly mode, my entire being feels weightless, like I'm levitating an inch off the floor. A rumble from the toes travels up the legs, fingers and arms, then ricochets inside the chest, ending with an implosion of euphoria in the brain. I close my eyes as the sensation caresses the pleasure centers. I feel cleansed of all worry and pain. I feel splendid. The music massages my soul.

"I want to be adored...I want to be adored... I don't have to sell my soul...he's already in me..I want to be adorrrred....I want to be adorrred...you adore me..you adore me...adore me..I wanna, I wanna be adored...I wanna, I wanna be adored..."

Someone taps my shoulder. It's the ponytail guy. I smile at him. The girl has vanished. "Would you like some champagne?" he asks. "Sure," I say. He hands me a half-empty bottle of expensive French champagne and suggests I drink from the bottle. I do. We exchange names. He's Charles. The woman is Nicole. They're British. He asks what part of America I'm from. "Los Angeles," I say.

"Daniel is a beautiful name," he says, then dangles a vial of white powder between us and asks if I'd like some. "Why not?", I yell. We repair to a less open spot and partake of the cocaine. It zaps me into the stratosphere.

He tells me I'm very cute. I tell him he's not so bad himself, but what about the girl? Doesn't she mind him picking up stray men?

"She'll like you," he whispers. His breath warms my ear. I suggest we dance. Squeezing through the hordes of people, we stop and neck. We touch tongues a little, swill more champagne, then dance. He's a good kisser.

Nicole reappears. Charles introduces us. She looks a little distant, a little aloof. We three move to the music and finish the wine. He hands her the vial. She smiles broadly and exits. My skin vibrates from the Percodan and Ecstasy.

He and I grope as we make out, lasciviously exploring one another. He rubs my crotch and suggests a three-way between he, Nicole, and me. I don't answer. He continues to run his hands over my body. It feels great. The proximity of the other people adds a dangerous edge to our triesting.

Nicole returns, beaming. Cocaine has that effect on people. She's giddy and more available. We three dance for a song, then Charles disappears. Nicole feeds me two more spoonfuls of coke after snorting a couple herself. She says I've got gorgeous eyes. We kiss. She tastes of cigarettes and champagne. Her small body fits inside my arms easily. We press crotches and chests and study one another's eyes. I see sadness and disappointment in hers. Why do I always see the pain?

I see a little of myself in her skittish eyes. Direct eye contact can be dangerous. There's always the possibility a stranger might see the secrets and pain behind the mask.

I shut my eyes and seal my lips across her mouth.

Charles returns with a fresh bottle of champagne. The club is packed. The music stops. A screen above the small stage at the end of the room appears, televising a festive gathering across town in Trafalgar Square. A tall, thin Norwegian pine is surrounded by thousands of people waiting to ring in the New Year. A cockney voice interrupts the music to lead the count to midnight.

Nicole traces figure eights on my back with her long nails. She has long, prehensile fingers. Chills shoot up my neck. Charles lays his right hand and arm around my shoulder.

The entire room shouts out the beats to midnight, as do the crowds on the big screen over at Trafalgar Square. We sway, share the champagne, and flirt outrageously. Charles has a dynamic, alluring smile and a certain mystery that intrigues me.

Nicole is cuddly and tender. Her touch gives me great pleasure. I feel greatly flattered, not to mention aroused, by their attentions.

We snort another round as midnight closes in. Ten, nine, eight, seven, six, five, four, three, two, one...Happy New Year. The entire club explodes with cheers and shouts. Nets on the ceiling unfurl, dumping hundreds of colorful balloons into the discoteque. We bat them and laugh like idiots. A silly fever infects us all. A conga line forms. Loud calypso music is piped in. Everyone sings and hollers "Happy New Year" to everyone else. The place becomes the friendliest party on earth.

Congratulations are in order all around. Slaps on the back, kisses from strangers, hugs and sloppy nuzzles are de rigeur. I lose sight of Nicole and Charles. Someone yanks me into the conga line. I shake my ass with the others as we snake through the masses, cutting through a narrow kitchen into the alley, then loop back through the upstairs bar.

The whole thing is so ridiculous and hilarious that I can't stop laughing. My side aches and head throbs. I'm on the verge of outright hysteria. Slow down, I remind myself, just slow down. Tears pour down my cheeks. Slow down.

Charles saves the day by pulling me off the line and into a protective bear hug. He asks me to leave with them now. I ask why. "Because we like you," he chuckles. "So we can have sex," I say.

"It's up to you, Daniel," he says quietly. "Its up to you." "Let's go", I yell. Why not? Nothing ventured, nothing gained.

He finds Nicole and pays a waiter to fetch their coats. I leave mine behind for no reason in particular. We sneak out into the alley. The conga line is bigger than ever. I feel squirrelly and tingly.

Nicole leads us to the street and into an unheated parking structure. The frigid night air and icy wind sobers me a shade. We pile into their leather upholstered Jag, me in back, Nicole at the wheel, Charles swilling champagne shotgun.

London is buzzing with thousands of pedestrians walking on foot, all spreading good cheer on the streets. We open the windows, turn up the heat, and scream inebriated greetings to passersby. There's a recklessness in the air. Anything could happen.

Charles passes his camels-hair overcoat back to me. It's lined with fur. I slide it on. The soft fur tickles my neck. I lie back in the cushy seat, smoke cigarettes, and think. I need to make a resolution right away.

Nicole turns toward Kensington while Charles complains about her excessive speed. She drives very, very fast. We turn down a tree-lined street. Without warning, I throw my stash of pills out the window. It lands in a big puddle next to the gutter. Quitting drugs will be my New Year's resolution, my new top priority. Tomorrow I'll try to go on the wagon.

Leaning forward, I kiss Nicole's soft earlobe and pull on the earring with my teeth. She smells of jasmine. I turn to Charles. His lips taste of smoke and alcohol. I've never made love to a man and woman at the same time. It might be fun.

Charles wishes me a Happy New Year and tosses the cocaine into my lap. I fall back and watch the streetlights flicker by. Nicole asks how I'm doing as she peers at me in the rearview. I force a big smile and swear nothing's wrong. Then I snort some coke and light a cigarette. Outside, a steady drizzle falls, rinsing the soot from the windshield. I watch the droplets roll down the window and wish the rain could wash me clean as well.

Chapter Two

The dream is frantic, hurried. Orson Welles sits on a golden throne, wearing a flowing black robe. He shouts "Just because he's feeling guilty doesn't mean he's innocent" over and over again while spooning chocolate ice cream into the mouth of a small dog sitting on his lap.

I run down long, empty hallways, trying to escape his overbearing presence. I fly up into the sky and down an avenue lined with huge billboards advertising my favorite drugs. The edges of the image are blurred, obscured by a psychic fog.

Alighting inside a shop with an old-fashioned soda fountain, I order a double-dip strawberry cone. Outside is a billboard ten stories high. It pictures a chorus line of shrimp-like creatures dressed in bright red tutus. They're performing a spirited can-can.

The copy reads "Come see the Marvelous, Magnificent, Magical Sea Monkeys." I lick my cone. The sea monkeys have heads that look suspiciously similar to chimpanzees. What in the sam hill is a sea monkey? I've never heard of such a thing.

The dream is hot and muggy. It's hard to breath. I fly with my cone and search for a quiet place to relax. Soaring above virgin forest and grassy plains, I land in a clearing by a river. Sitting on a stump, I slurp at the soft ice cream and watch an orgy. Men and women, dozens of them, lie scattered along the water's edge in various stages of fornication, fellatio, and so forth. I lose interest after a few seconds and dream myself into a cab.

The Arab driver nods when I suggest he drive me to the sea monkey show. The ice cream cone is nearly gone. I'm wearing a pair of khaki shorts and nothing more. Skin is tan, muscles toned and strong.

A sign welcomes us to the Sea Monkey Park. There is no one in evidence at the ticket booth. I walk through the turnstyle and down a cobbled street flanked by fish tanks as big as houses. Inside are massive sharks, whales, dolphins, and even an octopus. I don't feel afraid, just fascinated at the creatures' enormous size.

A wizened old man appears, selling donuts from a rickety cart. I buy an order of the warm, soft, lightly glazed crullers. They melt in my mouth.

I walk down row after row of carnival games and attractions, eating the crullers and searching for the roller-coaster ride. A fat woman wearing a tutu waves a pink wand and hawks the sideshow tent. She says they have the only dead sea monkey specimen known to man, as well as the world's smallest horse and a dead baby with an elephant trunk for a nose.

A young woman with a white parasol invites me to join her. She and her young daughter are walking to the lake to feed the fish. I tag along. I offer to share the crullers, but they decline.

The lake is ringed by willow trees and the water's silvery surface is placid. I sit on the grass and smoke a cigarette. The girl is four or five years old. She wears a pretty yellow sundress. She tosses small handfuls of popcorn on the water with great seriousness.

"What sort of fish are you feeding?" I ask. The sun is bright, but not blinding.

"Baby sea monkeys, if you must know," she says huffily.

The popcorn floats toward the center of the lake. I detect no movement from below the surface.

"Where are they?" I whisper.

"Sleeping, silly."

"Oh."

"You can feed them, but be very quiet. We don't want to disturb the little ones."

"What's your name?"

"Hilary. What's yours?"

"Daniel."

"Ssshhh."

"I think I see one, Hilary. Look."

"That's not a sea monkey, silly, that's a minnow."

"Oh."

"Sea monkeys swim very quietly, so hush."

"Okay."

"They must be sleeping. I have to go, Daniel."

"Goodbye."

A voice beckons me to a bridge that crosses the water. I walk to an arena. A midget wearing a tuxedo welcomes me, then shows me to a seat next to an indoor swimming pool. I'm the only one in the grandstand. The lights dim and circus music blares.

A trio of petticoated sea monkeys dance onto the stage, singing in high-pitched squeaks. I hear a phone ringing. The sea monkeys sound like dog whistles. I run for the phone.

A red phone booth stands outside the amphitheatre. I pick it up.

"Hello?"

"Hey, Daniel. Guess who this is?"

"I don't like guessing games."

"I know." Panic rises in my stomach. The dream is a deja vu. I'm frightened.

"What do you want?" I snap.

"Don't you remember my voice?"

"Yes, it sounds familar. So what?"

"It's David, jerk. Your brother."

"You're dead. I can't talk to you anymore."

"We need to discuss a few things."

"I have to leave. Goodbye."

"Time for your medicine, Danny?"

I slam the phone down and take to the sky, flying higher and higher, away from sight of earth. An inner compass tells me to dive down for a look. Below are fields of fertile farmland, barren in the cold of winter. In the spring corn will be planted. By August, the stalks will stand as tall as a man.

I cross entire states at a frightening speed. The town of Genoa Falls, Illinois appears. The house where I was born and raised, where my brother and I played, comes into view. A colonial-style residence with four white pillars and ten old oaks lining the driveway. Brown leaves scatter across the frozen ground.

David and I were born two minutes apart. He came first. We're fraternal twins. Our mother had hoped for a girl and got two boys instead.

He died in our bedroom three days before our eighth birthday. He had a virulent strain of hepatitis. He took a turn for the worse that night. My parents were on the phone with the doctor when he died. I was sitting on the floor of our room reading a book. I felt him leave the room, I felt helpless to save him.

I hover above the graveyard where he's buried. Gnarled old oaks guard the perimeter of the grounds, as does a black wrought-iron fence. Dozens of mangy crows sit in the barren treetops, watching me. Drifts of sooty snow dot the property, as do gravestones and monuments. I feel a chill.

Landing next to our family's plot, I locate Grandpa's marker. He was born in 1906 and died in 1988. David was born in 1960 and died in 1968. There's an empty hole between them. Its meant for me, waiting to take me. I fly into the trees, fighting as the gravity and sadness pull me down, down, down, into the hole and skidding down a dark tube of panic. Deeper and deeper I fall.

Soaked with sweat, I swim into consciousness. Where in the hell am I? Heart races. Reaching around me, I come into contact with human limbs and sheets. Oh yes, I remember. Charles and Nicole. I'm sharing their large bed somewhere in London. New Year's Eve. My cheeks burn. I've been crying in my sleep. How weird. I'd better get up. Stomach is groaning. It's been ages since I ate. What time is it?

Moving extra slowly, I slide off the bed and crawl across the floor toward a dim light. The bathroom. I open the door, stand, and tiptoe back to the couch at the foot of the bed, where I collect my clothes from amongst the pile.

Sealed inside the bathroom, I dress and wash my face. Black marble covers every surface. The sink's spigot looks like real gold. Next to the television set on the counter is a black leather case. I open it. Inside are several syringes, a plastic strap, cotton balls, Bic lighter, and two engraved silver spoons. Charles and Nicole must be heroin addicts. The glass ampules are filled with golden syripy liquid. My heart begins to panic. I have to get the hell out of this place.

A clock gives the time as four-thirty in the afternoon. The day has certainly whizzed by while I slept in a drugged stupor. I walk through the bathroom into the front hall and into another bedroom. I search for a sweater to wear on the way back to my hotel. Charles must have clothes in here somewhere.

Finally, I locate his dressing room and extract a wool cranberry V-neck from shelves piled high with sweaters of every color imaginable. The house is tastefully furnished with antique furniture and paintings of hunting scenes.

On a desk is a pad of paper. I write a quick note thanking them for a memorable evening and explaining the missing sweater. I sign the note "love, Daniel" and leave it on the floor inside the front door when I leave.

The weather is colder than yesterday and dark clouds hover menacingly overhead. The sweater is no match for the wind, but it helps a little. I walk for a block before realizing I'm across the street from Hyde Park. If I remember correctly, I can cross the park to reach my hotel off Piccadilly. My head is beginning to ache.

A search of all pockets yields no medication. I remember now, I threw the pills into the street last night. Stupid me. My intentions are good, but my ability to actually stop using the drugs is negligible.

Trudging across the soggy park, my legs begin to hurt from Percodan withdrawal. My body needs the drug to maintain sanity. Prickles of pain play at my temples. A bolt of hot lightning shoots into the skull. I stop next to a grove of birch trees and try to relax for a second. A stomach cramp is twisting my intestines, causing me to double over in agony.

This will pass, I've been here before. It will pass. I rip a piece of bark from one of the trees, then stuff the papery substance in my pocket as I move on.

Legs are rubbery. I wish I had a cigarette to smoke. I ran out last night. Dammit. The park is deserted. Everything is hibernating. Except for me. I walk on. Snow begins to fall. I feel like smashing something to smithereens. I'm enraged. I need some Percodan right now, dammit. I break an icicle from a bush and suck on it as I propel myself forward.

By the time I reach the hotel my legs are throbbing. The elevator ride to my floor takes an eternity. The cardkey is wedged between credit cards in my wallet. The mini-suite is dark, but clean. The bedroom is a whirl of clothes, luggage, and assorted purchases. I drop to my knees next to the dresser, then reach under a gap in the base. Behind the ornately carved detailing lie my bottles of pills, hidden for obvious reasons. An addict cannot afford to lose his life blood.

Heart races as I feel around for the plastic containers. Fingers locate one, remove it, then retrieve the second. Mission accomplished. I open one and dump dozens of yellow Percodans on the floor. Without missing a beat I stuff three in my mouth and walk to the bathroom for a glass of water.

As I wait for the drugs to kick in, I count all the pills, piling them in heaps on the tan carpeting. There are sixty-eight Percodan, fifteen Codeines, six Valium, and two Demerol. My dealer gave me the Demerol samples as a Christmas gift. I return the valuable tablets to the bottles, then hide them under the clothes in the two suitcases.

Dropping onto the bed, I scan the room service menu for appealing choices. I phone down an order for steak bernaise, baked potato, spinach, and a piece of chocolate cake. I'm ravenous. Just knowing the pills are in my stomach allows me to relax.

A short time later I'm soaking in a hot tub, smoking a cigarette, unwinding. The pills have improved my outlook and eased the sore muscles. After drying off I take another two pills and turn on the television. Outside, it is night.

Dressed in a hotel robe, I check the guide for television programs. The film "The Sweet Bird of Youth" is on. I always enjoy a juicy Tennessee Williams drama. Paul Newman plays a loser called Chance Wayne. He is dashing around a hotel room somewhere in the South, searching for an oxygen tank requested by a hungover movie star, Dolores Del Lago, brilliantly portrayed by Geraldine Page. She behaves like a stereotypical spoiled movie queen, ordering people around like peons. It's fascinating.

Dinner arrives. I eat and watch the film. Delores Del Lago smokes hash cigarettes, boozes it up big, and exchanges grandiose behavior for pathetic self pity with manic aplomb. At one point, Chance Wayne says, "The big difference between people is not between the rich and the poor, the good and the evil, 'cause the biggest difference between people is those who have known love and those who haven't."

I write down the words. They seem to pertain to me somehow. By the end of the movie, I'm drained. Tomorrow morning I leave London on a noon flight. I ring down and leave a wake-up call for eight. After brushing my teeth, I climb into bed.

What awaits me back home is a nice duplex, a beautiful garden, unemployment, a dwindling bank balance, and an expensive drug habit. I have friends, but no steady love interest at present. My prospects have narrowed the last few years.

While trying to fall asleep, my mind wanders. I picture David and me swimming in the river near our home the summer before he died. We both looked happy. Now he's dead and I'm numbing myself with drugs. Something went wrong along the way, but what? I haven't seen my parents in over a year. We had a falling-out after I told them I was gay.

My last visit to home last Christmas was fraught with tension. They were upset because a month earlier, I had told them I was gay in a letter. Spending a week with them was hell, pure and simple hell. How could I relax and be myself when they were obviously humiliated about my sexuality. If the world discovered they had created a freak for a son, they'd be finished, ruined.

They tried to dissuade me from being gay. I heard supposed quotes from the Bible condemning men coveting other men, I was told about the dangers of AIDS. I was patient at first, but their concerns quickly soured into bitterness and hostility aimed my way. I took tons of drugs to kill the pain. I felt rejected by them, again. After David died they sometimes avoided me. Their social life got busier, they took trips without the kids, they ran. When I decided to become an actor, they vehemently objected. I defied them and followed my dream.

They love me but don't respect me. I explained all these feelings in a long letter I sent to them when I returned to L.A. I told them I had decided not to see them for a while. I said I felt burnt from their nastiness over the gay issue. When they could learn to accept me and support me, then maybe we might talk again. They responded with letters and calls, but I didn't answer. I didn't know what else to do. How could I live with myself if I was bombarded by their constant negativity? Sleep obliterates these worrisome thoughts. I drift into a safer world.

Chapter Three

The plane circles LAX for ten minutes before beginning the final descent. This flight has been relaxing, even fun. I was upgraded to the half- empty business class, with a seat on the aisle next to an unused window seat. The airline woman who handled me in London mentioned how much she enjoyed the television program I used to act in. When she asked what I was doing now, I paused, embarrassed at the past three years of inactivity and sloth, then rallied. With assurance I told her several jobs were upcoming, then explained that I had taken taken a break from acting to tend to personal matters.

She took the bait and appeared stricken at whatever scenario her imagination conjured up. What could my very private crisis be? Death of a loved one, booze, severe bodily injuries, disease, anorexia, the options were unlimited. If I said I suffered from a severe erosion of self-confidence and became addicted to drugs as solace, she would have been shocked. The truth isn't always easy to hear, let alone say.

Across the aisle sits my mile-high floor show. The entertainers. They are a Scottish mother and son act. Mom weighs about two hundred pounds. Her pimply-faced boy weighs about the same. They travel in true culinary style, lugging containers of edibles in large carry-on bags. They haven't stopped munching since we left Heathrow ten hours ago.

They consumed the airline meals as well. Their constant chewing is dizzying. They're authentic eating machines. I can see the tabloid headline now, "Mom and Son Eat Themselves to Death." They must be unhappy to stuff themselves so excessively. Luckily for me, painkillers aren't fattening.

Their parade of yummies began with meat sandwiches and bags of crunchy chips seconds after take-off. Shortbread cookies, assorted chocolate and hard candies followed. So did licorice, raisins, cheese, slices of fudge cake, all packed in festively colored Tupperware boxes. I saw them gobble down nuts, apples, candy bars, and a lot of Pepsi. How can they eat so much junk and not get sick? But then, some might say the same about all the pills I ingest during a typical day.

I sat in my oversized chair, read magazines, watched the latest James

Bond flick, smoked cigarettes, ate the stuffed chicken, drank orange juice, and medicated myself into a state of bliss with the help of nine Percodan.

The only glitch in the flight occurred as we flew through a highly active electrical storm somewhere over the Atlantic. I was writing a list of reasons to quit drugs when we entered the storm. It was terrifying. Lightning shot near the plane, followed by deafening thunder. Flung into the eye of the storm.

As all hell broke loose outside, knocking the plane violently, I kept thinking I should swallow a few more pills to obliterate the fear. I realized then that my life focused on nothing but eliminating pain and sensation. The painkillers wipeout joy as well as pain and fear and self-doubt. I'm killing myself.

It struck me as funny and I started to laugh. I couldn't believe that I'd been wasting my life feeling unfulfilled and beaten instead of taking action to improve my feelings and build self-esteem to a healthy level. Painkillers shielded me from risk, loss, rejection and the good things like love and intimacy. Drugs provided a euphoric alternative to acting. Instead of revealing myself to the camera, I could cloak myself in a haze of narcotics.

When I quit working, some friends treated me like a total bozo. They couldn't believe I'd blow such a steady and lucrative job to do something as boring as finding myself. The entertainment business can be an addictive drug too. Most actors would have sold their sisters into slavery for the job I had on a series.

People didn't understand I was disintegrating under the hot movie lights, unable to reconcile the public persona with my tormented private self. I didn't deserve the attention, slight fame, big bucks, the success. Inside, I felt like a loser.

I couldn't live with myself under such conditions. Week after week I played a twentyish med student who marries an Italian girl. To save money, they live with her wacky folks in Brooklyn. I exuded a whole-some, hetero image that viewers felt comfortable with.

I felt trapped playing that wholesome guy day after day. It felt so phony. The back problems were a direct result of stress. Maybe I wasn't made to live my life in the glare of public attention. How can a person grow and find himself while living in a goldfish bowl?

I couldn't face acting any longer. I feared I was having a breakdown of some sort. I told people I needed a sabbatical, not that I had literally reached the end of my rope and I was ready to snap.

I looked to relationships for answers and possible escape. I dated here and there, but nothing serious until I met Howard, a handsome lyricist in his early forties. We started seeing one another a year after I left the show. We grew close fairly rapidly. There was a strong physical and emotional connection. We clicked. The sex between us was great. Everything was too good. I didn't trust good.

He knew I took painkillers for my back, but I did a good job of behaving normally most of the time. I was bruised goods, but fun, handsome, usually cheerful, and bright on the outside. Howard wanted to be around me no matter how sick or sad I felt inside. My increasing drug usage didn't frighten him away because he didn't see it.

After nearly a year of increasing intimacy and closeness, I put on the brakes. I didn't feel worthy of happiness, so I disabled our alliance with well-aimed torpedoes. I told Howard I was unhappy and needed to change my life. I said I couldn't see him anymore in a letter. I made a total break. I stopped returning his messages. I withdrew into my home and garden, numbed by increasing quantities of painkillers and buffered by isolation.

Shortly before I broke up with Howard, I finally got up the resolve to be honest with my parents. A few days before Thanksgiving, I wrote them a letter telling them I was gay. They called when they received it and said they'd love me no matter what. We agreed to discuss it further over Christmas, when I was scheduled to fly to Illinois for a visit. The entire trip was a disaster.

The first night, we sat in their woodpaneled library sipping cocktails and making small talk. During their second drink, Mom and Dad vowed eternal love and support for me. They said they would always love me, no matter what. We were all very friendly.

The next day they began to undermine me. It was reminiscent of their letters and calls after I quit the series. They thought I was crazy to give up the money and success. They couldn't be supportive because they were too busy attacking me.

They questioned my ability to make sound decisions, including this "gay thing." I said there was no question about it, I was gay and had been since I was a child.

They bombarded me with questions, comments, lectures. I tried to avoid them as much as possible. My older sister Linda lives nearby, so I escaped there as often as possible. For the entire week I medicated myself with massive quantities of Percodan and Valium, but nothing killed the loneliness and emptiness I felt.

The night before I returned to L.A., they became openly hostile at dinner. They condemned my "supposed" sexual preference. They refused to try to accept the situation or believe it was true. If it was true, that meant that they fucked up and created a monster, a freak.

I was accused of being selfish for sharing such disturbing news with them so close to the holidays. What did I expect them to do? Give their blessing to my sin? Their sudden religious posturing was absurd.

Mom told me I was in danger of getting AIDS. Dad stated I couldn't resist rocking the boat and should seriously consider spiritual and religious counseling.

Because I survived my more popular brother, because I became a disreputable actor, because I was gay, because I had quit my high-paying job against their advice, because I was different, my parents continued to feel justified in withholding approval and love from me. If they treated me kindly, that might be mistakenly interpreted as support for my bohemian lifestyle.

Flying home after that Christmas in hell, something snapped inside me. I decided to cut them off for a while. They didn't respect me or my life and I wouldn't allow them to treat me like a child.

I see a therapist now once a week. The process is helping me be more honest with myself. We explore my feelings and explore what it is I want from life and love. I trust the therapist, he doesn't ever tell me what to do. He guides me toward goals I set. Right now I'm telling him a little more about my drug habit. My aim is to forgive myself for being gay and an addict and seek professional help to quit the pills. A rehab hospital might be the right choice.

The therapy helps clarify my weak and strong suits. Other people's opinions and hang-ups have unduly influenced me. Disappointment, hurt, and abandonment don't have to be crippling. One of the reasons I rejected Howard was because I'm not fully accepting yet of my sexuality. I've been working on loving myself, but progress has been slow.

If I conquer this drug addiction, I'll be forced to confront reality with no barriers, no walls. The drugs won't be able to anesthetize and disguise the truth anymore. Intellectually, I know I'm not a bad person because I'm gay or addicted to pills, but emotionally I feel I failed. I've lived in suspended emotional animation for too long. Time to break out of the chemical cocoon and join the living.

The plane drops from the opaque clouds into pure sunshine. The Los Angeles basin is damp. A newspaper said Southern California received over four inches of rain the past few days.

Everything looks clear and clean, the mountain tops dipped in powdery snow. We dip to the left, allowing me a panoramic view of the coastline looking north toward Malibu. The Pacific is vast and blue. It's nice to be home.

The weather here beats gloomy old London. The time is just after three in the afternoon. London time is eight hours later. I don't feel tired in the least.

My plan is to acclimate to the time by forcing myself to stay awake until eleven or so and get up tomorrow at a decent hour.

By the time I collect the luggage and get through customs, the sun is setting in a swirl of red and gold. The temperature is in the sixties. I wait in line for a cab. My driver is Eastern European. When the Wall came down, hordes of these guys came to America and bought cabs. He tosses my bags in the trunk and takes the wheel. I say "Hello," give him the address to my house, and a few simple directions. He nods and pulls into traffic.

We're in the thick of rush-hour traffic. I suggest he take Sepulveda to Sunset Boulevard. I rent the upper half of a house up in the hills above the Strip. I've lived in the same place for seven years. I like the view of the city, the privacy, and the rooftop terrace and garden. It's home.

The driver ignores my suggestion and gets on the freeway, which is barely crawling. I tell him to please get off and take surface streets. I hate sitting in traffic. He balks. I tell him I would like to drive Sunset Boulevard and I'm paying, so please take Sunset. He looks at me in the rearview like I'm insane, then yanks us off the freeway.

As we're barreling up Sepulveda, I light a cigarette. "No," he says. I ignore him. "No smoking", he barks. "I want to smoke," I say. His eyes flash anger. Tough luck. I'm footing the bill and I'm unwilling to abdicate my smoking rights. I open the window to the bottom to air out the car.

"Look," I say as he shoots me another dirty look. "If you don't want me to smoke, drop me at the Century Plaza Hotel, I can catch another cab there." He grimaces and speeds on. What a drama.

We pass a caravan of limousines carrying a wedding party. The lead car is outfitted with white bows, ribbons, and "just married" signs. They honk as we pass. I wave out the window and shout good luck. The driver gives me the evil eye in the mirror.

The cool air smells of night blooming jasmine. The manicured lawns and gardens of Bel Air and Beverly Hills are picture perfect. Stopped at a light near the Beverly Hills Hotel, a woman in a red sports car beeps her horn. I pretend not to see her. She edges closer and yells my name. I turn and smile.

She has ash-blonde hair, cute upturned nose, big white teeth. I lean out the window and say hello like I remember her. She does look a little familar.

"Hello, Daniel," she says excitedly. "How are you?"

I nod and say, "Fine. What's new with you?" She says the pilot season has kept her busy. She asks if I've been working.

"Not recently."

"Let's get together and have dinner," she says.

I remember her now. She's the girlfriend of an actor I used to go to class with. Ronny something. We three went to Arrowhead for a weekend of water skiing two years ago. Becky is her name. She's nice, but a little pushy.

"How's Ronny?" I ask.

"Didn't you know? We broke up a few months ago."

"No, I didn't hear that. I'm sorry."

"Life goes on," she says cheerfully.

"Nice to see you," I say with false sinceri:y. The light turns green. The taxi moves forward. Becky's lane sits still. "Call me," she yells. "Okay," I answer, even though I have absolutely no intention of contacting her. I don't sleep with women anymore.

The ground outside my house is soaked. I lug the suitcases up the stairs and unlock the door. The smell of stale cigarette smoke is strong. I turn on a couple of lights and open all the windows for circulation. The predominant feature of my living room and dining room is four panels of glass that look across the entire city. To the left are snow-capped mountains and the Griffith Park Observatory above Hollywood. The center is dominated by the downtown skyline. During the day, Saddleback Mountain rises behind the sky-scrapers, a phoenix that dwarfs the shiny, man-made structures. A carpet of lights twinkle up at me. The sight of millions of colored lights is dazzling.

The answering machine on the desk in my bedroom lists seventeen messages. I drag the valises to the bedroom and undress, changing into my old terrycloth robe. A breeze from the bedroom window lifts a letter off the desk and drops it on the floor. My landlord kept an eye on things while I was in London. The mail is stacked in the center of the desk.

He's a retired rock-and-roll drummer. Now he manages a couple of properties and snorts a lot of cocaine. I buy my coke from him. I get a good price and he's certainly conveniently located downstairs. The house has four floors. I've got the top two. His place is larger, but lacks the rooftop garden.

I walk to the small den, which is wall-to-wall bookshelves, filled with first editions, most of which I've read during the last couple of years. I'm a voracious reader. Opening the French doors to the garden encourages circulation. This place is stuffy. The roof is crowded with oak barrel planters that house numerous species of trees, bushes, roses, and flowering annuals. It's very beautiful. Gardening is my hobby. Plants thrive up here. The two azalea trees are in full bloom, covered with salmon and fushsia blossoms.

Three sides of the roof are covered with trellising that supports bougainvillea and jasmine vines. Two rows of planters and tubs circle the center area, which features two chaise lounges and an old claw-footed tub converted to a pond filled with waterlilies and two koi, Ping and Pong.

Rose bushes lie dormant in terra cotta pots. A seven-foot-tall weeping mulberry tree has shed its leaves for the winter. In a few weeks it'll sprout new leaves and produce sweet-tasting berries. A pot of aloe is ablaze with a spiked beehive of orange blossoms. The waterlilies have a few tattered leaves and zero flowers.

The rainfall has adequately irrigated the garden. I empty a couple of buckets filled with water and remind myself to write a check for the rent. My bank balance is dwindling rapidly. All my earnings from three years on the show, plus residuals from reruns, are nearly depleted. What's left is about ten thousand in cash, another five or six thousand in bonds, and half ownership of a video store in Culver City. I'll be flat broke by the end of the year at this rate. The drugs are bleeding me dry.

I remove a pack of cigarettes from the fridge, light one, and return to the bedroom. As I listen to the messages on the machine, I take notes and admire the city lights.

There are two messages from my sister. One wishes me Merry Christmas, the other a Happy New Year. "Please call me, Daniel," she says. Five messages from my close friend Sally. She lives in Beverly Hills and is married to a rich plastic surgeon. We grew up together in Illinois and lost contact for years. Then she moved to Los Angeles to marry the doctor and we renewed our acquaintanceship. Her messages are rambling. She chatters on about a Geraldo show dealing with infidelity and wonders if her hubby is faithful or a cheating bastard.

On another message she sounds drunk. She parties quite a bit. We spend at least one night a week together, talking and doing cocaine, drinking champagne, smoking lots of cigarettes, and listening to music.

She owns a first-rate collection of jazz and blues CDs. Sometimes we party at my place so she can escape her husband. He's nice, but boring. She alternates between loving him madly and despising him for the slightest infraction.

I wonder what will happen to our relationship if I'm not ingesting all these drugs? Sober, she tends to be bossy, aggressive, selfish, and fairly negative. Drinking or ripped on coke or grass, she's loose, funny, and a pleasure to spend time with. Either way, Sally's a career drama queen. If there's not an emergency in her life, she creates one. She can be a dangerous, destructive person. Totally self-absorbed, but highly entertaining.

A hurried message from my last agent, asking me to call, something about a potential acting gig if I'm interested. Not really. Two messages from my drug connection, suggesting I call when I'm back in town. He's leaving for Aspen on the seventh. My dealer travels more than I do. He must do very nicely. Selling pills for three to five dollars apiece is obviously lucrative. I'm now spending an average of over two thousand dollars a month on drugs. I make a mental note to call him later.

I'm going to taper off the pills, decreasing my usual dosage by a pill or so a day. Cold turkey is too severe. I've been taking an average of about twelve to fifteen pills a day.

The rest of the calls are from assorted acquaintances, friends and leeches. There's also a message from Howard.

He sounds sad. He says he got the message I left for him on Christmas from London, but really missed talking to me in person. The last time we spoke was in November. He asks me to phone when I get the message and tell him how I'm doing. He quietly says he loves and misses me, then hangs up.

I press the erase button and sit at the end of the bed. I miss Howard. My attachment to him runs deep. I may even love him. I wish I knew. One day I'll be better equipped to have a relationship. Taking lousy care of myself is chore enough these days.

There are three boxes piled next to the desk. The address label lists my parents as the senders. Christ. What have they sent, Christmas presents? This is absurd. I didn't send them anything. The old guilt is triggered, causing my stomach to sink lower and lower. I grab a knife from the kitchen and sit on the bedroom floor, surgically opening the boxes.

The gifts are wrapped in cheerful poinsettia holiday paper. There is one card taped to the top of a box the size of my fist. "Merry Christmas, Daniel. We miss you. We gave you life and now you cut us out of your life. Our hearts are broken" it says. Blah, blah, blah. Same old broken record. I kick the packages around the bedroom, attempting to destroy the contents as well as my anger and rage.

I take the card to the garbage disposal and feed it to the grinding teeth, running the water at full blast, flushing it into the sewer with the rest of the dreck. Fuck-em.

"Fuck Christmas," I shout. "Fuck the New Year." My parents treat me like shit for years and years, so I stopped seeing them. They send a few lousy gifts and I feel guilty.

It's me, me, me. There's obviously something wrong with me. I'm the villain. I'm guilty. Round and round we go. When will I ever be free of them? Why can't they leave me alone?

I take a nap for two hours, rise, shower, swallow three Percodans, put on clean jeans and a blue shirt, and head for a popular club on the west side. My Jeep is clean thanks to the rain. The traffic is heavy. The moon is nearly full.

Stopped at the corner of La Cienega and Pico, I notice a series of rings around the moon. One is rust, then a wider turqoise band, then rust again. It looks like something from a sci-fi movie. The Percodan and nap have revived me. Thoughts of my parents are banished into an orbit a million miles from earth.

At eleven I'm seated on a barstool next to my new buddy, Lance. He's a cute college boy, a reformed surfer from Santa Barbara. We drink beer and talk about movies, girls, drugs, surfing, Santa Barbara versus Los Angeles, and music. He likes Depeche Mode, I don't. I listen to Crowded House, he's never heard of them. He's ten years younger than me and lives at a fraternity house at UCLA. He's studying business and partying a lot. He says I look like a guy who used to be on a T.V. show he names. "That's me," I admit.

He's impressed. He's shorter than me and muscular. I like blondes.

He's an all American boy. Probably raised on white bread and swimming pools of rich milk. Healthy.

Like so many surfers, he's tan. I'd like to take him home, no question. I'm not sure if he's straight, gay, bi, or what. I seem to gravitate toward hetero men. Lance looks too young to be married.

"Are you married or single?" I say, realizing my question lacks any subtlety.

"No, I'm not married," he laughs, then orders another round. His teeth are nearly as white as the shirt that partly covers his sinewy, browned arms. I like his smile. I'm very pleased he's a single man. He asks if I'd like to do some blow.

"Not here," I say.

"Let's go downtown. There's a new club we can checkout."

"Fine with me," I say.

We guzzle the rest of the brews and pile into my Jeep. He scoops coke from a vial using a car key, then holds it under each of my waiting nostrils. The coke tastes tart, but good. I get a buzz quickly. We're speeding down Pico toward downtown. I place my hand on Lance's thigh. He turns and smiles. We're gonna get along just fine.

Parked on a mostly deserted street about a mile from City Hall, I watch two alley cats in a lot littered with abandoned cars and trucks. The fat black one tackles the orange tabby, biting its flanks and kicking the soft underbelly. It's a vicious duel. Landing a blow to the tabby's neck results in a blood-curdling shriek and quick exit by the loser. The black cat stands on a bombed-out van, licking its front paws in delicious victory.

Lance is giving me head. It feels great.Rapidly approaching orgasm, I gently pull him away. It would be foolhardy for either of us to have unprotected sex. I had myself tested for HIV a few months ago and it came out negative. I've never been particularly promiscuous, but all it takes is one slip-up and I could have AIDS. I stroke myself to climax as we feed on one another's mouths.

He said he couldn't get off because of the coke. The drugs don't interfere with my ability to reach climax. I pull up my pants. We do a couple more keys-full of coke, kiss some more, then get out of the car.

Club Dump is the basement of an old warehouse. Lance says he's been here before but was too wasted to stay very long. We pass through a thick steel door manned by a husky dude wearing black. He asks for IDs then allows us to pass. Lance boxes with an imaginary opponent in front of us as we amble along a dark corridor and down a flight of stairs.

"This place is a riot," he says.

"We'll see," I reply.

The club is situated in a narrow room with a low ceiling and scores of seedy-looking people. Smoke fills the air. The walls are crumbling. The entire building should probably be condemned and razed. I don't belong here. In my mind, I dub it Club Slum.

People are dressed in ratty jeans, some with bell bottoms, plain and flowered shirts, and tie-dyed jackets. Retro-sixties-trash-can-fashion mixed with pure punk. I can smell a grungy body odor and it isn't pleasant.

Lance asks what I want to drink, then heads for the bar, wherever that is. I stand in the corner and watch the action. Some sort of heavy metal music screams from a bass-heavy sound system. The people look sleazy to me. Maybe I'm being paranoid. Coke can have that effect.

A young woman dressed in black halter, jeans, and thongs approaches. Gold sparkles are glued to her eyelids and black lipstick adorns an exaggerated mouth that slacks a little to the left. The topping on this upside-down cake is a head of white hair. She must soak it in peroxide on a daily basis. Her skin is alabaster. Her eyes look abnormally alert. I bet she's on speed or crack or something. There are grey bruises on her left arm. This chick doesn't worry about walking the streets at night, she looks like one of the undead. I can smell trouble.

She asks if I'll dance with her.

"I can't," I say. "I'm waiting for someone."

"Who would that be?" she says, trying to be probing but succeeding only at acting overbearing. She has zero finesse.

"I'm waiting for my date," I blurt, unable to makeup a better excuse. I want to be left alone. If I'm supposedly attached to someone else, she's bound to get the picture and move on to her next victim.

She walks away. I move toward a door. I'll hang out in the toilet for a few minutes. Inside the door is a vestibule and two bathrooms. I go into the one with the sign reading "Dicks Not Chicks." The place reeks of urine and God knows what else.

I take a quick leak into an overflowing toilet, then try to find my way back to the club. I'm a little stoned and feeling increasingly uneasy. This place and these people give me the creeps. I exit through a different door and stumble over someone's legs.

"Sorry," I mumble. Its pitch black.

"Don't worry, it's fine. Don't worry." A man's voice.

"I can't see your legs, is there a light?" I say in a shaky voice. The panic is rising inside my gut.

"No flame babe," the man says in slow, slurred speech.

I ease the Bic out of my right pocket. The flame is dim, but sufficent to see for a few feet. I'm standing in a nest of dope fiends or heroin addicts or something. My legs straddle a skinny black guy and a white girl. Their eyes are beyond glassy, they're marbleized, hard, cold, dead. Lifeless, like shark eyes.

It's obvious this is where the hard-core druggies hang. I back up and avert my eyes. Human wreckage. These sad sacks could be me. Percodan is an opiate like heroin. I don't want to end up like these people. How desperate they look. I get the hell out of there. The rest of the club seems like child's play in comparison.

The girl in white ambushes me as I cross a crowd of dancers. She asks if I want to get high with her. I tell her "No thanks." and keep walking. She falls in step beside me. She's not going to give up without a fight. Dammit.

"Let's get high dude," she yells. I shake my head no.

"Do you want to fuck? We can go outside," she howls.

"No thank you," I say. "I've already got a date."

"Oh, sure," she pouts. I turn in a circle, looking for Lance. This place is getting stuffy. My breaths are labored.

She starts screaming, saying I'm a faggot, scum, a homo. Where the hell is Lance? I scan the room, moving my head slowly so I don't miss a thing. It's time to get the hell out of here.

A hand grabs my left arm. I try to yank free. The man is a big bruiser, over six feet tall, broad shouldered, muscular, like a body builder. His head is large and bald. His mouth forms a menacing scowl. His teeth look grungy. The girl steps out from behind him and laughs. She's got me at long last.

"What's the problem?" I ask.

"Shutup faggot," charm girl hisses.

The bruiser tells her to blow off, he'll take care of things. She looks disappointed, but follows his orders and disappears. The bruiser gives me a shit-eating grin and places his hands on my waist.

"Let's dance, fag," he says, easily guiding us into a darker corner of the room near the back. I try to remain cool and not show fear. No one pays any attention to us, anything goes in this hellhole. My date pushes me, nuzzling my neck aggressively. His beard is abrasive.

"What do you want?" I ask.

"I want you to shut your trap, boy, and do as you're told."

"Why?"

"Because I'll damage your pretty face if you don't."

"You must be kidding."

"Try me, boy." I hold my tongue. I don't want to be beaten to a pulp. I hope he'll get bored with me after a dance or two. I'll wait him out.

A short while later the bruiser and I are shuffling to the loud music and inhaling poppers. I sniff very little, but pretend to be smashed. My heart races and I feel pretty good, all things considered. The bully is actually a decent dancer and the poppers help round out his considerable rough edges.

He pulls me closer, then brusquely rubs my crotch.

He squeezes tight. It really hurts. Brother. The other hand reaches around and squeezes my ass like he's testing a melon for ripeness.

"You're a pretty boy," he grunts. That means the world to me, coming from a such a fine person. What a pathetic specimen of humanity he is. He removes the hand from my ass and slides it inside my shirt, stroking my chest with large, insensitive fingers. He directs my right hand to his crotch. I try a perfunctory press. He shoves his hand against mine, forcing it right into his genitals.

He unzips his jeans and guides my hand in. Oh no.

He's not wearing underwear. I wrap a couple of fingers around his stiff cock. It's a real whopper. I'm simultaneously excited and repulsed. It's sexy in a demented, fantasy-rape fashion. He oozes danger.

I don't like to be bullied. He opens the poppers and sticks it under my nostrils. I pretend to take some, but don't. He snorts plenty. All the time I'm stroking his big dick. I ease a hand into my pocket and slowly finger my keyring. I have a plastic key with a razor blade on it. I got it at the car wash for free a few weeks ago.

As pigman massages my chest and grooves to the music, high on poppers, I extract the thin blade and pray it'll do the job. Some animals need to be severely felled or they'll turn and attack again. Kill or be killed.

He grins at me and forces his bad-tasting mouth on mine. The last straw. As his tongue invades my mouth, I throw my head back and jam the tiny blade into his hip. He screams like crazy. I step back. He drops to the floor. I look at him and he suddenly realizes it was me who stabbed him. He looks at me with a mixture of pure hate and intense pain.

"You little fuck," he says. "I'm gonna mess you up good."

"Go fuck yourself, asshole," I say, stepping into the crowd. They part like the scum that floats on the Red Sea. I feel triumphant, yet thoroughly disgusted. I've just stabbed a man. Me. I can't believe it. I don't have time to fret, I need to locate my date and get out fast. I don't see Lance. He'll have to fend for himself. I could be thrown into prison for what I've done. I hear the injured thug howl.

"Somebody get that faggot," he shrieks. Nobody responds. He's hobbled, harmless. A humbled bumble. Get me out of here.

Climbing into the jeep, I spit into the gutter. I can still taste that motherfucker. He should have left me alone. Fucking bully. I speed into the night, zig-zagging back to the freeway to avoid detection.

The moon is bright. The shadows from a row of palm trees bisect the perimeter of the mostly empty freeway. The windows are rolled down. Warm gusts whir around me. I wish I had a couple of Percodans, my head is throbbing. I can't relax. The coke, stabbing, and late hour combined have left me wired.

I light the umpteenth cigarette of whatever day this is, I can't remember. London time and West Coast time are a blur. I need to get home, where it's safe. I need a Valium to erase the tension in my back. It aches.

Looking into the rearview for flashing lights, I hear a distinct rustle from the back of the jeep. There are no cops on my tail. Another sound of movement.

Oh, no. What's next? My heart races like a bullet train, faster and faster. I look around and gasp. It's Lance, for Christ's sake. He's asleep on the back seat and breathing very softly. I'm glad he's with me and not back in that inferno.

Back at my house, we snort the remainder of his coke and listen to the stereo as we lie around the living room and talk about the stabbing. We cuddle on the couch, kiss a little, and rub bodies together. Lance has a firm, smooth young body. I like his hard ass and stomach. I like kissing him.

I excuse myself and fetch two Percodans and a Valium from my sock drawer. A dry Santa Ana wind blows. I open all the windows. I'm starting to unwind after my crime spree. While brushing my teeth, I find a splotch of blood on my right arm. The blood of the bruiser. I turn on the tub. A warm soak is called for. I dump in a container of scented bubble bath from the hotel in London.

Lance joins me in the tub. I roll a joint and put on the soundtrack from "Last Tango in Paris." I find it very romantic. Sitting in the oversized tub with four candles for illumination, I lather his chest, arms, and neck. He gets hard very quickly, as do I. His skin feels so good, so cool.

We're pleasantly high from the grass. We laugh about stupid things, then start to make love. We move our wet bodies to my bed.

After the sex I light a cigarette. The time is five-thirty in the morning. The sun will be coming up soon. I draw the blackout curtains and turn off the ringer on the phone. Lance is facing away from me. I smoke and stare into the dark, sealed room. What a homecoming.

I forgot to call my dealer. I'll call tomorrow. Tomorrow I'll start keeping a written record of my drug use. I'll start cutting down right away. Today I have taken about thirteen pills. Plus the coke and a Valium. What a night. Stubbing the ciggie into the ashtray, I spoon up to Lance's backside. His skin feels great. I get hard again just touching him.

The moon lights the room. A siren wails up the canyon, inciting a pack of coyotes into a yapping spree. They sound like hyenas. I fall asleep thinking of the dog that my brother and I got on our fifth birthday, a golden retriever named Mac.

We loved that dog with our hearts and souls. When he was run over two years later, we were crushed. That dog was warm, protective, and trusting. A real pal. I never allowed myself to cry when he died. I refused to give in to the pain. I built more walls instead of admitting I hurt. David did cry.

I miss David. I miss our dog. I miss who I used to be. What happened to the real me? Tomorrow I'll try to cut down to five Percodans. That's more than a fifty-percent reduction from my present level. It's a start.

Closing my eyes, I give in to sleep. I try to remember a prayer I used to say, but it slips from my grasp.

Chapter Four

The next day I struggle to reduce my intake of Percodan to five pills. Usually, I take two or three pills within a few minutes of waking up. Today, I will try to wait as long as possible before taking a Percodan.

The morning paper has a story in the Metro section about a mysterious stabbing at a downtown rock club. It says the injured patron, Anthony Anderson, suffered a single wound to his thigh. The wound was inflicted, it states, by another patron who disappeared before police arrived on the scene.

After reading the short piece, I return to bed. What a nightmare! What if the police track me down? What would I say? What would my alibi be?

At noon I take half a Valium to alleviate the craving for Percodan. Muscle aches accompany an overall malaise reminiscent of the flu, typical symptoms of Percodan withdrawal. I lounge in bed, then sun myself on the roof for about an hour, all the time trying to distract myself from thinking about drugs, but thinking of little else.

Lance is on holiday from classes, so he hangs out at my house, listening to the stereo, watching T.V., sunning on the roof, and reading my hardcover copy of Hollywood Babylon. It's impossible not to think about the damn pills. Something inside me is crumbling, eroding. I can't ignore the truth anymore: I'm a slave to painkillers. They control my life, not I.

By three-fifteen, I can wait no longer. It's particularly torturous trying to abstain when there are dozens of Percodans in my sock drawer. I break down and take two pills and eat a bowl of lentil soup. The Percodan stimulates my appetite, so I make a tuna sandwich half an hour later, after the pills have kicked in a little.

At five, my dealer stops by with the extra fifty pills I ordered, as well as a baggy of marijuana. I write him a check and attribute my sluggishness to jet lag.

Lance is down the hill shopping for dinner. He thinks I've got a cold and offered to go to the market. I don't want him to be here while I'm buying the drugs.

I smoke a joint before Lance gets back. It really improves my mood.

The effects of the two Percodans were short-lived. My tolerance to Percodan has ballooned. On a typical day, I would already have swallowed seven or eight pills. I barely feel the effects of two pills anymore. I need at least three pills to get a decent buzz.

Lance returns with two bags of groceries. He's got steaks, ice cream, wine, and various other goodies. We decide to get high and watch "Star Wars" on video. I roll a joint while he unpacks the foods. I put a U2 CD on the stereo.

We light up the reefer as he cuts vegetables on a chopping block I didn't know I owned. The bitter-tasting smoke alleviates the remaining tension. We eat spoonfuls of chocolate ice cream while he slices and dices, then retire to the living room for our film.

During the first half-hour of the film, Lance sits with his leg pressing against mine. The television is situated in a corner facing the view. The sun has dropped beyond the mountain. The lights of the entire basin are flickering to life. It looks magical. Lance reaches over and squeezes my leg several times. I slide closer and entwine my arm around his.

This escalates into heavier necking and groping. We pause the movie and move to the bedroom. I could definitely get used to having him around. It's been a long time since I've had a regular boyfriend. I feel comfortable with him.

After our intermission, he grills the steaks on the barbeque. I lounge on the couch, flipping channels on the T.V., smoking cigarettes, feeling relaxed for the first time in ages. We eat while finishing the movie. My head is feeling heavy and achy, so I take three more Percodans.

We decide to watch another sci-fi film. The Percs kick in fast. Stretched out on the couch watching spaceships zoom through the heavens, I feel no pain. I rub Lance's feet. We smoke the rest of the joint. The special effects are great. We have a fun time together. By eleven we're back in bed, making love again.

I sleep like a rock, waking early the next morning. Lance is already up, sitting in the garden reading the paper. He suggests a day at the beach. I instantly agree. My head hurts quite a bit. I hope I can cut down to four Percodans today. The sun is blazing overhead. Yes, a day at the beach might be a good thing.

By eleven we're stretched across towels on a sliver of sand up in Malibu. My legs are starting to hurt like hell. Drug withdrawal is a bitch. I brought along my allotment of four pills, two joints, and a Valium just in case the discomfort gets really out of control.

We brought a small cooler filled with club cocktails and water. The day is remarkably warm for January. The sun feels great. Lance is wearing blue-and-white speckled Speedos. He's got a really sexy hard body. I open a screwdriver and wash down the Valium. My muscles are freaking. They want the painkillers. I'll give them Valium instead.

The alcohol begins to loosen the sore joints. The orange drink is refreshing, but tastes artificial. Lance walks to the surf, where he engages two young surfers in animated conversation.

I'm trying to light a match from an oversized matchbook when it suddenly bursts into flame inside my cupped hands. The right palm sticks to the burning matches. My brain doesn't register the pain for a couple of beats. By then the damage is done. I let out a sizeable howl.

The pain is excruciating. Damn. I rip the matchbook from the skin and drop it on the sand. My hand is very red. The palm and several fingers pulsate in agony. I better do something quick.

I plunge the hand into the ice chest, allowing the cubes to quell the heat. Lance appears, asking me what's going on. I tell him what happened between winces. He asks how he can help. I calm myself and ask him to light me a cigarette. He does this and sits down. I smile and convince him I'll be fine. "It's just a little burn," I say. I tell Lance my threshold to pain is ridiculously low, that's all. I tell him I'm going to take a nap. He buys my act and returns to his buddies.

The burnt palm actually hurts like hell. I refuse to take any painkillers before three o'clock. I waited yesterday till three, so I'll do the same today. It's time to exhibit some willpower. My goal is four pills today, three tomorrow. I wrap the hand in a T-shirt and lie on my stomach. The warmth of the sun calms me. I try to sleep.

I open my eyes, forgetting where I am for a few seconds. The familar sound of waves rolling onto shore quickly jogs my memory. Malibu. According to my watch, it's nearly two. Thank God I put on sunscreen before I left the house. Where's Lance? I sit up. My hand is throbbing. It really hurts. .

Sunglasses cut the glare. My head is pounding. Sleeping in the sun can be disorienting. I spot Lance out in the ocean, swimming alongside a darker-haired guy with a surfboard. I wave, but he doesn't see me. I locate my stash and swallow two Percodans with the last swig of the screwdriver in a can.

After lighting a cigarette, I unwrap the hand for a quick look. The palm is one big red and white blister. It's a mess. It might be a second-degree burn. I may need professional medical attention. What a nightmare. Damn those stupid matches. From now on I'll use a lighter. I dress. I'm hungry and cold. Lance appears. He's soaking wet. "Let's go," I say. "I'm starved."

Lance offers to drive. Barreling down the coast highway, he lets it slip that he's still dating a young woman from school. He asks what I think of that. I say it's none of my business, he's got to follow his own path. I explain that I've been struggling to accept my own sexuality. "I'm gay," I say. "I've tried to be straight, but it doesn't work for me. Physical intimacy with men is what's natural for me." Lance says he doesn't know what he wants yet.

We sit at a wood table in a cafe called Patrick's Roadhouse on Pacific Coast Highway. The place is packed with body builders, beach bunnies, movie stars, nobodies, the usual mix.

I wrap my hand in a couple of paper napkins and hide it in my lap. What a klutz. Quitting drugs will never happen if I'm secretly sabotaging myself with painful little injuries.

The right eye feels spastic. I ask Lance if he notices anything funny about my eyes. He says my right eye has a slight tic. I wonder if I'm having a nervous breakdown?

We dine on cheeseburgers and fries. Tall glasses of iced tea cut through the grease. The meal tastes fantastic. The Percodans are kicking in, thank God. My head is lighter, the hand less tender. The pain is sapping my strength. He insists on paying for lunch.

Riding down Wilshire with Lance at the wheel, I start to nod off. I revive as we near Westwood.

"Your hand looks pretty messed up. Maybe we should take you to an emergency room," he says in a concerned voice.

"Maybe after the movie," I say, unwilling to alter our plans.

We sit six rows from the screen for an action buddy movie. I feel worse and worse as the inane movie unrolls. I hear myself laughing too loud or not at all.

The throbbing in the hand is vibrating into my head. It's exhausting. Lance gets treats. I eat a little popcorn, but lose interest after a few handfuls. I feel beaten. The movie is predictable. I drink a few gulps of the soft drink, cradling the injured arm on my chest, then close my eyes for a little rest.

Lance wakes me. "Stop that," I say. He's shaking me. "I'm fine. What's happening?"

"You need to see a doctor, Daniel. You're not well."

"It's my hand," I say, laughing like a fool. I feel light-headed. My hand feels demolished. I'm afraid to unwrap the bandage and look.

He drives me to a hospital near West Hollywood. An emergency room, for Christ's sake. Such drama. Lance fills out the forms. I sit on the waiting room couch, then pass out.

I dream of thousands of squawking parrots. I'm trying to join them in flight, but my body is heavy. I flap both arms, hop along the ground, but can't seem to fly. I wake in an examining room. A bearded doctor is taking my pulse.

"Hey," I say, "what's going on?"

"You've got a nasty third-degree burn on your hand. How's the pain?" he asks.

"Pretty bad," I say, unsure of how I really feel.

I remember pain.

"We're going to keep you here overnight. We've given you a shot of Demerol for the pain and applied a superb topical cream to the burn. You'll feel better in a day or two."

I thank him and wonder where Lance is. The M.D. calls a nurse and they load me into a wheelchair. The nurse rolls me into an elevator with shiny steel walls.

Ten minutes later I'm situated in a bed on the sixth floor. I have a view of the massive Beverly Center and much of West Hollywood. I'm tired but coherent. The Demerol has me flying. The buzz is similar to Percodan, but far stronger. I feel no sensation in my hand. It's miraculous.

An older woman, Gloria Maddox, is my nurse until her shift ends at midnight. We'll have nearly six hours together. She orders me a chocolate shake and brings a couple of magazines. I use the remote control with my unbandaged hand and tune in to a game show after she leaves on rounds. She treats me like I'm her favorite.

I call my house. The answering machine picks up. Where's Lance? I call the hospital switchboard and ask to be connected with the emergency room. The attendant there pages Lance. A few seconds later, he gets on the line. I tell him I've been moved upstairs and to come up. He asks what room. I check the panic button on the bedside table. "615," I say. He's breathing heavily. I hope this little adventure hasn't frightened him off.

The milkshake and Lance arrive in tandem. I turn to music videos and apologize for the hassle. He says it's no problem. Gloria pops in to say hello. She tells him he's cute as a button. I share the shake with Lance and fill him in on my activities.

I suggest he walk across the street and get us food from the Hard Rock. I feel like another burger, my insides are wrung out. Lance says that sounds good. I ask if he'd do me another favor and look after the house while I'm in the hospital. He seems pleased that I trust him. I give him forty dollars from my wallet and the keys to the house. I could call Sally to keep an eye on things, but I don't want to involve her in this little mess.

Lance leaves for the food. I place a call to my sister in Illinois. She sounds concerned.

"What's wrong Daniel?"

"Nothing, really. I'm in the hospital."

"Were you in an accident? Talk to me."

"I burned my hand. Third degree. It hurts."

"Oh no. Are you okay?"

"Sure, I'm fine. They're keeping me overnight just to be safe. They gave me a shot, I'm sort of dopey."

"What's going on with you? Don't you ever return calls?"

"I just got back from London."

"I didn't know that. You're so secretive. What's going on?"

"Nothing. London was a last-minute thing. I burned my hand this afternoon, but I'll be fine. I wanted to call and say Happy New Year. How's the baby?"

"Fat and sassy. Can I do anything to help, Daniel?"

"No. I'm fine. Everything's under control. I'll call you soon."

"You'd better," she says.

"How are Mom and Dad?" I ask.

"Fine. They miss you. I think they realize they've been shits, Daniel. Maybe you can forgive them at some point."

"Maybe. I better go. Goodbye, Linda."

"I love you, Daniel."

"Thanks. I love you too."

Hanging up the phone, I feel tremendously alone. No one understands my loneliness and pain. I can't explain it because I don't understand it myself. I press the button to summon nurse Gloria. It's time to finagle additional pain medication.

The next day, at four in the afternoon, I'm sprung. No more injections of the wildly euphoric Demerol. Lance drives me home. He's stocked the fridge with frozen foods, vegetables, eggs, milk, a few basics. He says he can stay and look after me while I convalesce. I assure him I'll be fine in a few days. I'm taking antibiotics and the doctor gave me a prescription for fifty Percodans. I'm set for the moment, pharmaceutically speaking.

My withdrawal from painkillers is temporarily sidetracked.

I'm relieved and disgusted. I distract myself by taking three more Percodans and a hot bath. Lance joins me.

As I'm soaping his chest he asks if I take a lot of drugs. I look into his eyes and blink. What should I say? He should know the truth if he's going to hang out here a lot. It's only fair.

"Yes," I say. "I'm addicted to Percodan. It's a strong painkiller. I'm trying to quit, but it's not going too well."

"Thanks for telling me."

"I like you."

"Why do you take them?"

"Because I'm hooked.

"Go to a hospital."

"I just got out of a hospital. They gave me even better drugs."

"Go to a rehab center."

"That scares me. I'm afraid."

"Of what?"

"Being told what to do and think."

"My brother went into rehab to stop snorting coke. He said it wasn't bad at all."

"If I can't do it on my own, well, I'll have to think about it."

"Have you tried to quit before?"

"Sure, a dozen times, easy."

"Why didn't it work?"

"I couldn't handle the withdrawal pains and depression."

"Check out rehab centers, Daniel. You're too smart to take that shit. Getting high once in a while is one thing, but those painkillers are bad news."

"Where did your brother go for rehab?"

"Rancho Mirage. The Betty Ford Hospital."

"Really? Was it expensive?"

"I don't think so. He said it was the best thing that ever happened to him."

"No kidding?"

"That's what he said."

"How long does it take?"

"He was there a month."

"Did you see the place?"

"Sure. I went to visit with my folks once. It wasn't anything fancy. A lot of it's AA-oriented. The guys in my brother's group were really cool."

"I always assumed it was a country club deal, swarming with rich movie stars and idle fatcats."

"Nope. It's for everybody."

"Anybody that's hooked on drugs."

"Like you."

"Sad, isn't it? Yes, like me," I say, scratching my ear with the bandaged hand. Look how far I've fallen. Drugs, stabbings, burns, the hospital, needles, more pills. What a disaster I've become.

The next morning I wake with a headache and a bandaged hand furious with pain. I immediately remove two Percodans from a bottle in my sock drawer, then swallow them while I take a leak. Lance is gone, but I find a note taped to the inside of the front door.

Good morning, Daniel. I'm off to do some errands. I'll
call this afternoon. Maybe we can play tonight. How's
the hand? Don't forget to take the antibiotics like the
doctor said. Don't forget to think about hospitals.
Leave a message on my machine if you need to.

Love,
Lance

What a sweet guy. I carry the note to the bedroom, then take a penicillin tablet and light a cigarette. Removing the phone from the cradle, I call information for the number of the Betty Ford Center.

I dial the number. A woman answers. I slam the phone down. Maybe I'll call later. I'm not ready for this.

Screw it. I'll do it now. This is what the damn redial button is for.

"Betty Ford Center," a woman answers.

"Hello?"

"Can I help you?"

"I'd like some information on your ... services." Sounds like I'm speaking to a house of prostitution.

"Certainly. Just a moment please." She puts me on hold. I could hang up, but don't.

"Would you like us to send you our brochure?" she says when she comes back on the line.

"Please."

"Would you like to have a counselor phone you back?"

"That's a good idea. Sure."

I reluctantly give my name, address, phone number. It's time to stop being afraid. How can I get help if I can't tell an operator my name? She may think this information is for my wife or brother or a friend. She carefully explains that someone will phone me back for a more in-depth interview in a few days. My name is on a list.

"How long before a person could start the program?"

"The waiting list is several weeks long," she says. My heart sinks. If I don't start soon I may lose the nerve. She reassures me that someone will definitely get back to me. I thank her and hang-up.

The rest of the day is spent watching television and floating on an opiate magic carpet. Lance calls but I don't pick up. I'm feeling sore from the burn, even through the pills. My mind is preoccupied with this rehab business. Should I or shouldn't I? I want to end this addiction, but I'm afraid. I take a total of ten Percodans before going to bed at one in the morning. I feel like my life is a waste.

The next day a heatwave hits L.A. By noon the temperature has soared to ninety-two degrees. A summer day in January. The paper predicts another winter rainstorm in a few days. I'm supposed to clean the burn wound once a day and slather the white cream on it three times a day. The pain is lessening, thank God.

Lance has left two messages this morning. I don't feel like talking to anyone right now. I feel afraid. I'm trying to direct my energy into maintaining the resolve to go into a drug dependency treatment center.

The phone wakes me from a sweaty nap at three. I'm wearing shorts. I turn over, and listen to the machine. It's a man calling from Betty Ford. I grab the receiver.

"Hello?"

"Yes, I'm calling for Daniel from Eisenhower Hospital."

"Yes, this is Daniel."

"Daniel, this is Frank. What can I do for you today?"

"Well, I'm addicted to painkillers and I'd like to stop. Someone suggested Betty Ford. I'd like to get started soon."

"What medication do you use?"

"Painkillers. Percodan mostly."

"How many a day?"

"Anywhere from four or five to fifteen or sixteen a day."

"For how long now?"

"Three years or so."

"Have you tried to quit on your own?"

"Sure, many times. I can't do it on my own."

"What we do is get some information initially, then we devise a treatment plan. You'd come out to the desert for about a month," Frank says. He sounds competent and non-judgmental.

"Sounds good."

"Do you use cocaine?" he asks.

"Occasionally."

"Hallucinogenics?"

"A few times."

"I need to make a profile, that's why we ask these questions."

"Sure."

"Have you ever used heroin?"

"No."

"That's good. We don't treat that here anymore."

Frank describes the rehab program. A month living at Betty Ford, no drugs, a lot of AA and twelve-step philosophy, group therapy. They rarely give drugs for withdrawal, but Eisenhower Hospital is next door if it becomes necessary for medication or hospitalization.

The Betty Ford Center has a staff of doctors and nurses that evaluate the patient when they enter the program. I feel relieved to hear they don't believe in treating addiction with other drugs. It's frightening to consider a rehab program where they keep the addict doped on new drugs to ease the withdrawal process. I want to quit all drugs.

He tells me the cost, which is under ten thousand dollars.

"Count me in," I say. "When can I come down and check in? Tonight?"

He laughs and says the waiting list is a month long right now, but he'll see what he can do. He suggests sending a check as a deposit.

I write the info on an envelope from the trash basket. I explain that I'm trying to cut down my intake of pills and getting impatient. He says for me to hold tight, he'll phone back in a few days with additional details.

I feel energized by my decision to kick the drugs.

It's time to reinvent myself as a healthier, more honest man. I change into jeans, sport shirt, and athletic shoes, then drive to the bank and arrange a cashier's check for the rehab program. I mail the check and a brief letter to Betty Ford. The time has come to grow up.

I call Lance from outside the post office and get his answering device. I say I've taken his advice. I'm going into rehab. Call me later.

Hearing myself tell another person I'm checking into a hospital for treatment of my addiction is difficult, but I feel a little less ashamed.

I drive toward the Beverly Center to catch a bite of lunch and a matinee. The heat is irritating the burn. I steer with the left hand and awkwardly shift gears with the right wrist. I'm getting pretty good at it.

Driving up the ramp into the parking lot, I realize a heavy weight has been lifted from my shoulders. I'm looser and freer somehow. The decision to put myself in the hands of addiction specialists means I won't be alone with this drug problem anymore. I'll have support and guidance.

It dawns on me that my life will never be the same once I enter a program. There will be no going back to these pills. If I'm going to heal, I must say goodbye to my pharmaceutical companions. I think I'm ready.

Chapter Five

I n the dream, my twin brother David walks in the distance, sprinkling handfuls of yellow Percodan pills on green grass. He's naked and surrounded by a golden halo.

I can't see his face, but I follow him.

I walk to a wide, wide river. A group of men, women, and children are gathered a few feet from shore. They are entirely naked. In the center is a bearded man with glowing eyes. He holds a baby in his arms and says a blessing in Latin. The sun streams through wisps of pale ivory clouds, while menacing clouds gather on the horizon.

The preacher dunks the baby under water. Several women cry "Praise Jesus" again and again. The holy man passes the blessed infant to the women, then turns to me. He welcomes me with extended arms. I shed my clothes as the naked crowd watches, unembarrassed by the intimacy of the moment. There is nothing to be afraid of here, in this place, with these people. I wade in. The people part to let me through. We float to the middle of the river. The preacher holds me close, then kisses me on the mouth.

He sprinkles me with river water and speaks more Latin. I start to cry and laugh. I release the pain. He dunks me under. I swim away, deep into the murky river. I can breathe here. I pass into the open sea. Groves of willowy sea plants sway along the sandy bottom. Salmon-colored coral stalagmites rise like undersea high-rises. Fish of every hue glide by.

My arms and legs metamorphose into fins and flipper tail. I swim like a dolphin or sea cow. Smooth and graceful. Sunlight drops a veil of spidery shadows on the ocean floor. A pod of three whales silently passes in the distance.

I stop to harvest three yellow pills from inside a clam shell. Out of nowhere appears a pack of crazed, snarling midgets. I can hear them cursing even at this distance. They're armed with crossbows and spears and swim fast. I kick myself into escape, but I feel too heavy to move.

My hands and feet revert to their human form. I lose speed and agility. I start to sink. I hear the midgets shout as they get closer and closer. I dog paddle to the surface.

When I wake from the dream, the alarm clock is buzzing. The time is five thirty a.m. Right. I slide over and turn it off. It's dark outside. I feel exhausted, not remotely rested. Nobody said quitting drugs was easy.

I've been trying to wean myself from the Percodan in preparation for entering rehab. I've managed to limit my Percodan intake to five pills for several days. The muscle and joint discomfort from withdrawal makes me edgy and depressed most of the time.

Frank from Betty Ford called yesterday. He said there was a last-minute opening. Could I check in tomorrow? "Absolutely," was my reply. The sooner the better. It's been ten days since I placed the initial call.

Lance agreed to water the plants and bring in the mail while I'm away. By noon today, I'll be a patient in a drug treatment program.

I feel humbled beyond belief. Either I'll get straightened out or continue to live the sorry life of a tormented addict. I know I need help. I feel very low. "The end of one thing is the start of another," my mother always used to say. There's a certain sense to that. What will replace who I am now?

I listen to the stereo and pack a duffel with enough junk to last a month. We're not allowed to bring books, but I pack a couple of paperbacks I've been wanting to read just in case. I hate to go anywhere without reading material. No medications are allowed. No alcohol, no cologne. I have a carton of cigarettes and basic toiletries, too.

While soaking in a hot tub, I write my sister to detail where I'm going and why. I tell her she can write to me there if she likes. The letter is two paragraphs long. It's all I can manage.

The bathroom is littered with all my drugs: Percodan, Codeine, Valium, grass, everything. I know what I must do. I open each prescription bottle and empty the dozens of remaining pills into the toilet bowl. Some melt, others slowly corrode. I dump the primo baggy of pot in, too. Without missing a beat, I flush the toilet. I'm big on symbolic gestures to firm up resolve. I take the empty bottles outside to the trash can. Then I place the letter in the mailbox and raise the red flag.

Sitting in the back of a taxi speeding down La Cienega towards the airport, I realize I've never felt so sober as I do right now. The morning is cool. The sun is climbing above the hills that separate the airport from the city. Oil pumps hammer the damp ground, slaves to a rhythm mandated by unseen masters.

It's a few minutes after seven. Traffic is extremely light. The driver swerves to avoid striking a heavyset Mexican woman standing in the road. Next to her is a disabled van. A man lies under the vehicle. What is she doing out in the street?

I smoke several cigarettes before arriving at LAX. My arms are hurting again. Withdrawal. The bandage on my hand has come off, the burn has healed fairly well. It's still tender, but covered with new skin. It itches constantly.

After paying the driver, I check my duffel, get a boarding pass, then throw up last night's dinner in the men's room. Nerves of steel.

I could have taken a few pills to make the ride smoother, but that didn't seem in the spirit of beginning a drug-free life. I don't see myself arriving at Betty Ford stoned out of my mind. No thanks. I want to put my best foot forward, no matter how sick I may feel.

The flight to Palm Springs is quick and uneventful. There are only a few other passengers. My head is swimming with questions about the next month. Will I be allowed to make phone calls? Will I have to discuss all of my deepest, darkest secrets in front of total strangers? I know they emphasize group therapy. What will that be like? How will I manage the emotional turmoil without Percodan? Am I strong enough to do this?

Getting off the plane in Palm Springs, I'm greeted by a rather warm morning. I clean my sunglasses with a sleeve, then stand in the sun and smoke a cigarette.

Entering the heavily air-conditioned terminal, I shiver. Withdrawal from Percodan involves wildly fluctuating body temperatures. One minute I'm burning up, the next my teeth are chattering from cold. I stop in the coffee shop and order eggs and toast. I can barely swallow the food, I'm too anxious. I read the paper and smoke cigarettes. The weather section says the temperature will climb into the high nineties today.

I'm due to arrive at Betty Ford at noon. That leaves me with another two-and-a-half hours to kill. I eat a few more forkfuls of the bland eggs and read the entertainment section.

I wonder whether this is the beginning of the best part of my life or the start of the worst. My guess is life will get easier without drugs to complicate it. I find it hard to be optimistic with my legs aching. I wish it would stop.

I haul my bag outside and hire a cab. The driver asks where I'm headed. I pause. I don't feel like admitting I'm a hopeless addict to this guy.

"Take me to Eisenhower Hospital please," I say.

"No problem," he answers. "Would you like the fastest route or the longer scenic route?"

"Oh, let's go the scenic route. I'm in no hurry."

It's been a couple of years since I last visited Palm Springs. Howard and I came here for Thanksgiving one year. We stayed at a hotel and had a great time. We almost always had fun together.

There are golf courses everywhere. Condo complexes seem to have sprung up on every corner. Change. The area is still uncluttered and open compared to L.A. Palm trees grow in profusion along the roads. A sign on the highway suggests stopping at a local restaurant for their world-famous "Date Shakes." I love the name, but hate the idea of drinking liquified dates. The mountains that separate Palm Springs from Los Angeles provide a dramatic backdrop to the flat desert. Beyond the snow-capped mountains lies the big bad world.

I chain smoke and try to keep collected. I feel very afraid. The superflu symptoms have grown more pronounced. I guess the drug withdrawal is shifting into high gear. It's been over fifteen hours since my last dose of Percodan. By nightfall I'll be climbing the walls.

"We're here, buddy," the driver says. The car is parked at the entrance to Eisenhower Hospital. I feel ashamed at my embarrassment. I'm acting so weird.

"I'm going to the Betty Ford Center, actually," I croak. My throat is dry.

"No problem." He coasts down a drive that connects Eisenhower Hospital with a cluster of low buildings on the other side of a large lake. The road is lined with red and white flowering oleander. Sprinklers spray a fine mist across the lawn. A trickle of water rolls down the street gutter. I light another smoke.

The complex of buildings is pretty non-descript. Typical desert-style stucco exteriors, nice landscaping, courtyards and paved paths connecting the larger structures with barely visible buildings in the background. Everything is painted in earth tones. It looks just like it did in the brochure they sent me. I wonder where the pool is?

I get out of the taxi. The driver places my duffel on the sidewalk. I hand him the money. He smiles and says, "Good luck, man," before returning to his car.

He starts to drive away, stops, and leans out his window. "God bless you," he yells. I wave and can't help but laugh. What a nice thing for a stranger to say.

Smoking a cigarette, I scan the immediate area. The reception area must be inside the large building with mirrored doors. I can't see in, dammit. I step closer to a hibiscus bush for shade and a little cover. I feel so exposed, so vulnerable.

I look past the side of a building, across the lake at Eisenhower Hospital. Perhaps this is a mistake. Maybe I'm not ready to spend four weeks in an institution, for God's sake. What if I can't make it? That would be humiliating.

I must do this, I must.

"Hey. Don't worry...it's not so bad," an unseen man shouts.

"What?" I don't see anyone.

"Over here. To your left."

"Hi," I say. A bearded man, aged forty or so, stands next to a patio outside a low-slung building, smoking a cigarette, wearing only a pair of shorts. He's sun bathing, I suppose.

"Whats your name?" he yells.

"Uh, Daniel."

"I'm Gary."

"It's a pleasure, Gary."

"Yah, I know. You're thinking about leaving, right?"

"Sort of."

"You remind me of me when I arrived."

"When was that?"

"Two weeks ago."

"And how is it?"

"Best thing that ever happened to me. No shit."

"Well, it's been nice talking to you."

"Don't leave, Daniel."

Hearing this strange man's concern vibrates deep inside me.

"I won't leave."

"Promise?"

"Promise."

"The people here are good. Get inside that office."

"I will."

"Are you a smoker?" he asks. What a bizarre question.

"Yes, I am."

"Good," he hoots, then disappears behind the patio wall.

I try to smoke another cigarette, but my heart just isn't into such an obvious ploy to kill time. It's getting hot out here in the sun. I feel sick to my stomach. I wish this day were over. I'm a grown man, for Christ's sake, I should be able to waltz into the Betty Ford Center like anyone else. Fuck it. I'm going in.

Duffel in one hand, cigarette in the other, I approach the glass doors, which sense my presence and swing open. I enter and immediately drop the cigarette in a tall ash cannister. A woman stands behind a counter. She looks friendly enough. I give her my name. She asks me to take a seat, someone will be with me in a few minutes.

"I can come back later. I know I'm early," I stutter. I know I shouldn't consider leaving, but I'm afraid.

"It's no problem. There will be someone with you in just a few minutes."

"All right."

I sit on one of the big chairs that are grouped around the lobby. The room is pleasant. Plants are everywhere. The people I see look normal enough. It doesn't look like a mental ward, though it's what happens behind closed doors that builds a funny farm's reputation.

A cheerful Asian nurse leads me to a room, where we sit and talk. She asks questions and writes as I try to answer. How many pills did I take a day? Did I drink? Did I mix the pills with alcohol? What about my cocaine use? They want to know everything. She asks questions about my health and history of illness. She asks when was the first time I remember drinking alcohol? When did I first smoke pot?

I keep no secrets. I answer honestly, no matter how uncomfortable I feel. I blush a lot during the hour we spend together. I feel like a mess, but force myself to stay composed and pleasant under the emotional pressure. I can survive this, I can, I can.

I tell her about the death of my brother, about a pneumonia I had three years ago, and my back problems. She asks if I was ill when my brother got the meningitis that killed him. "No," I say. "I wasn't physically ill. I got very depressed after he died. It was like I died too. I felt doomed. We were twins." I laugh for no reason. A knot of anger pulls at my throat. I feel like crying, but don't.

Why do they need to know all this shit? How can it help me? My willful nature hasn't served me very well recently. I suppose I need to place my trust in these people.

The nurse is very nice. She isn't at all judgmental or pushy. Her attitude and behavior suggest someone very accepting. She asks about my history of trying to quit the pills. I describe my usual withdrawal symptoms. I explain that the discomfort usually makes me so crazy that I return to drugs for relief. She asks whether I ever have thoughts of suicide. "No," I answer truthfully.

She tells me they have a new device, a patch that adheres to the arm and releases tiny amounts of an anti-withdrawal medication. Supposedly, this patch helps alleviate the worst physical side effects of Percodan withdrawal. I tell her it sounds like a good idea and admit I'm afraid of facing withdrawal in new surroundings, among strangers.

She explains that people rarely die from opiate withdrawal. They don't believe in giving drugs to patients here unless it's medically called for. Some alcoholic patients are given sedatives to offset the DT's, which can cause heart attacks and death. Patients here are educated on techniques for coping with stress without chemicals.

She promises to talk to the nursing staff about getting me a patch. She says I'm the only painkiller addict out of eighty patients at Betty Ford. What an honor. The rest of the inmates are coke addicts, alcoholics, and potheads. The creme de la creme.

After asking if there was any diabetes in my family, she takes my blood pressure and says she hopes I'll apply myself and learn the program. I say I'm here to get well, whatever it takes to succeed. She says I'll do just fine.

She explains that the worst of the withdrawal occurs during the first five days. It's usually quite a bit easier after that. I tell her my withdrawal is usually a week of hell, followed by a couple of weeks of depression and moodiness. She says to try to manage the pain on a daily basis.

"Try not to be too hard on yourself over the next week, Daniel. Percodan withdrawal is difficult. You'll feel overwhelmed with emotion at times. If you have any problems, come to the nurses' station. We won't give you medicine, but we'll suggest other methods of pain management. I know we've got cold and hot packs. Don't be afraid to ask. No need to be shy. Okay?"

"Okay."

She leads me down the hall to another room. She says the duffel will be delivered to my room in a short while. I wonder whether they'll search it? Why wouldn't they? She says a doctor will be giving me an examination in a few minutes, then wishes me luck and leaves.

A man in a white coat shuffles in. He introduces himself, then asks me to lie down, he will be evaluating my physical condition. He pokes and prods for a few minutes, then asks me to dress and join him in his office across the hall.

We proceed to the question-and-answer portion of the interview. He grills me on my drug use. Where did I get the Percodan? Did I work doctors? Did I buy the pills from pushers? Did I ever use heroin? Did I do cocaine? How much? How often? Where did I get the money to buy drugs? How long have I taken Percodan? Did I use Demerol? Codeine? How many a day? A week? Have I ever tried to kill myself?

I answer these personal questions more easily the second time, though my hands are shaking. He's more aggressive than the nurse. Do I smoke cigarettes? What about pot? How is withdrawal for me? Do I have headaches? Ulcers? Diabetes? He tells me that addiction is a disease and that there is new evidence to suggest that some people are born with an X chromosome that predisposes a person toward alcoholism or addiction. Interesting. I never really thought of my problem as disease, more like a scourge that was the direct result of moral weakness and a lack of willpower.

He suggests I follow the full exercise routine here. I tell him about the burn on my hand. He examines the wound. He asks if I ever injured myself while high. "Not really," I truthfully answer. When I burnt my hand I wasn't drugged. That's the truth.

Twenty minutes later I have a silver-dollar-sized patch affixed to my shoulder. The nurses say I'll wear it for about twelve days. What a curious invention. I really hope it helps.

A middle-aged man wearing a plaid shirt and a moustache approaches me, introducing himself as John. He's soft-spoken and attractive. He's a counselor at McCallum Hall, the place where I'll be living for the next month. The brochure said they have two all-male dorms, one all-female, and one co-ed. McCallum is boys only. That's certainly good news.

He asks where my bag is. I say I left it with the nurse.

He retrieves it and leads me outside to a sidewalk that curves towards a building above the lake. What will I do with myself in this place for a month? I'll go crazy.

There's a mother mallard and seven tiny ducklings swimming near the edge of the water. Hidden sprinklers pop into action, spraying water across the grassy banks that slope to the lake.

John asks if I'm all right. "Sure," I lie. "Just looking at the ducks. The sun feels really hot here." There's a sign on the building. It says McCallum Hall. My new home. I'm not ready to walk in just yet. John asks how many Percodans I took a day. I tell him. He says he took Percodan a few times and really enjoyed the high. His drug of choice was cocaine. He's been clean for nine years.

"How did you do it? How did you quit?" I ask.

"One day at a time, Daniel."

"What does that mean, exactly?"

"The idea is to break life down into easier-to-digest chunks. Live in the present. One day at a time." That makes sense. It really does. One day at a time. I have to remember that.

It's a relief to discuss our addictions so openly. We're cut from the same dysfunctional cloth, it seems. He suggests we go inside McCallum. "Why not?" I answer. We pass through a small lobby and a big room outfitted with tables and chairs, sink, microwave, and coffee pots. A set of glass doors leads from this lounge area out to a large patio overlooking the lake. A large living room with couches, chairs, and fireplace is located down a few steps from the lobby. Everything looks clean and easy on the eye. No harsh colors. He leads me to a pleasant office that overlooks this entire wing.

John sets my bag on the floor and offers me a chair. He sits at a desk, opens a file, writes a few notations, and fiddles with a Polaroid camera. He says they need a photo of me for the record. I feel puffy. Maybe that's the point, to have a visual evidence of my appearance to show me in a month. I force a smile and the camera flashes. How glamorous I must look. He asks if I have any questions. "Not yet," I say.

He asks me to answer a questionnaire. I grab a pen and begin. There are dozens of inquiries into my drug use, work habits, personal life, family and background, suicide attempts, criminal behavior, pressing legal matters, and so on. How many times do I have to go through this? It's obviously part of the program to force us to face the unsavory consequences of our addiction. I admit that drugs have damaged many areas of my life.

He asks whether I'm hungry. I hear the sound of many men talking and laughing through the walls. John explains that the morning group therapy has ended. The residents of McCallum will go to lunch in a few minutes. He explains that everyone gathers outside the front doors before every meal and activity for something called "circle." I nod my head and try to assimilate this information. My head is foggy. I've got a splitting headache.

He'll show me my room after lunch, he says. Someone named Parker will be my roommate. He reminds me that it's integral to my recovery to keep close to the McCallum people. Striking up conversations with other patients isn't encouraged. He calls it "fraternization." Rules, rules, rules. I suppose I need more structure and discipline in my life, but I feel beaten by the thought today. My legs are hurting badly. There are no phone calls allowed in or out for the first five days. That's fine with me. I probably won't be feeling particularly sociable this next week. I'll be feeling too physically ill to give a shit about the phone. I appreciate being shielded from the world for a few days. Withdrawal is a bitch.

I ask when he'll search my duffel for contraband. He rises from his chair.

"That can wait until after lunch, don't you think?" he says with a laugh.

"Sure. I don't have anything very interesting anyway."

"Let's introduce you to your peers." My peers? What a strange word that is. Sounds so clinical.

I follow him outside. The glare is intense, so I put on my shades. The pain in my skull is getting worse. About fifteen men stand in a loosely formed circle. They talk and a few smoke cigarettes. John introduces me to two older men, Alan and Ron. Alan is in his fifties. He's about my height, has grey hair, wide wire- rimmed glasses, and wears navy slacks and a red sportshirt. He looks as though he's waiting to play a round of golf. Ron is slightly younger and has a dark beard and a gap between his front teeth. Another guy with a beard stares at me from behind mirrored sunglasses from the other side of the circle. I can't recall why he looks familiar.

A young man wearing jeans, Lakers T-shirt, and sneakers calls the unruly group to order. "Let's get into circle guys, let's go," he orders in a friendly, yet firm, voice.

John says he'll see me back in the office after lunch.

He points to the guy in the Lakers shirt. "That's your granny," he says and returns indoors. Granny? What the hell is that? This is unsettling.

The ragtag collection of men draw into a circle, shoulder to shoulder, arms wrapped around one another's waists. I awkwardly place my right arm around Ron's slightly slumped shoulder, the other curved around a bearded Hispanic's neck. Three men with beards. What does that mean? Do men grow beards as masks? Is facial hair another barrier to intimacy? I'm obviously in for some serious exploration of male bonding the next few weeks. The sun is blinding.

The young man in the Lakers shirt begins to speak. The rest join him in reciting a prayer of some sort. Something about God and serenity. Accepting the things we can't change, finding courage to change. The rest is a blur, except for the vaguely religious tone to the proceedings. I've been told that this program is based on AA principles. That's fine, but it makes me nervous to have too much religion forced down my throat. The rebel in me has always been suspicious of organized religions. I don't want to be told how and what to think and feel. I realize I need to make some changes here and there, but I'm inherently mistrustful of authority. I'll try to be co-operative and keep my mouth shut for a while.

Obviously I have lost my way and need help making fundamental changes in my thinking, feelings, and behavior. I've been drifting away from my fellow man and God, whatever that is, for years. I've been unhappy for a long time. The pills obliterated some of the pain and loneliness. I'm having difficulty concentrating. Too much stimuli. My brain is starved for drugs.

"We've got someone new with us," the leader says, looking directly at me. I feel a blush coming on. Hot flash. The spotlight has shifted to me. Can I handle the pressure?

"Let's go around the circle and identify ourselves," he says, then starts with himself. His name is Paul. He's a coke addict and binge eater. In a week, he graduates from this establishment. He looks healthy and alert.

The rest of the men seem decent enough. Each gives his name, then identifies himself as addict or alcoholic. Two men in their early twenties appear shell-shocked, but they may be on medication. Getting to know these guys will be quite a project. Just remembering their names will be a herculean feat.

The familiar bearded guy has blonde and red hair. He gives his name as Gary. It clicks. I laugh a little. Gary looks at Paul and says we met earlier. It's the guy who told me not to leave when I first arrived.

He's more handsome up close. I'd estimate his age at somewhere around forty. I feel instantly attracted to him. He grins and picks his teeth with a toothpick. I try to listen as each man introduces himself, but my mind keeps returning to Gary. I can feel him looking at me from behind his sunglasses. He's wearing loose-fitting shorts, T-shirt with the name of a French sports manufacturer emblazoned across the back, and mirrored shades. Things are definitely looking up at Betty Ford. The men seem friendly. We all interlock arms and they shout this cheer.

"Two four six eight, after drugs and alcohol, do it right, McCallum Hall, HEY! Heeeerrreee'ssss Daniel."

Hearing my name shouted by these guys cheers me. I realize I'm smiling in spite of the agony in my legs. I've been initiated into their exclusive club.

We march en masse up the sidewalk toward the big building where I first checked in. Paul shows me the ropes in the dining hall: Where to pick up an orange plastic tray, how to slide said tray along the steel shelf, how politely ask the kitchen help for one of the hot entrees, how to serve yourself a drink, dessert, fresh fruits or veggies, and so forth. The food looks quite edible. I'm not really hungry, my stomach is upset from nerves and withdrawal. I get a hamburger, fries, and milk, then follow Paul to a table. He explains that we all eat together at every meal, at these same three tables.

We unload the plates and dishes of food onto one of the assigned tables, then deposit the empty trays on a rack near the soft drinks. Paul explains that we all have duties to perform each day. Would I mind taking responsibility for keeping McCallum's ice buckets full? "Sure," I say. "That would be fine with me."

He tells me the ice buckets are in the freezer at McCallum. I should bring one with me at breakfast or lunch, set it on the dishwasher's window in the alcove behind us before eating, and it'll be filled with chipped ice by the end of the meal. I try to listen and eat. I'm getting very tired. So much to remember. Ron sits with us, as does the Hispanic guy with a beard, Roberto. He's friendly, but his eyes slide side to side in a suspicious manner.

Ron is polite, intelligent, and casually mentions that he used to beat his wife after they got drunk together. Days of Wine and Roses material. Makes me feel like my addiction was a mere inconvenience.

Roberto talks about his first day here. He's an amphetamine and coke addict. He says he arrived at Betty Ford totally wasted. He couldn't eat for nearly two days, he was so wired on a powdered speed he snorted called crank.

He asks my age. "Thirty," I say. "You look so much younger," he exclaims. I don't feel like fielding comments on my appearance. I feel like I'm thirty going on seventy-five. My joints are getting more painful. My dining companions ask what my drug of choice is, was. I tell them about Percodan. They ask how many I took each day and what the high was like.

Roberto points out my roommate, Parker, sitting at the table behind us. He's the tall one wearing a turquoise shirt. He's very lanky and good-looking. He's probably close to my age. He has a bad-boy aura about him. He's very much the center of attention at his table.

"Watch out for Parker, Daniel," Roberto warns, his eyes shifting side to side.

"Why?"

"Don't let him bully you."

"Is he a jerk?"

"Not really. He can be bossy, at least with me. We have our ups and downs."

"How's your burger, Daniel?" Paul asks.

"It's fine, thanks."

"I've gained seven pounds since I checked in," Paul says. "Do you remember how skinny I was, Ron?"

"You looked dreadful, Paul. Emaciated." Paul does look thin around the cheeks.

"Look at these love handles," Roberto says with a conspiratorial wink, lifting his shirt and pinching his middle. He's a funny character. "Please, not at the table, Roberto. Where do you think we are?" Paul says.

"The pig sty," Roberto laughs, displaying his mouthful of chewed-up food for us to see.

"Stop this," Paul half-heartedly warns, laughing very hard. People at the other tables turn to watch us. I eat a few fries and enjoy being a spectator. I realize I'm having fun.

I get up and snag a refill of lemonade from the machine. I'm terribly thirsty. There are other groups eating lunch now. McCallum eats first, I guess. I like that.

The other McCallum men eat impressive quantities of food. I manage to consume half the burger and a few fries. Roberto says we arrive first at the cafeteria for all the meals. Breakfast is at six-fifty, lunch at eleven-fifty, and dinner at four-fifty. My teeth are aching from stress.

After lunch, Roberto and I walk back to McCallum and smoke cigarettes. There is no smoking indoors anywhere at Betty Ford. It's a smoke-free environment. I don't mind having mine outdoors.

I'm exceedingly tired. I thank Roberto for the talk and return to the office at McCallum. John shows me to my room. It's a double at the rear, with a sliding-glass door opening on a walled-in patio that runs along this end of building.

"The Swamp is next door," he says, hoisting my duffel up on the bed nearest the window. There are two desks opposite the beds. One is covered with books, papers, notebooks, and lots of pamphlets on cocaine addiction.

"What's The Swamp?" I ask, leaning against the wall.

"Like in MASH. It sleeps four guys."

"I like this just fine."

"There are closets over there and the bathroom is near the door."

"Okay."

"Oh, you're scheduled to get x-rayed over at Eisenhower this afternoon at one-fifteen.

"Oh, sure. I can remember that."

"How are you holding up?"

"I'm survivng. My body feels like it was thrown off a fast-moving train."

"Hold in there, buddy."

"Did you know I got a patch for the withdrawal?"

"No, I didn't."

"Wanna see it?"

"Sure."

I lift my shirt and expose the shoulder and patch. John examines it.

"Pretty interesting, Daniel."

"The nurse says it's filled with time-released medicine."

"Why don't you unpack your stuff?"

"Sure."

"A few other rules you should be aware of. We make our own beds every morning before breakfast. Try to keep things tidy. Dirty towels go in the hampers next to the laundry room. We have coin operated washers and dryers if you have clothes to clean."

I'm embarrassed to realize it's been ten years since I washed my own clothes. I always take mine to the dry cleaners. I've ironed a shirt maybe three times in my life. There are two dressers on either side of the beds.

My bed is stripped down to the mattress. I pull piles of hastily packed clothes from the duffel and dump them on the bed. I open my toiletry kit. He seems especially interested in that. I removed all contraband last night. He digs around and confiscates a tiny bottle of cologne. No alcohol is allowed. A desperate alcoholic might find it and swallow the contents. He removes a travel-sized tin of aspirin too.

Otherwise, I check out just fine. I begin transferring the clothes to the drawers of the empty dresser. John reminds me to be outside the main reception area at one-fifteen. "I'll be there," I assure him. He asks when I had a Percodan last.

"Yesterday afternoon at five," I say. "I've been trying to cut down somewhat."

"Good for you. If you feel crazed, come talk to me or any of the other counselors—or your peers. Don't isolate. These guys have been through the same things as you. They can help. You'll see. Good luck. Come talk to me anytime, okay?"

"Thanks, John." He pats me on the back, smiles, and exits.

He didn't swipe my paperbacks. One is "The Razor's Edge," the other is "Loving Yourself." I guess the material isn't considered subversive to their teachings.

The room is pleasantly air-conditioned. It's cool but not cold. I make the bed and lie down for a brief rest. My body is aching badly. Outside on the patio are several clumps of lantana bushes. They're covered with colorful yellow and red flowers. A hummingbird hovers nearby, feeding from of the tiny blossoms. A quiet invades my consciousness, gently neutralizing thoughts and resistance.

John wakes me quietly. It's after one-fifteen. I'm late for the x-ray appointment. I get up, grab sunglasses, quickly brush my teeth, and run over to the main building. A woman directs me outside. A golf cart with five people sits under a palm tree. Doesn't look like there's room for me. I smile and step closer. An older man, in his sixties or seventies, slides out from behind the steering wheel. He introduces himself as Bill. "Climb aboard, Dan," he says. Next to him sits a blonde woman and a black man with a beard. Another bearded man. I nod at them both.

In the back seat sits a middle-aged woman wearing huge sunglasses, green blouse, and black jeans. She looks familiar. She smiles and pats the space between her and an elderly woman with her arm in a cast. Everyone looks withdrawn and tense, except for perky Bill. I sit down where I'm told.

Bill starts the engine and we're off. He says we're getting the scenic tour today. He drives down a road, slowing to point out various buildings and sights. All I can think about is the pain in my legs. I need some drugs, I'm feeling terrible. The woman who looks familiar takes hold of my hand.

"I'm Amanda," she says. Of course, that's who she is. Amanda Douglas, the actress from all those great movies. She looks beautiful. I wonder how old she is now? Her career started in the Fifties and peaked in the Sixties. I haven't heard of her for years. I thought she was married and living in South America.

"I'm Daniel," I reply. "Nice to meet you."

"This is my first day, Daniel. I'm very nervous." She sounds totally assured. She became famous portaying difficult, emotional women in her films. It's hard to believe this talented woman is a slave to drugs or booze just like me.

"I'm nervous, too. I like the lake. It's a pleasant feature of the grounds." I don't know what I'm babbling about. I'm on some sort of automatic pilot.

"I love it, too. Look at the ducks." She points to a nearby willow tree that hangs over the water. The mother duck and six babies are visible. What happened to the seventh?

Bill careens around the end of the lake and over to the Eisenhower Hospital side of the property. Amanda asks what I'm in for.

"Percodan."

"Those are strong." She sighs. "I'm here for alcohol and sleeping pills."

We introduce ourselves to the lady with the pin in her arm. She's very quiet. She's probably withdrawing from pills or booze, too. None of us probably feels too fantastic today. Bill shouts "Last stop" and parks near the entrance.

"They're expecting us," he says, then hops out and leads us inside. We troop to an elevator that deposits us a floor below at the x-ray department. We sit in a waiting room, watching soap operas on a color T.V. that hangs in a corner.

After the x-rays, we're returned to Betty Ford. I walk back to McCallum and take another nap. John wakes me at four o'clock. I'm expected at the nurses' station. Part of my schedule the next ten days requires several daily visits to the nurses' station. They want to take my pulse and blood pressure to monitor my withdrawal. As I walk to the main building, I realize my step has no buoyancy, no lift to it. I feel like death warmed over.

The bearded man with the red eyes is sitting outside the nurses' room. We shake hands and introduce ourselves. He's Richard from Los Angeles. We're both in McCallum Hall. The conversation is uneasy. He looks really tired.

The nurse checks my vital signs and reminds me to return after dinner. They need to see me four times a day. I trudge back to my room. My roommate, Parker, is hunched over his desk. I saw him at lunch, but we never actually met.

"You're Daniel," he states. "Do you prefer Daniel or Dan or Danny?"

"Daniel's good," I say. His eyes are hazel.

He tells me he's a coke addict. A voice comes over the PA system. There's a speaker in the hall right outside our door.

"Five minutes to circle for dinner, gentlemen. Five minutes to circle," a man's voice says.

"Who's that talking?" I ask.

"Ronny baby. You smoke, right?"

"Yes, I do."

"Good. Can I bum a cigarette?"

"Sure." I remove several from the pack in my pocket. He shakes his head.

"Just one for now. I'm trying to cut down."

"Fine."

"Do you want to eat together?"

"Sure."

"Are you hungry?"

"Not really, but I should try to eat something."

"You're the Percodan addict, right?'

"Yes, I'm the Percodan addict."

"Someone told me you're going through withdrawal. What's that like?"

"A real nightmare. Lots of aches and mood swings. I hate to be dramatic, but it's like a part of me is dying. It sucks."

"That's one good thing about kicking cocaine, there's no physical withdrawal. The emotional withdrawal is a bitch, though."

"How long have you been here?"

"Fifteen days."

"Does it work, whatever it is they teach you?"

"Sure it does. The first week was the worst for me. If you need to talk about anything, just holler."

"I should tell you something," I say.

"Oh?"

"Well, just in case somebody says something. I'm gay."

"That's cool, Daniel. I have gay friends. Just don't get any funny ideas about me. I may be the sharpest-looking gent in this place, but I like girls." He laughs and squeezes my neck.

"Just kidding, Daniel, don't look so serious. Chill out. I'll keep an eye on you."

"Shouldn't we go?"

"Dinner, right. We'll sit together. The other boys will be so jealous," he whispers in a slightly camp tone of voice. His posturing amuses me.

At dinner I sit with Parker, Ron, Roberto, and a man that checked in three days ago, Lester. He's a big guy with a beard. Ron rushes through dinner, explaining that he's expecting a call from home at McCallum's pay phone in ten minutes. Lester asks Ron what his drug of choice is. "Booze, Lester. I'm a lush. See you all later." He leaves the table. Oh no, I forgot to get ice. I better go back and get the buckets. I don't want to appear irresponsible on my first day. I'll try to eat a little more, then take care of the ice.

Listening to Lester eat is an exercise in sheer terror. He breathes noisily as he consumes extra portions of the chicken and mashed potatoes. I feel sick to my stomach at the sight of his feeding. I've never seen someone eat niblet corn with such gusto. The urge to gag is strong. I excuse myself, explaining that I forgot to fill the ice buckets. Lester nods goodbye as he stuffs a roll in his gullet. I'll try to remember not to eat with him too often or I'll waste away to nothing. He's a natural appetite suppressant.

After fetching the ice, I meet another of our counselors, Randy. He's cordial on the surface. I sense a potent anger seething just under the surface. He asks me why I left the television show. I tell him. He responds more judgmentally than the other counselors. He says he's a recovered alcoholic. He doesn't seem like a happy person to me. He drills me with a whole battery of questions about my drug use, then asks me to fill out another questionnaire. Then I join the rest of the McCallum men outside for circle, the cheer, and a walk to the main building.

We sit in a small auditorium and listen to a lecture by a doctor. The topic is the cycle of the recovery process. He talks about overcoming denial and accepting our sickness. Seeking help is the next all-important step. The staff and fellow patients provide support and fellowship during this frightening period. Sobriety takes hard work. "We're all in this process together," he says. He's very upbeat, even irreverent at moments.

The lecture includes a few words about how each patient is given a master plan, devised by our counselor and the entire staff of Betty Ford. I'll be studied by doctors and mental health therapists, exercise people, everybody but Betty Ford herself, it seems. Mrs. Ford usually makes a personal appearance at least once a month. She talks to patients about her experiences in recovery. She's very much respected and appreciated here. The staff seem capable and responsible. I feel like I'm in good hands. They have a good reputation. I paid under ten thousand dollars, a bargain considering the tens of thousands I've spent on drugs the past few years.

After the lecture, we hang around the lounge, drinking decaf coffee, smoking cigarettes out on the patio, socializing. I walk to my room and lie down for a few minutes. My body feels wrung out. Parker follows.

"How's it going?" he asks.

"Fine," I say.

"Right," he says. "You look miserable, Daniel."

"Maybe I'm a little tired."

"Can I bum another smoke?"

"Of course."

We stand on the patio and smoke. The sound of the Beatles singing "Sexy Sadie" comes from the Swamp next door. Parker smirks and taps on their window. Gary opens the sliding glass.

"Yes?" he asks, winking at me.

"Turn that shit down, asshole," Parker says.

"Sure thing, asshole."

"How're you doing, Parker?"

"Fine. Do you know Daniel?"

"Yes, we've met. Hey."

"Hi, Gary."

"Is tonight AA or NA?" he says to Parker. I light up.

"Want one?" I ask Gary.

"No thanks, I've got my own. Just a second." He walks back inside and returns with a pack of Marlboros. I stand next to the flowering lantana and look up at the stars.

The desert is so clear. No bothersome city lights to ruin the view. The night is cool, but I feel chilled to the bone. I'll put on a sweater before the AA meeting at eight.

"AA or NA?" Gary asks.

"AA."

"Right. This your first time at an AA meeting, Daniel?"

"Yes, it is."

"How are you holding up?" he inquires in a gentler voice.

"I'll survive."

"Percodan is definitely bad news. Very addictive."

"Trés addictive man," Parker adds.

"What are you here for?" I say to Gary.

"Speed and coke."

"When did you arrive?"

"The same day as this butthead." He punches Parker's shoulder. Reminds me of high school. I sit on a chair and smoke my cigarette, trying to keep my eyes off Gary. He's handsome. I feel a definite spark between us, unless the withdrawal is playing havoc with my sexual radar as well as everything else.

"Don't be afraid," Gary says after Parker disappears around the wall.

"I'm not. Well, I'm a little scared."

"That's natural. I remember my first day, I was a disaster. What do you do on the outside, Daniel?"

"I'm an actor. I used to be an actor. I don't know what I am anymore. What about you?"

"I develop and sell real estate."

"Where?"

"Up in San Luis Obispo. That's north of Santa Barbara."

"It's beautiful there."

"I love it."

"Do you have a family?"

"I was divorced about a year ago. I have two kids that live with my ex."

"I'm sorry."

"Don't be, I'm not." We both laugh.

"What are your children's names?

"Matt and Niles."

"Great names. How old are they?"

"Six and eight."

"I bet they're nice. You're nice."

"So are you."

"Thanks Gary."

"Are you gay?" Ah-ha. His antennae are operational.

"Yes, I am."

"So am I."

"You said you were married. I guess that doesn't mean anything, really."

"Well, I'm bi-sexual."

"Really? That's all right with me." What is he trying to say? Is this a blatant pick-up or is he simply giving information?

"Thanks for telling me, Gary. It'll stay between us. I'm not a big gossip. Well, let's say I'm a discreet gossiper."

He laughs. "We'd better get going. I'd like to get to know you more, Daniel."

"I've got plenty of time," I say. He smiles and squeezes my arm as we exit the patio and walk to the front of McCallum Hall. The men form a circle, arms interlocked. I have Gary on one side and Roberto on the other. We repeat the serenity prayer again, then walk back to the lecture hall next to the cafeteria. McCallum sits in the left rear quadrant of the room. Paul sits on my right, Gary behind me, Parker to the left. I feel protected, yet emotionally naked. A woman begins the meeting by having us go around the room and introduce ourselves. "Hi. I'm Gary and I'm an addict" is a typical greeting. Amanda rises and says "My name is Amanda and I'm an alcoholic." There are no last names here.

When they get to me, I stand and say, "I'm Daniel and I'm an addict." My face blushes. I feel so exposed. I feel proud for speaking. It's a small step, but it feels good. The honesty of admitting I'm an addict to this roomful of people is a big relief.

A woman AA launches into her life story, sparing us no unseemly details. She shares the story of her disease. Her enslavement to the alcohol wrought car accidents, injuries, heartbreak, divorces, financial ruin, lost homes, ill health, the works. She's a study in triumph over alcoholism. Here she stands, looking very pulled together, sober for nine years now. Wow. That's a long time from where I sit.

The hard plastic seat hurts my butt. The withdrawal pains are escalating in intensity. I'll try not to think them.

After her time is up, a succession of patients gets up and speaks briefly, including Paul and Gary. Parker whispers that I don't have to get up until I want to.

I focus on the other patients and speakers and our common interest in healing. There's a spirit of brotherhood. I feel vibrations of warmth and caring.

My fear of withdrawal eases, allowing a part of me to open. Sitting in a room with eighty addicts and alcoholics is reassuring. I'm not alone here. This is a good place to be. I can learn things here.

The atmosphere is one of support and safety. One of the basic tenets of AA involves the anonymity of its members. That's why we share only first names.

After the meeting, I walk to the nurses' station for one of my mini check-ups. A new nurse is on duty. She's a friendly woman. She says she's a recovering person, just like me. My pulse and blood pressure are fine.

I tell her I feel terrible. She makes a notation on my chart to ask about scheduling a relaxation class with the exercise lady.

I return to my room. Parker is not around. I shower and dress in sweats. The room is too cool, my muscles hurt. I need heat. I step outside where it's warmer.

Alan and Ron are sitting at the other end of the patio. I light a cigarette. They call me over.

"Want some coffee, Daniel?"

"Sure." I hate coffee, but love the aroma.

"Well, we've got a secret to share with you. Betty Ford is a caffeine-free establishment, as you might have already heard, but we have some of the real stuff."

"No kidding?"

"Once an addict, always an addict. The pot's the one on the right in the lounge. Help yourself."

"Thanks, I will."

"Come back and join us, will you?"

"Sure. Thanks, Alan. Thanks, Ron." I walk to the lounge and get a cup of coffee from the prescribed pot. My first day and I'm already sneaking coffee. I feel shy, but force myself to be sociable.

I sit with Lester on the communal patio for a few minutes. He tells me about his years of smoking cocaine and drinking vodka. He doesn't say a word about the food. Maybe he'll face that problem after he conquers the drugs. He's interested in my career. Why did I quit the television show? I tell him I'm not exactly sure.

Roberto calls Lester from the swamp.

I return to the patio at the rear and smoke cigarettes.

At eleven I hit the sack. I wake again at one-thirty. The floor is quiet. My legs are cramping worse now. I take a hot shower, which helps relieve the soreness, then put my sweats back on and walk to the lounge. There's someone sitting in the office. It's Bill, the man who drove me to Eisenhower for x-rays. I wave hello and step outside.

My cigarette tastes stale. I perch on the patio wall that looks across the lake. The sprinklers over at Eisenhower hiss as they spray water across the expansive lawn. The full moon lights the water. The stars look amazing. The air smells clean. A peaceful night in the desert.

I ponder the idea of writing my parents a letter explaining where I am and why. I can hear them when they find out I'm in Betty Ford. They'll be humiliated that their boy is not only gay, but a dope fiend to boot. I don't care what they think anymore. It's time to look after myself and quit using their disapproval as an excuse for failure. Time to move on and become an adult. Enough of this teenage angst. I don't want to be a reincarnation of James Dean. I'd rather be a survivor, like Paul Newman.

A couple of cigarettes later, I return to my room. There's a lull in the leg aches, so I slip into bed and try to sleep. I feel tingly all over and stiff as a board. Head is heavy and dull. I hope I can make it through a week of these withdrawals.

Parker snores very softly. I listen to it for a few minutes, then clear my throat. No response. I clear it again, louder. He snorts and turns over. The wheezing stops. I close my eyes and smile. This is a little like summer camp. I try to remember a prayer I used to say as a kid. I stopped saying it after my brother died. It was written on a cup he was given one Christmas.

The prayer we recite during circle reminded me of it. I start to remember, "The truth, oh Lord, is yours to say. Give us love on every day and in every way. Give me strength." The air conditioning hums. I snuggle under the covers and let myself drop into sleep.

Chapter Six

I open my eyes. The left calf is gripped in a muscle spasm. I try to keep quiet, but a groan escapes. I sit up and knead the knotted ball of muscle in an effort to stop the pain.

Parker turns on the light next to his bed. I give a grim smile and apologize for waking him. The withdrawal pains are making me miserable. He nods, then gets out of bed and sits next to me. He massages the leg with his hands. We're both in our underwear.

"Hand me a cigarette, would you?" he asks. I reach over to my dresser and grab my smokes. I light two and insert one into his mouth. He gives me a dopey grin and rubs the sore leg.

"How's that?", he asks.

"Much better, thanks. What time is it?"

"Four-ten. You've interrupted my beauty sleep. How can you stand these menthols?"

"How can you stand those dirty-tasting regulars?"

"Habit, son."

"I like 'em."

"They're okay, if you're gay."

"Shut up." We both laugh. I like him. He's not such a show-off in private. During lunch and dinner, I got the impression he was trying hard to impress the world. He reminds me of Chance Wayne, the character Paul Newman played in "Sweet Bird of Youth." Always searching for respect, anxious to be loved and admired.

The pain subsides. I thank him. He stops, stands, and steps onto the patio. I hobble after him, my leg still constricted by the spasm, unable to accept my full body weight.

"That's a real bitch," he says, watching me hop on one leg. The calf is tender to the touch.

"They tell me a person can't die of Percodan withdrawal, but it feels horrible."

"Bummer. You're an actor, right?"

"Uh-huh. What do you do?"

"Limo driver by day, singer by night."

"Great. What do you sing, what sort of music?"

"Rock-and-Roll."

"Do you have a band?"

"Sure. Call ourselves Departure. We just cut a demo."

"Good luck."

"Thanks. You used to be on a series, right?"

"Right. Until about three years ago."

"What happened?"

"Oh, I don't know, really. I lost faith in myself and started taking drugs."

"Sounds like low self-esteem, Daniel. Everybody here suffers from that."

"Apparently. Anyway, thanks for the medical assistance. You're a nice guy, Parker."

"I don't know about that. Time will tell. Thanks for the smoke. Good night." He slaps my leg and rises. I avert my eyes from his underwear. Even in the throes of withdrawal, I'm checking out his body. I should probably feel ashamed of my lascivious thoughts, but I'm not.

"Good night, Parker."

"Don't burn the place down. I paid good money to stay in this dump."

"Right."

"Who's your caseworker?"

"I don't know yet."

"Everybody gets a counselor. Mine is Bill. You may have Molly. She'd like you."

"I don't know."

"If it's Molly you'll be sorry. No, just kidding. She's a pretty lady. 'Night."

My skull feels pierced by dozens of razor-sharp needles. We climb back into bed. My sinuses are draining from the withdrawal. I get up several times to blow my nose in the toilet. I can't stop tossing and turning, so I get up. I throw on my sweats again, grab the information sheets John gave me and walk to the main lounge. I sit at a table by myself.

A typed instruction sheet lists my duties and obligations during the next few days and weeks. I'm instructed to discuss my reasons for coming to Betty Ford with three McCallum men a day for the next three days.

This is the hard part. Baring my soul is not only difficult, but potentially painful. In the stack of papers is a blue notebook. I'm supposed to write a paragraph or two every day describing my feelings. Feelings? Yes, it says feelings. The notebooks are collected and read by the patient's caseworker each day. I'm to leave the notebook on a desk in the corner of the sunken area below the lounge. They call this room "The Pit."

I scan the paperwork for mention of my counselor. Parker was right. They've given me to Molly. There are pamphlets titled "First and Second Step Worksheets" that I'm to read, then complete the written question section at the back of each. They're due in two days, time. They don't joke around when they say this program is a lot of work. I don't mind. I want to know how to get better and these exercises are obviously designed for just that purpose.

The instruction sheet says I'll be meeting with Molly in the next day or two. She's still on vacation. Oh, that's rich. I'm up shit creek with these withdrawals and she's out of town. Big help. I may have to complain. Maybe I should have a male counselor. I'm feeling very cranky. Nothing would satisfy me at this moment. I'll reserve my opinion until I actually meet her. If Parker doesn't like her, I probably will. Maybe he's threatened by women in positions of authority. Some men are like that. I'm like that sometimes.

Mondays through Fridays I'll participate in twice daily group therapy sessions. I'm in the "B" group. I can't wait to be peeled like an onion. There's a pamphlet called "Low Esteem and You" I'm to read right away.

Staring at a blank page of the notebook, I decide to write a few friends and explain the details of my situation. I'm learning here that supportive friends and family are integral to recovery. That means sharing my problems with people who care about me. I need to take chances and reach-out.

I borrow a pen from the bulletin board across from the coffee pots and sit back down. The darkness outside is edging toward dawn. I have a feeling I may be able to successfully kick the Percodan. I feel safe here. I can focus my energies on feeling physically stronger and learning to stay sober without outside interference. I have hope. A window of opportunity and light opens inside my brain. I can choose to win or to lose. I have a choice.

The initial flush of courage got me through the doors to Betty Ford. I must make it. I'm too good to be polluting my body and brain over with chemicals. It must stop now.

I pen brief letters to Sally and my parents. I say I'm an addict, have been for years, and now I'm in Betty Ford trying to get well.

To my parents I add that I'm sorry for shunning them these last years, that their rejection of my sexuality was terribly painful. I don't blame them for our rift, I simply state that I didn't know how to be with them and protect myself. I've been running from pain for so long, yet I dwelt on every little pain and every hurt feeling. I write that I love them and hope we can mend our fences one day.

My temples throb with a craving for painkillers. The suffering isn't nearly as bad as when I was at home alone. Knowing the other rooms are home to countless addicts and alcoholics is reassuring. There is safety in numbers. I feel optimistic, even through the wretched withdrawal.

I finish the letters and pace. My legs are cramping again. It's hard to be still and serene when searing pain is shooting up your knee or thigh. It's a terror unlike any I've ever known. Truly horrific. I will endure the unpleasantness because I'll feel better in a few days. I will, I will, I will.

As the sun rises behind McCallum Hall, I walk to the lake and sit on the ground facing the desert. The grass is damp from dew or sprinklers. I knead my knee and calve. The pain is driving me insane. I smoke cigarette after cigarette. I'm tired but wired from my body's desperate longing for Percodan. My throat is parched.

I walk to the lounge for a can of juice. One of the senior patients rustles up a pot of coffee. I say "Hello." He looks like a marine. Big shoulders, square-cut jaw, square-cut everything. Blonde and well built. I can't remember his name. The juice tastes great. He smiles.

"Hello, Dan. How're you doing this morning?"

"Not too hot. I'm sorry, I can't remember your name. "

"Tom."

"I'm not feeling very well."

"I've heard. Pain pills, right?"

"Percodan."

"That's right. What are you here for?"

"Booze."

"Did you wonder if you'd be able to stick it out when you first got here?"

"Sure. I wanted my security bottle, man. Fuck everything else. I was mad all the time. Angry. Alcoholics have a lot of anger, Dan. It's scary when I think back on some of the things I did. The people I punched, the cars I totalled, I was a mess. Fucked over good."

"Sounds intense."

"But look at me now. I've reformed. Hard to believe, eh?"

"Good for you. I bet it was a lot of work."

"Damn right. Have you got your master plan yet?"

"No. My case worker's on vacation."

"Molly, huh?"

"Yes."

"I like her. Some guys think she's a ball buster because she's strong. She'll be good for you. She's smart."

"When the pain in my legs gets really bad, it makes me want to leave."

"So you can go home and get some drugs."

"Yes, that's right. I don't want to feel crazy like this, but I do."

"It's the drugs, Dan. Chill out while your body detoxes. You probably have a lot of that shit in your system."

"No doubt. When do you leave?"

"Saturday. Don't leave, Dan."

"I won't, really. I just panic and there's nobody to help."

"I was here. Didn't our talk help, even a little?"

"It helped a lot, Tom. Really. I go up and down like a seesaw."

"You're doing fine."

"Maybe it would be better to have some medication. Maybe I should check in to Eisenhower for a few days, until the withdrawal subsides."

"You'll make it, Dan. Don't leave, trust me. Just try to hang on and you'll feel better in a few days. How long does the withdrawal go on?"

"The worst should be over in a week or so. It gets easier after that, supposedly."

"You can do it. You are doing it. How long has it been since you took any drugs?"

"Well, it has been awhile. Almost thirty-six hours."

"That's an accomplishment, Dan. Give yourself credit. In a few hours, you'll be two days clean and sober. One day at a time is what they teach us. It works for me."

"I'm willing to give it a shot. I'm here, aren't I? It's damn difficult to be philosophical when my body feels like its being squeezed through a meat grinder."

"I don't want to sermonize, buddy, but hear this. A lot of what you feel is fear of the withdrawal pains, right?"

"That's probably very accurate. Yes."

He leans close, his face turned down in thought.

"Basically, the Big Book teaches us, me, you, that God, whoever that is, never gives us more than we can handle at any given time. You got through yesterday and that was impressive. Now, you'll find ways to make today endurable. You can deal with today, Dan. Just keep away from looking too far forward, it breaks the normal flow of living, seems to me."

"What do you do out in the world, Tom?"

"I'm a swimming instructor."

"I bet you're an excellent teacher."

"I'll be better sober. God, I could be a cranky bastard when I was drinking."

"Are you married?"

"Sure. My wife was here last week for family week."

"How did it go?"

"Good. Painful. We aired a lot of problems, but we're gonna try to work things out. It's tough. We've been together for eleven years. We might not make it to twelve. I'm not sure of anything anymore. I think I still love her, but we may not make it."

"Any kids?"

"One daughter."

"How old is she?"

"Seven."

"Sounds nice."

"They're the best."

"Thanks for talking."

"Anytime, buddy."

I return to the patio behind our room, where I pace and smoke. The sun is rising rapidly. If it weren't six a.m. I'd go get my shades. The wake-up time is six-fifteen. I don't know how they wake us up, but they do. It says so on my schedule. My stomach is begging for food. Scrambled eggs and bacon would be good. I wonder what they usually serve? Dinner wasn't the bland institutional gruel I had expected.

I'm in the shower jerking off when I hear someone open our door and announce "This is your wake-up call, girls." Parker moans "Kiss my ass." I continue stroking my dick with shampoo. The sexual stimulation is deliberate. I need to feel better. I fantasize having sex with Gary. Reaching orgasm makes me feel human again.

After breakfast, we meet outside McCallum for the meditation walk. This is a forty-five-minute segment before the nine a.m. lecture. We can walk or sit in the grass or meditate or whatever. The point is to get in touch with feelings. Most the guys change into shorts, T-shirt, and athletic shoes. I wear my jeans but change into a short-sleeved shirt. I prefer being warm to getting the chills. The sun is already blazing.

Paul hands me a small book and asks that I read the meditation passage. I flip through the pocket-size paperback. Each page features a day and a quote, followed by a longer paragraph. I scan today's entry to familiarize myself with the material.

The men of McCallum straggle in bit by bit. We draw into a circle and I begin to read. My voice feels craggy and sounds uneven initially, but settles into a steady, warm rhythm. I sound healthier than I feel. The words tumble out without any big effort.

"Is the inventor of the ear unable to hear? Is the creator of the eye unable to see?"

Psalms 94:9

It's hard to believe I'm reading quotes from the Bible to a bunch of strangers. I think of myself as religious, yet I don't sanction organized religion. I like to think for myself, usually. I believe there is some sort of spirit or force uniting and connecting all living creatures, not some super being floating around waving a magic wand and giving orders. My reading continues.

"The way we have been restored to our spiritual path is partly a mystery. Our willingness to accept mystery in our lives has taught us we are part of a larger whole. There is more at work in the world than we can ever know. Acceptance of the larger whole restores us to health.

We are not just separate beings with a private world. Our existence is a part of a larger process. We came into being with no control and no forethought on our own part. We arise from a past that no one remembers.

It was when we didn't see our place, as part of creation, that we were in the greatest pain and difficulty. Now each day, each hour, when we remember we are not in charge, and our will is not in control, we are restored again."

Wow! That certainly hits home. We all clasp arms and bodies. Paul, our granny, is on my right; Tom, the swimmer from last night, is on my left. I feel safe. The understanding and acceptance I feel, here in this place with these people, is undeniable. In unison, the men of McCallum repeat the words.

"God grant me the serenity to accept the things I cannot change, the courage to change the things I can, and the wisdom to know the difference."

When a patient graduates from the program, he or she is presented with a medallion inscribed with the serenity prayer on one side. I'll have to memorize the words soon.

I walk with Morris, who has been here for two weeks. He wears white over-sized shorts, white T, and black tennis shoes. He tells me he's seventy-two. This is his second stay in a rehab center. The last time was three years ago. A day after finishing that program, he was boozing again. It occurs to me as we speed-walk around the lake that the hole in my chest feels less hollow today. My legs, stomach, head, and arms may feel like shit, but I'm feeling fairly happy. It's weird.

We walk around the lake and talk. Morris has been married four times, twice to the same woman. His present wife is the third wife's sister. He lives outside Las Vegas. He enjoys gambling. He's worried about the beating his health has taken from alcohol. A series of blackouts in recent months scared the hell out of him, so here he is, getting sober at Betty Ford.

I decide to tell him about my Percodan addiction. "Tell three peers a day the circumstances that led you to seek treatment," my instructions state. Here goes.

I tell him about the drugs, the promiscuous sex, the falling-out with my family, trying to accept being gay, Howard, the death of my brother, the works. We cover a lot of ground fast.

He says I shouldn't worry too much about anything but the program. I should focus on getting well. He tells me I'm a fine young man who lost his way. He thinks I'll make it. We circle the entire property. There is an established walking path that rings the compound of buildings, the lake, and runs along the outer perimeter of Eisenhower Hospital. There are many flowering shrubs and trees. As Morris and I approach the parking lot on our second lap, he points to a bird on the lawn. It's a roadrunner.

Its long legs facilitate a speedy sprint across the wet grass. We laugh as it shoots out of sight.

We pass an out-of-breath Amanda and another woman from her dorm. Everyone says hello. We're not supposed to fraternize, so we continue our walk. He tells me I'm the first gay man he's ever talked to. I remind him that most gay people are masters at blending in with straights. He's probably spent time with gays and didn't know it. He says I'm probably right, he never really thought about it before.

We see the mother duck and her brood. There are only five ducklings today. Where are the babies disappearing to? I ask Morris if he has a theory about the missing ducklings. He's heard that several huge fish live in the lake. They nab the ducks quite easily. Supposedly Roberto witnessed a duckling murder a few days ago. The exercise relieves the muscle pain in my legs.

The day is a constant buzz of activities. Lectures, personality tests instead of group therapy, lunch, lecture, more paperwork instead of afternoon group therapy, exercise, dinner, another lecture, the daily AA meeting. By nine o'clock, I'm a zombie. I've gone two days without a single Percodan and haven't climbed a wall yet.

I've discussed my reasons for coming to Betty Ford with more than the prescribed three men. I've talked things over with Alan, Ron, Morris, Parker, and Gary since I arrived. Soon I'll have told everybody. These guys are all so supportive that it makes me forget my nervousness.

The newness of everything is overwhelming at times, but I'm managing. The male nurse who took my vital signs after dinner said the patch should be operational by now. I hope so. I feel like shit.

I'm trying to avoid talking with Gary much. He's too attractive. I feel too shaky. For now, the less we interact, the less chance there is for sparks to fly.

At dinner, which was a delicious goulash dish and chicken, we sat at different tables. While eating, I looked over and caught him staring directly at me. He grinned. I felt excited. Heat rushed into my face and my heart raced. Without the drugs, everything feels bigger.

I sit on the patio off the lounge and socialize with the hard-core caffeine junkies: Alan, Ron, Gary, and Morris. I sip a mug of the bitter-tasting brew and marvel at its popularity. It tastes awful. Sure, the caffeine provides a boost, but I can't drink much. It overstimulates me. Speed and cocaine were always on the trying side. Painkillers zipped me awake, but didn't make me wired and tense.

This brotherhood of addicts provides a surprisingly effective core of support and understanding. If I were at home quitting the pills on my own, I'd be half crazed.

I dump the coffee down the drain and return to my room. Parker is hunched over his desk, writing a paper on his history of drug abuse. He asks if I'll proofread it for him. "Sure," I say, perplexed that he's looking to me for academic assistance.

"I'm not exactly a model student," I say.

"You're probably smarter than the rest of these goons," he says flatly.

"Well, I don't know." I feel flattered. I know I'm intelligent, but I was always bored in school. After I quit the show three years ago, I devoted most of my time to reading. I bought and read hundreds of books. Biographies on dozens of historical figures like Napoleon, the works of Hemingway, the short stories of F. Scott Fitzgerald, the plays of Tennessee Williams, and countless novels. I took drugs and read books. It was nuts. I was searching for answers to my problems on those pages. I learned plenty, and found many truths, but enlightenment eluded me. I was enriched, but still a hopeless addict. I didn't know how to position myself get happy. The books couldn't teach me that.

"Oh," he says, turning around. "I was thinking about your leg cramps. Maybe you should eat a couple bananas a day until it improves. The potassium might help."

"That's an excellent suggestion. Thanks. I'll try that."

"As a matter of fact, I brought you something." He says, removing a banana from his desk drawer.

"I thought we weren't supposed to take food from the cafeteria." I sound like Pollyanna.

"No, we're not SUPPOSED to, so what?"

"Thanks, Parker."

"Anytime, guy."

I scan his paper and find several errors. I can sense he feels a little threatened accepting my corrections, but he behaves graciously. He thanks me and grimaces, explaining that he doesn't want to rewrite the paper, he feels lazy tonight.

I read the pamphlet on the first two steps of AA. The first step says:

"We admitted we were powerless over alcohol—that our lives had become unmanageable."

That certainly applies to me, no question. Dangerously out of control. At the AA meeting tonight, one of the patients said the principles of AA were her higher power for now. That makes sense to me. Someone else said it was key to recovery to find a higher power to visualize, whether it's a doorknob or the kitchen sink.

The second step of AA says:

"We came to believe that a power greater than ourselves could restore us to sanity."

That sounds nice. I've played my own God for so long its hard to give up the reins of power. I read on. The third step says:

"We made a decision to turn our will and our lives over to the care of God as we understood him."

"As we understood him" is underlined. So, it's open to interpretation. I like that. Hmmn. This one's tricky. It sounds awfully similar to the second step. I'm reticent to fully turn my life and inner self over to anything just yet. I'll have to think about this some more.

In a sense I already did the third step when I finally sought help and walked through the doors of Betty Ford. I put my trust in getting well by whatever means will work. The God I was raised with abandoned me when my brother died. That was a betrayal I've never forgotten. I took responsibility for my own destiny then, cynical of anyone or anything that promised easy answers. I'd like to trust life more. For now, my higher power will be this program.

I decide out of the blue to write a letter to Howard explaining my situation. I should have told him long ago, but I was too ashamed. He deserves to know why I broke up with him. I was such an asshole. He may despise me when he gets the letter. I hope he'll forgive me. I'd like us to renew our friendship. I miss him. I think about him every day. It's weird. Perhaps my feelings for him were deeper than I realized. With all the drugs it was hard to be sure. Maybe I really loved him.

An iciness invades my loins. I'm surprised at how well I've managed to cope. My spirits are good, all things considered. I throw on jeans, thick cotton sweater, amd white athletic socks, then climb under the covers to finish the letter.

Parker is still hunched over his desk when I turn out my light. I say goodnight. He asks how I'm doing. "Okay," I say. "Let me know if you need help during the night," he says, then turns back to his homework.

I wake in a cold sweat at three-thirty. Damn. Four lousy hours of sleep. How will I survive if I'm deprived of adequate sleep?

My legs are hard as tree trunks. My dreams were upsetting, I remember searching for Percodan. Even in my sleep, I crave the drugs. At least I didn't swallow any pills in the dream.

Today is Saturday. I retrieve my schedule from the desk and walk to the bathroom. I sit on the toilet lid and read. No group therapy today. The television in the pit is turned on, after AA. Pool exercise in the afternoon. Meals are served at the usual times. Tomorrow is our one free day, as well as visitor's day. Thank God I can't have guests until next Sunday. I'm barely able to face the patients, let alone outsiders.

I shower and walk my letters to the office. Then I sit on the big patio and smoke a cigarette. Someone from another hall is feeding the ducks on the grass next to the lake. I count four babies. And then there were none.

After lunch I meet with a staff psychologist. He's a dour soul, ear-to-ear seriousness, humorless in the extreme. He doesn't act like he wants to be in the same room with me, let alone interview and evaluate my mental health. Poor guy. He's working on a Saturday. I am friendly. I won't allow him to spoil my halfway decent mood. Hell, I'm the one in withdrawal. He should be beaming with smiles and good will, the butthead.

He asks me questions about David, his death, what it's like being a twin, my parents, being gay, my drug dependency. I emphasize my enthusiasm for making a success of this rehab program. I give completely honest answers, no mattter how painful or awkward the truth seems.

He asks why I stopped acting. I think it over for a few seconds, acting, for me, was a compulsion, a need and ability to process emotions in front of an audience. You could dispaly happiness, sadness, boredom, all the emotions that swirled inside of me in real life, and get paid for it. Pretty amazing. Acting made me feel vital.

I take a deep breath. There's a simple answer right in front of me. The reason I quit working was because I was afraid. I think of the list of "feeling" words John gave me when I checked in. Afraid means fear. "I was fearful of everything," I say. "I felt very bad about myself. So, I quit working and took drugs."

For an hour he probes. I coax the truth out of myself, break down some walls, pry open a few self-defense mechanisms. He seems particularly interested in my childhood and David. He jots on his pad. At the end of an hour, we shake hands and he wishes me luck. I feel relieved.

At three the men of McCallum troop over to the pool, wearing swimming trunks. Gary looks good in his blue and white shorts and black sunglasses. I feel very scrawny. I know I look fine, but the withdrawal makes me feel wrung out.

Lester looks very pasty and fat. He must be self-conscious about his weight problem. He's wearing a baggy T-shirt and floppy shorts. His neck is very wide. I saw him eating a Twinkie in the laundry room last night. I'm going to be nice to him and get over my hang-up about overweight people.

I walk with Lester the last twenty yards to the outdoor pool area. He asks if I want any of his sunscreen. "No thanks, Lester. I want to get as much color as possible," I say.

All seventeen of us climb into the shallow pool. We perform warm-up exercises right in the water. Body bends and stretches are followed by running in a circle clockwise around the pool. Dashing through waist-deep water isn't easy. Many of the guys struggle. I have plenty of energy. The activity warms my legs.

The pool is relatively small. I would have thought an Olympic-sized job would have been more in order. Turning and running the opposite direction, my calves begin to throb. A charley horse grips the right foot. A ball of pain implodes in the foot. Sharp rays of pain shoot up my leg. I'm paralyzed. I try not to panic, stifling the urge to scream bloody murder while scrambling out of the water. I sit on the top step and massage the damn knot. My sunglasses drop into the pool.

I try to pretend the pain isn't bad. The female instructor asks what's going on. I explain that I'm in withdrawal. She nods and asks if she can help. "Thanks, but I'll be fine," I lie. It's time I learned to grit my teeth and live with a little pain.

Gary swims over. He retrieves my shades and asks how I'm doing. I say I'll be fine, it's just a silly leg cramp. He has a good physique. His chest is well developed. He must lift weights. He leans close, slides the shades onto my nose, then rejoins the group running around the pool. Pool volleyball begins.

I wait a few minutes and rejoin the game. The teams are A group versus B group. When it's my turn to serve, I totally lose co-ordination, slamming the ball way up in the air and over the fence.

Roberto hoists himself out of the water and fetches the damn ball. I feel totally lame. I have little control over my body. Either I hit the ball too hard or too weakly. Daniel the spaz.

By nine p.m. we're free agents for the night. I sit on a couch in the pit between Lester and Gary. About ten of us are gathered around the television set, watching an episode of "The Golden Girls." I've been drug-free for over three days now. I try not to press my knee against Gary's. Lester is breathing very heavily between guffaws. He sounds like he's snoring.

The antics of the geriatric girls make us laugh. I've been enjoying myself a lot for someone in the throes of withdrawal. The laughter is a release. My arms hurt. All day I've experienced a series of grim little headaches. I've had some nasty stomach cramping, too.

After the show, I join Ron and Alan outside on the patio. Alan smokes constantly. He lives in Atlanta with his wife and teenage son. He's a successful import/export businessman and travels around the world constantly. This is his second rehab effort. His drug of choice is gin.

Ron is a doctor from Des Moines. He and his wife are separated, but they're attempting a reconciliation. He has a girlfriend the wife doesn't know about. They have two sons in college. Ron is trying to quit using alcohol and drugs after twenty-five years of heavy use.

He asks me to take a walk. We circle the lake as he tells me his life story. He grew up dirt poor and suffered physical abuse at the hands of his alcoholic father. When he was ten, his mother committed suicide. Ron found her dead body.

Because of a serious stutter and shyness, he was thought to be mentally retarded until he was a teenager. His family treated him abysmally. In high school he discovered his intellectual abilities and excelled. He escaped his poor family with a scholarship to a fine college. That's when he began to drink socially.

He found he couldn't drink just a little. It was either total abstinence or alcoholic annihilation.

After college, a hitch in the army, and med school, he met his wife, married, and tried to settle down. He drank less for a few years, but fell off the wagon a couple of years ago. In recent months, he began experiencing regular blackouts when he was drunk, including one behind the wheel of a car. Luckily, he didn't cause bodily harm to himself or anyone else. He came to Betty Ford to save his health, his career, and his sanity.

I tell him my story as we sit next to the lake. I smoke cigarettes and talk. He's very understanding and accepting. He's not at all shocked by my sexuality. He says I'm a very special man and should never feel ashamed of anything. Sharing our pasts bonds us. I feel close to him. It's funny, telling a virtual stranger things I couldn't share with people I've known for years. Go figure.

I'm drained after our talk. I go to my room and brush my teeth. My body feels like a truck has run over it. I undress and climb under the covers. Parker is nowhere to be seen, so I masturbate in the dark. The release relaxes me.

The moon casts a dim glow across the bushes outside my window. I can hear a wind whistle through the palm trees. The distant sound of men's voices reminds me I'm in Betty Ford.

Chapter Seven

I wake in a total panic. Legs are knotted, arms feel prickly and heavy, head is pounding. I feel empty inside. The time is a few minutes past four. It's Sunday morning. Parker is asleep, snoring softly. I dress and walk to the nurses' station.

The male nurse takes my pulse and blood pressure. He says my blood pressure is low. I explain how terrible I feel. He asks how the patch on my shoulder is working. I tell him it's impossible to tell. He gives me a pill of the same substance that's inside the patch: Clonidine. I feel so low.

He tries to make me feel better by saying this is probably the very worst of the withdrawal. In a day or two I'll be significantly improved. Right. It's hard to believe I'll ever feel decent. I'm being cracked open like a nut.

I return to my freezing room, fetch my cigarettes and tiptoe to the patio for a smoke. My brain is buzzing. My entire being screams for relief. Without the painkillers, I feel everything.

I take a long, hot shower. The warmth of the water soothes the raw nerve endings and sore muscles. The withdrawal medication might be helping, it's hard to tell. My stomach is growling for food, but I have no appetite.

Dried and redressed, I move to the lounge. The place is quiet. The man who drove me to Eisenhower Hospital for x-rays a few days ago, is sitting in the office. We chat for a few minutes. He asks how the withdrawal is going. "Badly," I say. "Hang in there, Dan. Hang in there."

I grab an apple from the fridge and walk to the lake. The sun is rising behind McCallum. The temperature is slightly cool. I sit on a bench under one of the trees and stare into the water. Are there really gigantic fish in there?

I hear the doors from the lounge squeak. Footsteps. I turn. It's Richard. Parker told me that he's really Richard Montel, a popular singer. His records are usually love songs and romantic ballads.

He's headed this way. We've barely spoken since our x-rays excursion the first day. We say hello every day, but that's it. I've been watching him. He's very guarded most of the time. I like him, but sense he's having a more difficult time here than I am, if that's possible. He's wearing black sweat pants and an oversized red sweater.

"Hey, Daniel," he says. "How're you doing?"

"I feel lousy, but happy," I reply, simulating cheerfulness with a phony smile.

He sits next to me and lights one of his long European cigarettes with a heavy gold lighter.

"Nice lighter," I say to keep the conversation rolling. "I woke-up feeling rotten. I'm better now."

"I can't stop thinking about getting high."

"You used coke, right?"

"Right." Parker told me that cocaine is the hardest drug to quit emotionally."

"He's probably right, Daniel"

"You cut off your beard, Richard. That's what's different about you. You look great. You've got a handsome face, it was a shame to hide it, in my opinion."

"Thanks, Daniel. You're a sweet guy. So you're a Codeine freak?"

"That's me. Codeine and Percodan freak. Percodan was my drug of choice."

"Serious medicine. I took Percodan after a root canal surgery a few months back. They made me dizzy."

"How many did you take a day?" he says, blowing smoke out of his nostrils.

"Oh, it varied. The last year or so I was up to ten to fifteen a day. Some days I took less or combined them with Codeine and Valium. The most Percodan I ever took was eighteen a day."

"Did you worry about OD-ing?" I take out a cigarette. He lights it. "Sure," I say. "At times I worried that I was going too far, but I knew I had a high tolerance."

"No offense," he says, "but you're not exactly a big guy. I'm surprised you could take that much."

"I managed. Tell me about your addiction, Richard. Do you prefer Richie or Richard?"

"Richie to my friends. Richard to the world. Well, Daniel, let's see. About a year ago I was working on a record down in Atlanta. I'd been using drugs for years. When we were making this record, I had just started smoking it."

"I freebased coke once and thought I was having a heart attack. It's too intense, too speedy. It frightened me." I say.

"I hear you, I hear you. I would smoke before working in the morning, then call in sick because I was too high to sing. It was crazy, Daniel, crazy. So one night I'm driving back to this house I was renting. I ran a yellow light and two cops pulled me over. To make a long story short, I got busted."

"For what?"

"Possession of several grams of cocaine and an open bottle of vodka. They hauled my ass to jail. I phoned my manager. He flew out from L.A. and bailed my ass out of that jail."

"What a nightmare."

"There were stories in the papers about my arrest, it was embarrassing. My lawyers got the charges dropped because of technicalities."

"Did you try to quit using afterwards?"

"Not really. I went into a drug rehab program, mostly to shut up my family and manager and agent and the record company goons, but my heart wasn't in it."

"At the AA meeting last night they were saying how addicts and alcoholics usually have to hit rock bottom before they seek help."

"That makes sense to me," he exclaims.

"I used to watch you on Living and Loving. You're a good actor. What's going on with your career?" He stubs out his cigarette and immediately lights another as he waits for my answer.

"Oh, I freaked out. I couldn't handle the attention and success. I quit after two-and-a-half seasons and devoted myself to drugs. "

"I hear you, man. I love singing and making records, but I hate the constant attention."

"Do you think about using a lot."

"All the time, Daniel. It's a bitch. I keep telling myself to hold out for another day."

"What prompted you to go into rehab again?"

"I finally realized drugs were making my life miserable. I have no real friends anymore, just people I get high with. I'm almost forty and I have no personal life outside of smoking coke."

"If you've chosen to come here of your own free will, that's a big step, right?"

"I guess. The problem is, I don't really want to stop one hundred percent. I like getting high. We'll see how that goes. How did you get your ass to Betty Ford?"

"Because the pills were running my life. I haven't worked in three years, I don't even speak to my parents anymore. My life is shit. I have no self respect when I'm getting stoned every minute of every day. I was obsessed with the pills. I've wasted enough time with drugs. I'd like to do something with my life again."

"We're twisted souls," he says, looking into the distance.

"Do you want to go to breakfast? I'm starved."

"No breakfast for me today, babe. I'd like to lose lose a few pounds while I'm here." he says, pinching a love handle.

"Why don't we eat brunch together?" He lights another cigarette.

"Sure." His eyes are clearer than two days ago. He's actually very handsome up close, particularly without the facial hair. He's very accessible and friendly. I like the way he uses his eyes and laughs. He's pleasant.

We climb the hill back to McCallum. I carry the apple core in my right hand. I noticed that my hands trembled when Richie lit my cigarette.

"It's gonna be hot today," he says. "Hey, after brunch we could get some sun on my patio." "All right." I reply. " Sounds like a good plan." We cross the patio and enter our dorm. I toss the apple core towards the trash canister and score a direct hit. Bingo.

The clonidine pill the nurse gave me is easing the withdrawal pains significantly. After the chat with Richie, I go to the cafeteria and eat some oatmeal sprinkled with raisins.

The tables are mostly empty. I sit by myself. Amanda enters with a thin, dark-haired girl I haven't seen before. They approach my table. We exchange good mornings. Amanda introduces me to her new roommate. I tell her she's come to the right place. Amanda looks a little careworn. They head for the food line.

After finishing my oatmeal, I walk back to the lake and search for the ducks. They're nowhere to be seen. I feel tired, but upbeat. Tonight will mark four days without a single Percodan. I return to my room and lie down. Parker is still sleeping. Unable to go back to sleep, I lie in bed and read the first and second step worksheets.

At noon there's a loud rap on the door. I stop in the doorway. Richie comes in, sees Parker asleep, and quietly moves towards me. He asks if I'm ready to eat.

"What's up?" Parker moans, throwing the covers back, revealing his face. "Morning," Richie says.

"Hello boys," "I'll meet you in the hall in five minutes," Richie says, then reaches down and squeezes Parker's ankle. "See you later, sleeping beauty."

"Bye, doll," Parker lisps. Richie and I laugh. "See you in five," I say, crossing to my desk. Richie slips out.

"Daniel?"

"Yes, Parker?"

"Still love me the best?"

"Of course I do. Don't we sleep together?"

"But not in the same bed.."

"Not yet..."

"Shut up," he yelps and tosses a pillow at me. I enjoy playing with him. I wonder if he's a repressed homosexual? He certainly does a lot of mincing around, talking and playing the part of an effete gay. Maybe this is his way of making me feel comfortable and accepted.

Brunch is buffet style. One of the cooks carves roast beef and turkey. Richie and I slide our trays down the racks. I serve myself mashed potatoes, broccoli, corn, and a pile of sliced turkey. My refreshment is the usual: a big glass of lemonade with crushed ice. Outside the air-conditioned dining hall, the sun is baking the desert. The temperature is in the nineties again.

As we're moving down the line, Richie tells me a storm is expected tonight or tomorrow. A couple of tables are occupied by patients from other halls and their guests. Unlike the rest of the week, the seating is open. Tables are already set with placemats, linen, and eating utensils. Betty Ford is certainly putting its very best foot forward today.

Lester appears a few minutes after we sit down. I start to chew more rapidly. As Lester is waiting for the beef, he takes a wad of dollar bills from his pocket and sniffs. I scrunch my face at Richie. He asks what's wrong. I nod towards Lester.

"What in the hell is that boy doing?"

"Smelling his money."

"What's he gonna do, eat it?"

"That's what I'm watching for."

"How sick. Look, he put the bills back in his pocket," Richie says, cutting off a bite of turkey and inserting it in his mouth. He has very respectable manners. Lester pushes his tray down the line, loading it with goodies. I eat faster and faster. I know that when he arrives, I'll be able to eat very little, if at all.

Lester sets his tray on the table and begins to unload his meal. "Hi, guys," he says. "Hey, Lester, how's it going?" Richie says. I give a low-wattage smile and chew on a slice of beef. I don't have the energy to pretend great joy.

"What's going on?" I mumble. Lester has a big plate piled with beef, turkey, veggies, and mashed potatoes swimming in gravy. There is a side plate crammed with white bread and another with two pieces of chocolate cake. Seeing this grotesque amount of food makes me want to gag.

Lester sits and begins to gorge himself. Between bites, he tells us he's expecting his family at two. Richie asks if they'll be wanting to eat. Lester isn't sure but says he can always come back with them and have seconds. I'd like to say he's already got seconds and thirds in front of him, but stop myself.

He's wearing a nice-looking pink sport shirt that is two sizes too small and extremely tight-fitting blue slacks. He looks like a stuffed sausage. I'm learning that food can be a drug too. I have to remind myself that I'm no better than he.

Lester quizzes Richie about his career. He listens to all of Richard's records and won't shut up. Richie is gracious and kind, answering the questions patiently. I push my plate away and turn toward the window. I don't feel up to this.

The cafeteria is half filled by the time we're done eating. We wait for

Lester to finish, then the three of us leave. Lester asks what we're doing this afternoon.

Richie tells him we'll be tanning on his patio. Lester says his mother is a big fan of Richard's. Would he mind meeting her at some point? This sort of behavior isn't encouraged by the staff, I've been told. Celebrities are to be treated the same as everybody else . Richard tells Lester he'll think about it.

The communal areas of McCallum are crawling with visitors by two o'clock. Lying on the white towels we're issued, Richie and I sun ourselves on the grassy courtyard outside his room. It's surrounded by a wall covered with bougainvillea, except for a slim opening onto the lawn. There is a definite sense of privacy. Richie and his roommate, Fred from Albuquerque, share their patio with Morris and Dave in the room next door.

Morris and I are buddies, but I've only met Dave in passing. He's about nineteen and nice, but dense. I catch him looking at me quite a bit. I think he's intrigued by my faded celebrity and sexual persuasion.

Visitors enter the main building, sign in, then someone calls our office here at McCallum. A counselor then pages us over the PA system. The patient walks up to the main lobby and escorts the guest back to McCallum, or to the cafeteria for brunch, or around the grounds. The private rooms are strictly off limits, thank God.

I have on a pair of red UCLA shorts Lance gave me. Richie wears a black string bikini. He looks like he belongs on the French Riviera. He's a large man, standing six feet tall, weighing about two hundred pounds, with broad shoulders, thick legs, muscular arms, and a round, tight ass. A long silver earring hangs from his left earlobe.

His roommate has a portable cassette player that we listen to. The radio station plays a motley assortment of classic rock, pop, and R and B. I begin to relax. The sun and music soothe me. The withdrawal pains ease to a dull ache. The sky is cloudless and deep blue. The mountains are brown with wisps of white snow along the upper ridges. I turn over onto my stomach.

A car cruises up the drive on the other side of the wall. More visitors. A song of Richie's comes on the radio. He sighs. I laugh.

"Love will come, baby...try to light a fire, baby...kiss me, hold me, baby..," his voice sings in an intimate, knowing voice. "Lord, turn that thing off, save me," he kvetches.

"Oh, hush. I like this song. You have a wonderful voice."

"Thanks, babe." he says softly.

The music lulls me into sleep.

Lester's voice wakes me.

"Hi, guys. What's up?"

"Hey, Lester." Richie says. I pretend to be asleep.

78

"My mom and sister are here."

"Good. You having a nice visit?" Richie sounds so even and kind.

"They brought cookies and ice cream. Want some?"

"Maybe later."

Lester is trying to lure Richie out into the lounge to meet his family.

"I'd really like my mother and sister to meet you," he pleads.

"I'll come out and say hello in about fifteen minutes, how's that?"

"Great. Thanks Richard. I'll save you some cookies. Bring Daniel if he's awake then. My sister has a big crush on him. She was really excited to hear we're all in rehab together."

"See you in a few minutes."

"Okay, Lester."

I hear him open and close the door near the laundry room. Richie breathes deeply and coughs, then lights a cigarette.

"Save me some cookies," I whisper.

"I thought you were asleep."

"I was. Lester woke me."

"So you heard the rest. Want to meet his family?"

"Gee, I think I'll pass."

"Oh, come on, Daniel. We can brave Lester's family together."

"Sure. Maybe he'll give me some cookies, too," I say in a deliberately insinuating tone.

"Shut up. Ten minutes, okay?"

"Ten minutes to Lester. Okay. Count me in."

Lester's mother is on the hefty side, but his sister is positively skinny. We sit outside on the patio for a few minutes and make small talk. Lester's mother has brought a medium-size crate of cookies. The wooden box has layers and layers of thick, chunky chocolate chip cookies. I eat two, then get a glass of water inside.

A second crate of cookies sits on the counter near the coffee. Taped to the side is a sign saying "Help Yourself," I don't mind if I do. I wrap half a dozen in a sheet of paper towel, then stash the baked goods in my room before returning to my surrogate visitors.

Lester's sister gushes on and on about how much she loved me on the television show. She asks when I'll be on TV or the movies again. I politely tell her I haven't made any plans, but I hope to work again soon. My head is throbbing.

I excuse myself and walk inside to the pit. The TV is turned on, but nobody is watching. I change channels till I find "I Love Lucy." Stretched across one of the couches, I watch an episode where Lucy and Ethel hitchhike to Florida with an eccentric old woman. It's hysterical. Richie joins me in time to see Lucy and Ethel changing a tire. I laugh so hard my side aches.

Gary appears near the end of the show with his sons, Matt and Elliott.

They're very cute kids. A shade withdrawn perhaps, which is understandable under the circumstances.

He introduces us to the boys. Matt is seven, Elliott is five. Gary beams in their presence. Both are sandy-haired and toothy. Matt is studied, quiet. Elliott is a charmer, a born manipulator. Elliott gravitates to Richie, who offers him a seat for the next sitcom. Gary and I exchange sly smiles.

"Stop it," I say.

"What?" he says, grinning.

"Flirting," I whisper. Matt is looking through a magazine on a table in the pit. Gary and I stand on the steps to the lounge.

"You love it, Daniel."

"Your kids are here. Behave."

"You're so fucking cute."

"I have to get my kids outside. Their mother is leaving. I wanted you to meet them."

"Thanks, Gary. They're cute boys."

I watch them leave. A woman with short brown hair, long legs, a tight smile, and very dark sunglasses meets them on the other side of the doors. Maybe he's hopelessly hung up on her. Time will tell.

The leg pains are still driving me crazy. I try to keep distracted, but it's difficult. My fuse is short. I tell Richard I'll see him later, I need a nap.

At six we have the patients-only AA meeting. It takes place in the cafeteria with Amanda's dorm. Our granny, Paul, leads the meeting with Dolores, the granny of Amanda's group. When I enter, she waves me over.

"Let's fraternize," she says. "I saved you a seat." I force a smile and sit next to her. I feel dreadful. My head is gripped in an invisible vise and my limbs feel sore.

I try to be friendly. Amanda introduces me to George, another new arrival at Betty Ford. We shake hands. I welcome him. He asks why I'm here.

"I'm addicted to Percodan." It gets easier and easier to say with repetition. George's palm is sweaty and cold. The meeting begins. We go around the room introducing ourselves and listing our addictions. It's an effective ice breaker. We're all united in our addictions.

We take turns reading from the big book out loud. I try to pay close attention, but my concentration is shot. When my turn comes, I manage to read a paragraph fairly well.

One of the McCallum men is leaving Betty Ford tomorrow. Henry from San Jose. I've spent time talking to him. I told him my reasons for being here on the second day.

He's a pleasant, middle-aged man with a wife and kids. He came to Betty Ford to end his drinking binges. He seems very together the few days I've observed him.

After the meeting, we return to McCallum. Dinner is a plate of sandwiches from the kitchen. Paul takes orders for pizzas. Lester orders a deluxe large. Tom asks if I'll split a medium pepperoni with him. I say "Sure."

We gather in the pit and watch more sitcoms. My favorite is "Married With Children." The family is hilariously trashy and tacky. Tom sits on my left, Richie sits in a chair on the right. He squeezes my arm during particularly outrageous moments.

At nine, the TV is turned off for the burning of Henry. Everyone gathers in the pit. The couches and chairs are pulled into a circle. Paul sits on the center sofa and holds a tape recorder. He passes around copies of paper. On it are written the words to Jimmy Buffett's "Margaritaville." Henry sits beside him. The order of seats is strictly regulated. The A group fans out to the left of Henry, the B group to the right. The patients with the greatest seniority sit closest to Henry and Paul. As the junior members of both groups, Richie and I sit side by side. Lester sits on his other side.

Gary is three seats down from Paul. Parker is on my side, as is Alan, Roberto, Will, Morris, and Tom the swimming instructor. Paul speaks into the tape recorder, giving today's date, the time, and the reason for the circle: Henry's Burning. He passes the recorder to Alan.

"Hello, Henry, this is Alan."

"Hello Alan," Henry says as though he's greeting an old, dear friend. Alan reminisces about Henry and his stay here at Betty Ford.

He says Henry was a belligerent drunk when he arrived, but has blossomed into the nicest, kindest man he's ever met. He obviously cares for Henry and expresses himself naturally and sincerely. What will I say when the recorder gets to me? I don't want to sound like a total boob

After Alan is done, he passes the recorder and stands, as does Henry. They meet in the center of the room and hug tightly. I feel very touched by their obvious affection. I want to be a part of this. I want to love and be loved. I want to fit in.

I want my damn calves to stop aching all the time. When the recorder gets to me, I take a breath and improvise.

"Hello Henry."

"Hey there, Daniel."

"Well, this is my fourth day here. I think you're a very nice man and I hope you can stay sober because you seem very happy and together. Good luck to you. Thanks for making me feel welcome."

We meet in the center and hug. He squeezes pretty hard. The intimacy is scary, but comforting. He wishes me luck and says I'll do fine at Betty Ford.

"Work the program and you'll succeed," he promises.

"I intend to," I reply.

After the tape recordings, we move outside to the patio, where a big metal canister sits. I always thought it was a big ashtray. Gary stuffs newspaper in and lights it. The night is brisk and clear. The stars are out in full force.

The burning commences. We circle the fire. Paul sits on the short block wall overlooking the lake with the tape recorder resting on his knee. Henry stands beside him, feeding papers from his month into the flames. Notebooks are torched, as are numerous addiction pamphlets, hand-written reports, tests, even the plastic I.D. bracelet they give us on the first day. Mine fell off in the shower yesterday.

Henry talks about the resentment he held inside for years and years before coming to Betty Ford. Anger from childhood, job disappoint-ments, frustration, low self-esteem. He calls himself a textbook alcoholic. He says a great deal of healing took place during family week with his wife and children.

His words fill me with sadness for the relationships I've run from or destroyed. I feel sad. I miss Howard. If Henry can put his life back together, then there's hope for me to do the same. Something gives way deep inside me. I'm overwhelmed with emotions.

Tears roll down my cheeks. I hope no one can see me. I'm standing toward the back of the group, away from the glare of the fire. Tom puts his arm around my shoulder. He doesn't say a word, he just holds me. I tense, then relax. A chunk of my loneliness and pain disappears. I feel stronger. I realize that I'm going to make it, I really am. I'm going to make a success of this program. I place my hand and arm around Tom's waist and stare at the guys' faces in the reflected glow of the fire. I'm not alone.

Chapter Eight

It's five-thirty on Monday morning. I've been awake for two hours. Both legs are in excruciating pain, as is my entire head. The room is cold. I grab a shirt and cigarettes, then go outside. An owl hoots from a nearby tree. I smoke a cigarette and pace. I feel like I'm going to jump out of my skin from these withdrawals.

The night air is warm. The high yesterday was ninety-five degrees. At six I take a shower. At six-fifteen, our wake-up messenger, Roberto, delivers the wake-up call. As I'm drying my hair, I glance at a copy of the week's schedule I've taped to the mirror. The line-up is pretty much the same Monday through Friday:

Wake up at 6:15 a.m.
Breakfast at 6:50
Meditation Walk at 8:00
Morning Lecture from 9:15 to 9:45
Group Therapy from 10:00 to 11:30
Lunch at 11:50
Group Therapy from 1:00 to 2:00 p.m.

Between 2:00 and 3:00 there is either exercise class or a lecture.

Between 3:00 and 4:30, three days a week, there is what's called "Peer Group." This means that the A and B groups meet separately, without counselors. We read homework assignments or discuss topics assigned to us by the counselors. The other two days this time slot is used for exercise.

Dinner is at 4:50.

In the evening there's a lecture followed by the daily AA or NA meetings. They really keep us busy. I just hope I can keep up. I feel like crud.

While the rest of the B group is involved in the morning group therapy, I'm meeting with Molly. Starting tomorrow she will be facilitating our B group's sessions.

She's about five-two in height and has a well-proportioned figure. I'd guess she's about my age. Her brown and blonde hair touches the top of her shoulders. A generous mouth and wide green eyes highlight a bright, open face. My favorite feature are her slender hands. From the moment we meet in the office I'm hyper aware that she's studying me. She's friendly, but no-nonsense. She isn't the type to waste anyone's time. She's going to make me sweat.

Her desk faces a wall. I take the chair that looks toward the window and into an enclosed courtyard. A leafless tree dominates the little garden. It looks as bare as I feel. The withdrawal makes me feel extremely vulnerable, a fact I suppose Molly is fully aware of. I tell myself to relax. I need this diminutive woman's help. I really have to forget my shyness and pride and trust her.

She opens a file and starts asking questions. I recount some pertinent details of my addiction, personal life, David's death, the estrangement from my parents, sexuality, my therapy before I came to Betty Ford, fear of intimacy with Howard, my career, the probable end of my acting career, my constant sense of failure, fears and pleasures. I don't censor myself.

She asks how many drugs I used on a daily basis. She asks me to list all the different chemicals and mood-altering substances I can recall ever ingesting. I try not to leave anything out. I tell her about taking Ecstasy on New Year's Eve. She asks if I became sexually promiscuous while high.

"The few times I took Ecstasy, sure. On New Year's Eve I slept with someone I wouldn't have normally." I go on, telling her about Charles and Nicole. It was dishonest for me to have sex with a woman. My inhibitions were tampered with by the chemicals. Ecstasy does that. The two previous times I took it, I also behaved irresponsibly. Those times, I had sex without using a condom. Stupid. I could have gotten AIDS. She asks if I realize how out of control my life has become. "Yes," I say. "I know it's a mess." I feel embarrassed for myself.

She opens a printout from the medical lab, a screening for drugs in my bloodstream. She reads the results. The bloodwork shows varying levels of Percodan, grass, Codeine, and Valium. She asks if I lied to her about my drug use. "No," I say. "I don't think so."

She says it shows I've used Valium. She doesn't remember me mentioning Valium. I automatically feel guilty of the charge. Then I remember telling John and the nurse I sometimes used Valium when I first arrived. I don't want her to think I'm hiding anything. I say I wasn't hiding the Valium, I simply forgot. I tell her I've been trying to be honest and forthright about everything.

She says she believes me. I feel like a scolded child. She asks how the withdrawals have been. I tell her. She asks if I would like for her to arrange a one-on-one relaxation class with the exercise lady, Rita.

"Sure," I say. "I feel tense all the time."

"You're doing remarkably well. Opiate withdrawal is very traumatic," she says. "You've been taking extremely dangerous amounts of chemicals, Daniel. You could have killed yourself. It'll take your brain and body some time to expel the toxins. I'm glad you're here. Not a moment too soon."

She's like a bossy older sister. She won't take any bullshit. I respect her. She can help me get well, I think.

We spend over an hour talking. She writes several pages of notes. While the rest of the guys are in afternoon group, I'm scheduled to take a memory test, she says. It's important to know whether there are brain deficiencies. I feel a chill at the suggestion of permanent damage. Could that be so? My memory seems fine. What if I've ruined a part of my brain? I'm horrified.

She launches into a sermon on the evils of Ecstasy. She rails against designer drugs. No one knows their full effects on the brain. Ecstasy is believed to burn small holes in the brain tissue. I appreciate her passion. She says it's a decidedly dangerous drug, a hallucinogenic amphetamine. It speeds the heart and induces a touchy-feely craving that often results in reckless sexual behaviors. I feel like scum. Our meeting is like a great purge. She now knows my secrets.

Molly promises to have my master treatment plan ready tomorrow. She asks what homework I have done so far. I tell her I've read and completed the first and second step pamphlets/worksheets for AA.

She instructs me to leave completed assignments in her mailbox in the office. I tell her I've been writing in my daily feelings notebook. She says she'll be reading my entries later today. I explain that I've discussed my reasons for coming to Betty Ford with nearly everyone by now.

"Have you told them you're gay?"

"Yes, as a matter of fact, I have been explaining that I'm gay. Why?" I sound totally defensive.

"It's important that you be honest about that, too, Daniel. Learn to like yourself. You're a likeable, lovable man."

I know she's right, but it's damn hard to change without a struggle. She asks what I might like to do with myself if I wasn't acting.

"Something creative," I answer. "Maybe write a novel."

"Why don't you?"

"I never finished college, I'm not the intellectual type."

"Says who?"

"Well, me, I guess. I've written a few stories, but I don't always have confidence in myself."

"I bet you'd be a terrific writer. You're very perceptive. You only shortchange yourself with that attitude."

"I'll work on it."

"Good. I'd like you to read a list of your positive qualities in group tomorrow. I better let you out of here or you'll be late for lunch."

After lunch I take the memory test. It seems pretty easy. Then I meet with Molly again. She and I discuss how unmanageable my life has become. She asks how much money I've been spending on drugs. I estimate two thousand dollars a month. Now I'm nearly broke.

"Do you see how insane that is?" she asks.

"Yes, I do."

"Let's talk about your goals."

"I'd like to stay sober."

"Good. Go on."

"Okay. I'd like to live an honest life."

"Okay."

"I'd like to act again, I think."

"Okay."

"A meaningful relationship would be nice. I'd like to be more comfortable with myself."

"Good."

"I'd like to be more comfortable with the fact I'm gay."

"Yes?"

"I need to increase my self-esteem. I'd like to quit hiding from my feelings."

"Anything else?"

"I want to get myself in better physical shape. Oh, I'd like to be on better terms with my parents."

"Have you told them that you're here, Daniel?"

"I wrote them a letter."

"That's a good first step."

"Uh-huh."

"What about inviting them here for family week?"

"Why?"

"You tell me."

"I'll think about it, really."

"I think it's very important. Did you and your parents ever discuss your brother's death?"

"No."

"Maybe it's time. You have several family issues that need to be addressed. If you don't deal with them here, with our support, it might impede your recovery when you leave. I'd like you to consider letting us contact your parents and inviting them here."

"I'll think it over and let you know. If you try to force me to invite them, it won't mean a damn thing. I need to do it because I decide it's the right thing to do."

"We'll talk about it in a few days. How long has it been since you last took any drugs?"

"Nearly five days."

"Congratulations, Daniel. That's an accomplishment to be proud of."

"Thanks. I am proud of it."

I feel emotionally spent the rest of the day. The evening lecture is terribly appropos for me. The speaker addresses something we all have in common: low self-esteem. Drugs and alcohol only intensify and exacerbate problems. Alcohol is a depressant, as are many of the pills I used. Addicts often choose a drug or substance because of the particular high it delivers. I chose Percodan because it allowed me to maintain a normal exterior while suppressing urgent emotional needs and hang-ups.

I've always disliked drinking for the most part. People act so sloppy and stupid when they're boozing it up. I lose respect for drunks. Sally often calls me when she's been drinking. It's excruciatingly painful for me to listen to her incoherent ramblings.

More than a drink or two makes me depressed. Alcohol was never fun like painkillers were. Percodan provided euphoria without drastically altering my behavior or appearance. I liked cocaine because it induced a powerful buzz of self-confidence that superseded my shyness and allowed me to open up with nearly anyone.

The lecturer mentions cross addiction. When an addict or alcoholic can't get their drug of choice, they find substitutes. The effect of Valium isn't totally dissimilar from that of alcohol. Both stimulate similar pleasure centers of the brain. Codeine and other painkillers work in much the same way as Percodan, thus, these drugs could be as addictive for me as Percodan. A cross addict can easily get re-hooked to Valium, painkillers, booze, cocaine, food, sex, speed. It sounds as if I'm basically a walking time bomb.

Later, after the Narcotics Anonymous meeting, Gary and I take a walk around the lake. He started family week today. He says he's got a splitting headache, but seems relaxed compared to me. I feel like a bundle of exposed nerve endings. I tell him a little about Molly and my day. All this soul-searching is trying. He says it was difficult for him at first, too, but it gets easier with practice and time. Patience isn't one of my stronger suits. That's why I liked drugs, they provided immediate results.

We smoke his filterless cigarettes and sit on the damp grass at the opposite end of the lake. The night is still except for the crickets. A storm is expected to break loose later. There are a few clouds hovering over the mountains, but nothing terribly ominous.

He asks where I grew up. He says he wants to get to know me better. I tell him about the death of my brother and the estrangement from my folks. He suggests I invite them for family week. I try not to scowl. He asks whether if I've been dating anyone. Not lately, I say, then tell him about Howard. He listens, then grasps my hand in his. The blood courses through my veins, velocity increases, I get flushed.

We continue holding hands. By the light of the full moon I can see the green-grey of his eyes. His beard is a mixture of brown and blond. I'd like to grab hold of the whiskers with my teeth and pull. He's very masculine and yet there's a sensitive side that's very appealing. The sound of approaching footsteps forces us to drop hands. It's Parker and Roberto. They ask what we're doing. "Talking," says Gary. Parker looks at me suspiciously. I smile, but reveal nothing. I cloak myself in the night. They continue on their walk. Gary says we should get back. He has a paper due tomorrow.

As we're walking back toward McCallum, I ask if he's ever been involved with another man. He says he had sex with a guy he got high with. They'd snort coke and then his buddy would give him a blow job. Gary says he's known for years he was attracted to other men, but didn't have the guts to really do anything about it. I ask if he gave his friend blow jobs. "No, I didn't. We never even kissed. I let him do it for drugs. I was a whore. I've never really made love with a man I cared for."

He asks how long I've known I was gay. "Since I was about five," I say. "I always knew I was different. I liked girls and had sex with them, but it was mechanical. I couldn't love them the way I could men."

I ask if he's committed to coming out or just considering it. He says he's not sure yet. Perhaps, in time, we'll have a physical and emotional relationship. I'm tremendously attracted to him.

I get into bed just after eleven. I'm exhausted, but the leg aches are less intense. Today's activities distracted me from much of the physical discomfort. Changes are under way that I'll never be able to forget or ignore. This is a turning point in my life. I'm beginning to change my behavior , which Molly says will lead to fundamental shifts in my thinking. I'm dealing with emotional issues that have frightened me for years, yet I don't feel broken. I fall asleep feeling satisfied with the day.

I wake at four-fifteen the next morning. It's my longest night's sleep since I arrived. I have a splitting headache, but I feel better. I have more vitality and spunk. "One day at a time" is a fine credo for me. I can deal with problems and pain more easily in smaller pieces. My spirit is lifting. The lady with the cast on her arm told me at dinner last night I had the nicest, warmest face in the place. She made my day.

The cycle of pain and unhappiness of the last few years seems to be broken. The hollow space in the middle of my chest is shrinking. Healing is taking place. I feel less anxious. That's enouraging. I hear myself laughing more. I can see and feel people responding positively to me.

I get up and shower, then take pen, paper, and cigarettes to the bench next to the lake. I write a letter to Howard. Both arms are dull and heavy. I've had some cramping in my stomach, too.

I share the full scope of my addiction with him. I apologize for the way I treated him when we broke up. I write that I miss him and would like us to be friends. I end the letter by saying I totally understand if he'd rather not re-connect with me.

The morning is quiet, except for a mockingbird that sings from atop a nearby bougainvillea bramble. The buttery hues of the rising sun spreads across the water.

I spot the mother duck and her brood drifting in the muddy shallows near the shore. There are still four ducklings. I feel greatly relieved they've made it this far. There's hope for us all.

At breakfast, Ron, the doctor with a wife and mistress from Des Moines, asks me to partner with Alan to write his going-away song. After each goodbye burning, we sing one or two songs. The required song is "Margaritaville," The optional is a song written by peers using memorable details from the graduate's life story. The emphasis is on humor.

I'm flattered. I've only known Ron for a few days. We've had some great discussions about everything under the sun during our late-night coffee klatches. He's liberal, funny, and totally accepting of me and my sexuality. I feel authentic support from him.

I instantly agree to help. They both have burnings on Friday night, then leave on Saturday. I'm going to miss my Betty Ford surrogate dads.

I accompany Richie and Roberto on the morning meditation walk. We discuss Lester's eating habits and the current gossip. I'm anxious about my first group therapy session at ten, so I listen more than I talk.

At ten sharp, the B group assembles in Molly's office, forming a large circle with our chairs. We, the patients, dictate most of the agenda, Molly says. We're encouraged to share whatever we like. It's open. Structured, but flexible. It encompasses us all, forces us each to participate on several levels. Constructive communication is stressed, but outright criticism is not welcome. The emphasis is on honesty, not pain and hurt feelings.

Several men discuss their addictions. Fear seems to be a common denominator. Fear of abandonment, fear of intimacy, fear of pain. These fears unite us. We have dysfunction in common.

Molly focuses the group's attention on me. It is traditional, she says, for a new patient to be evaluated by his peers. She passes out a mimeographed list of hang-ups and problems that might get in the way of my recovery. She gives us two minutes to complete them. I'm on the hot seat. She stands and scribbles columns across the blackboard.

Each guy reads their evaluation of me while Molly keeps a running tally on the board. At the top of the hang-ups column is my estrangement from my family and Howard. I feel a little violated. How dare they tell me how to conduct my life?.

Several say I blame my parents for my pain. They say I need to forgive them. David's death wasn't their fault. They say it sounds like my parents and I love each other, but it's been lost in hostility for years. It does pain me to be separated on such bad terms from my parents. Maybe I can handle seeing them without drugs. I don't know.

Their comments indicate I need to take responsibility for my own pain, my own problems. They have a point. I try to look calm and unruffled. Hearing these things is difficult, but I force myself to listen and accept their suggestions like a soldier.

Parker says I'm a people pleaser. He's right. I sometimes say something just to fit in and keep the peace.

It's mentioned that I tend to isolate and that could be a detriment to recovery. The list of problems and negatives seems like it goes on forever. I have to agree with all the comments, they're accurate.

Molly strongly suggests I spend more time with my peers here. It's important to open up and allow these guys to get to see the real me. I thought I was being damn sociable already, considering the frigging withdrawal, but I do see their point. When I did drugs, I often engaged in activities by myself. It was undemanding, safe. Molly suggests that group is the place to talk about pain or fear or whatever needs to be addressed. She says that we all need to understand that feeling pain is natural and not necessarily destructive.

We move on to listing my positives. Molly says that addicts and alcoholics have a tendency to only look at the negative, not the positive. I'm trying to act and think more positively every day. It's one of my goals.

Alan says I'm intelligent, perceptive, interested in other people, and so forth. It's all too damn much to absorb in one sitting. Everyone else is wearing short-sleeved shirts. I'm draped in a black, long-sleeved sweatshirt and I'm still chilly. It's the withdrawal. It plays havoc with the body's inner thermometer. I careen from hot to cold constantly.

During the break between group and lunch, I sun on my patio, and think. It seems like emotions have ruled my decisions and thinking for as long as I can remember. Rational thoughts had little to do with anything. No wonder I felt out of control so often.

Now I'm learning to change that by consciously adjusting my usual reactions and responses. I can let go of the past and step into the future. Change doesn't have to be bad. Maybe my mother was right. The end of one thing might be the start of another. I'm very optimistic.

I bask in the warm rays, waiting for the announcement for lunch. I think about the ducks. I remember when I bought an incubator in the seventh grade. I hatched five mallard eggs. It was February. I was thirteen years old. I'd been home sick off and on for several weeks. I was constantly depressed. I felt like I didn't belong anywhere and it was eating me alive. I suffered from horrendous stomach aches and headaches.

Finally, my parents put me in the Genoa Falls Hospital for tests to find out exactly what was ailing me. They didn't want to carelessly lose their remaining son. I watched the ducks hatch a few hours before I was driven to the hospital.

My mother was a good sport. She took excellent care of the ducklings while I was gone. Three days later I returned home armed with medication to treat the ulcer and migraine headaches they diagnosed.

We treated the symptoms, but not my underlying unhappiness or problems. We never spoke, my parents and I, of my growing sense of isolation and sadness. I couldn't articulate the devastation I still felt at losing my brother. I was secretly ashamed because I knew I was a homosexual and felt powerless to change it. I didn't know how to tell people how I felt. I was too afraid.

I became expert at covering up my true feelings. Where my parents regularly vented their feelings, I bottled mine up. Occasionally I'd explode in wild rages, but usually I was a cool customer. I controlled my behavior pretty well for an adolescent.

I was constantly involved in wildlife projects. I rescued injured baby birds and nursed them back to health. Neighbors brought me shoe boxes of motherless rabbits, which I bottlefed with an eyedropper or doll's bottle. I once found a dead possum next to the highway by the woods. Poking at it with a stick, I discovered two tiny tails protruding from the belly of the corpse. I pried open the marsupial's pouch and found seven baby possums. Two months later I carried the four surviving critters to the woods behind our house and released them.

My favorite pet was Ruby, the German shepherd I was given six months after David died. She was my friend until she got hit by a car, just like our first dog Mac. I cried when she died. It was weird. I couldn't cry at David's funeral because the pain was too great. If I gave in, it might have swallowed me into a dark pit. I couldn't stop crying for days after Ruby died, the pain was too great to ignore.

The next morning, just before group meets, Molly presents me with my master treatment plan. It lists the numerous pamphlets I'm supposed to read, including ones on addiction, cross-addiction, alcoholism, and grief. Tomorrow, I'm to tell the afternoon peer group of my life story.

Parker told his life story yesterday. It took nearly an hour. Molly tells me I can use an outline while telling my life story.

I'm also assigned to write papers on each of the pamphlets, as well as topics such as "Why I'm An Addict," "Drug and Alcohol Use in My Family", and "How Death Has Affected Me." What a pleasure cruise the next three weeks are going to be. I've gone six days without a Percodan. The muscle discomfort is still fairly constant, but the headaches have lessened considerably.

Molly asks how I'm doing with the withdrawal. "I'm managing," I say. A few minutes later, in group, the topic is confronting our irresponsible behavior while using. We go around the circle and give examples. A few men mention driving while drunk or high. When it's my turn, I freeze, unable to reveal anything.

"Secrets will only lead you back to drugs, Daniel. Let go of the secrets here, where it's safe." Molly says. My face burns.

"Fine," I say. "What do you want me to say, Molly?"

"Give an example of your drug behavior."

"Fine," I say louder. "Let's see. A few weeks ago I fucked a man and woman while I was wasted on painkillers and Ecstasy and cocaine. I had sex with them both. Yes, I did it because I was ripped. I was messed up. As you know, guys, I'm gay. I don't normally have sex with women, but the drugs affected my usual thought processes." I feel so ashamed and angry.

I look at the floor, then out the window, averting my eyes from Molly.

"Can you see that your life was out of control, Daniel?" she says.

"Yes, I can."

"If you're gay why did you have sex with the woman?"

"Because. At the time I thought it might make me happier.

"I think you need to keep working on accepting your sexuality, Daniel."

"Yes, I do."

"Did you use protection?"

"No, it was stupid, I didn't. I justified it by saying they were probably clean beause they're a married couple."

"What if they were HIV-positive?"

"Well, then I'm out of luck."

"What if you were HIV-positive and infected them both?"

"I'd feel like shit. It's irresponsible, I know. I don't take pride in my actions. No question about it, the drugs influenced my thinking. I know. That's why I'm here. The morning after we had our fling, I found needles in their john. I guess they were junkies." I realize how emotional I sound by the ring in my ears. The guys look a little taken aback. They probably didn't expect such intense emotions from a seemingly rational person.

Molly says a few words about the evils of Ecstasy. Like other chemicals, it alters our moods and decision-making abilities. We're definitely impaired when using. She turns to me again.

"Why did you take the Ecstasy?"

"Because I wanted to feel happier."

"Addiction is a disease," she reminds us. "It isn't rational or predictable."

Morris mentions one of his drunk driving convictions as an equally appalling, irresponsible action. Parker describes a car chase with his cocaine dealer. Facing our wreckage is a sobering exercise.

The body conditioning class later is fun. My outlook is brightening by leaps and bounds. I feel a little better each day, as my emotions and moods rise to a sunnier realm. The group therapy is exhausting work, but healthy. I feel unburdened.

All seventeen of us exercise together, except for Tom, who has dispensation to jog around the campus two days a week. Lester sits on a mat next to the equipment bins and does nothing.

The exercise instructor is Rita. She's in her late fifties or early sixties, but has the body of a much younger woman. She tells us she's a former June Taylor dancer with twelve years of sobriety. She's very together and hip.

We start with stretching, then do some aerobics. The music emanates from a record player at the front of the room. She is partial to the disco hits of the seventies. Donna Summer and the Bee Gees. Mirrors cover the walls. A row of stationary bicycles lines the back wall.

Gary is wearing his pink shorts and a white T-shirt. He looks very sexy. I like his legs. They're strong, like a runner's. We perform a series of arm movements using giant rubber bands. As we're swinging our arms in and out en masse, I edge closer to Gary and whisper "nice ass." He turns and grins, then returns to watching Rita in front of us. Lester is passed out, asleep, behind a rowing machine.

While on the floor performing a series of donkey kicks, I see myself in the mirror. I look pretty good. My skin color is better, eyes are clear, whites are white. I look different. Gary catches my eye in the reflection and winks. I wink back. Roberto is next to me. I see his eyes following us in the mirror. He gives me a look that says he knows what's going on and heartily endorses it.

I dropped by The Swamp last night. Roberto and Gary's beds are on one side of the room, Lester and an empty bed on the other.

Gary, wearing the same shorts, was lying on his cot reading. Roberto was sitting at his desk, diligently putting pen to paper. He threw down his pen and complained that his lawyer was bombarding him with paperwork concerning an upcoming legal proceeding. Seems he was arrested a few months back for writing very sizable checks that were very rubbery. I haven't gotten the full scoop, yet. He told me at breakfast that he's supposed to tell his life story on Friday. I'm interested to hear the details. I'll bet he was wild.

Back to The Swamp. Gary offered me some pistachio nuts. "Sure," I said. He poured some into a Dixie cup. Lester wasn't around. I asked how things were going. They both made faces. Roberto couldn't stop himself from elaborating. He told me that Lester drives them crazy. He turns the thermometer way down to freezing at night and is constantly munching on snacks.

Roberto shot across the room and yanked open Lester's dresser drawers. "See?" Roberto said." See?" I crept closer. The second drawer was stuffed with food. Candy bars, chocolate chip cookies, nuts, chips, beef jerky, crispy pork rind treats, even cans of soft drinks. I asked where Lester procured such a windfall. Roberto and Gary looked at one another

and said, in tandem, "His mother." I laughed very hard. We all did.
The two crates of cookies his mother brought were obviously only the
tip of the culinary iceberg. The drawer was chockaaablock full of edibles.
It's damn gross.
His mother epitomizes codependency. Gary says it's sick, very sick.
I have to agree. Roberto is hostile toward Lester. He admits he's bitter
about their nightly air conditioning duels. All night they take turns
adjusting the thermostat. Up and down, up and down.
Rita jacks our pulses up for about twenty minutes. Then we perform
some cool-down stretches. Lester is fast asleep. Gary has a red face.
Parker is shirtless. I like his slender, but well-developed physique. He's
a hot-looking man.
I'm winded by the end of class. My legs actually feel better. It's been
ages since I have really exercised. We take our pulses, wake up Lester,
and then head back toward McCallum. Richie and I walk with Roberto.
They're both soaked with perspiration. The desert sky is dark with rain
clouds. The heat has broken, replaced by cool and a moist breeze.
Everyone takes showers before dinner. I eat with Gary, Ron, and
Tom. Hunk central. Amanda and I exchange "Hellos" as I'm getting a
refill of lemonade. She's drinking iced tea.
The rain begins to fall during the Narcotics Anonymous meeting. I
hear it softly tapping on the roof. I like this meeting a lot. A man and
woman from Palm Springs both tell their life stories. Drugs, drugs, drugs.
It's comforting to hear other people admit their failings. I feel less
ashamed of my disclosures during group earlier.
At the tail end of the meeting, patients take turns saying a few words
from the podium. We're all encouraged to participate in the AA and NA
meetings. Gary, Parker, Tom, Ron, and Morris all stand and say a few
words. I decide the time has come for me to do the same. Feeling a good
deal of trepidation, I jump to my feet and stride to the podium.
"Hi. I'm Daniel. I'm an addict."
"Hi, Daniel." The other seventy-nine patients answer back.
"Well, this is my seventh day of sobriety and I feel like a new person.
I'm not exactly sure why it's easier to quit drugs here, but it is. I feel better
every day. Maybe by the end of the month I'll be able to understand
exactly what's going on, maybe not. For now, I just feel thankful this
program is working for me. Thanks."
Everyone claps, that's part of the process. I like the positive
reinforcement. I return to my seat. My face feels heated to two hundred
degrees. I did it! If I can admit to this roomful of people I'm an addict and
admit my powerlessness to them as it says in the AA book, then I can begin
to get well.
Gary pats my back as I slide into my seat. Tom turns and gives me
the thumbs-up sign. Richie reaches over and squeezes my knee. "Way to

go, Daniel," he whispers. I feel like one of the big boys now.

After the meeting, we run through the downpour. It's raining buckets. The water soaks my skin. It feels wonderful. I get back in time to make my first phone call.

There is a sign-in sheet to reserve phone times on the bulletin board in the lounge. I signed up for the nine-twenty slot. Each guy is allotted ten minutes. No more, no less.

I drop a quarter in and dial Howard's number. A recording clicks on, demanding more change. I feed it more quarters.

He picks up on the third ring. Butterflies flop around inside my belly. The rain is slowing to a drizzle. I love a good storm. I wonder if it's raining in L.A.

"Hi, Howard. It's me." My voice sounds tentative.

"Daniel. I was just thinking of you. As a matter of fact, I've thought of little else since I got your letter this morning."

"Oh."

"Thank you for telling me. I'm proud of you."

"Why?"

"Because you're getting help."

"Thanks."

"It helps me understand part of the reason we couldn't get closer and why you broke up with me."

"Yeah, well, I was obviously preoccupied with my stupid drugs."

"How's it going?"

"Pretty well, actually."

"You said in your letter that the withdrawal was difficult."

"My body feels like it's been run over by a Mack truck."

"That'll get better with time, right?"

"That's what they say."

"You sound down, Daniel."

"I feel sad."

"About what?"

"You. Us. I was a jerk."

"Don't distract yourself. I'm fine. Don't worry about me. You just concentrate on getting well. What can I do to help.?"

"Just be my friend."

"I never stopped being your friend, Daniel."

"I guess I feel guilty because I haven't been much of a friend to you lately."

"Hey, you've done the best you can. Hopefully, your best will get better." We both laugh. I relax a little.

"Howard, I've been thinking about us, our relationship."

"And?"

"And I think it was a good thing. I really cared for you."

"And me for you, Daniel."

"Do you still like me now that you know now I'm an addict?"

"Yes," he laughs.

"You're my first phone call."

"What do you mean?"

"We can't use the phone the first five days. You're my first contact with the outside world."

"I'm touched."

"I think of you often."

"That's nice. I think about you surprisingly often, too."

"I have to get off soon. We only have ten minutes and I'm running out of change."

"Can you have visitors?"

"Sure. On Sundays."

"I'd love to see you. Would you like me to drive down this Sunday?"

"That would be great if it's not too big a hassle."

"What time?"

"Visiting hours are from one to five. We can have lunch here."

"Great. I'll see you at one. Can I bring you anything?"

"Oh, no. Well maybe. How about a carton of cigarettes."

"Sure. The usual?"

"Yes, thanks." I'm surprised he remembers what brand I smoke.

"See you Sunday, Daniel."

"I look forward to it. Thanks. Is it raining in L. A.?"

"Not since this morning."

"It just started pouring here."

"I've really missed you, Daniel."

"I've missed you, too. You know what?"

"What?"

"I've recently realized I love you."

"Is that scary?"

"Yes, a little. No, that's a lie. It scares me a lot."

"Why?"

"I'm afraid if I love someone they'll die or abandon me. I'm trying to learn how to trust again."

"Good. I've always felt that you loved me, Daniel. Even when you were a little shit, I knew you cared deeply. I think you'll be a much happier man when you rid yourself of those demons. You're growing up."

"I think you're right. It's hard to believe."

"You have my support, Daniel. You never lost it."

"I thought you'd get mad at me for being an asshole and stop caring."

"It's not that easy to get rid of me."

"I'd better go," I say.

"See you Sunday, Daniel."

"I love you."

"I love you, too."

I write in my feelings notebook that I'd like to be free of anger and resentment toward my parents. That would be nice. I write about my conversation with Howard, how good it feels to mend the fences. Then I sit on our little patio with Alan. There's a lull in the storm. The desert smells so clean and fresh. We try to formulate a song for Don. The goodbye songs are sung to the beat of the classic Army drill tunes. We write sentences and then read them aloud. I tell Alan about my call to Howard. "Good for you," he says in his deep baritone. "Good for you."

At midnight I hit the sack. The rain breaks loose again about an hour later. Magnificent bolts of lightning flash between heaven and earth. The thunder rattles the window and shakes the walls. Parker and I sit up in our beds and watch the electrical activity. After a few minutes, we move to the open door and stand in the dark, smoking cigarettes in our underwear.

The rain floods the patio. I hear a duck quacking. A series of electrical bursts momentarily blind me. I gasp in awe. Three deafening thunderclaps follow, sending chills up my spine.

We stand there silently and watch the sky. The lightning reminds me of fireworks on Fourth of July. We climb back into our beds. The steady patter of raindrops hitting the glass lulls me into a calm sleep.

Chapter Nine

By the next morning, the winter storm has moved on. The sky is tinted a rich azure. The air is warm and wet. Gary and I team for the morning meditation walk. We smoke one of his cigarettes, allowing our hands to touch as we pass it back and forth. We look for the big fish that is supposedly terrorizing the ducks, but see nothing. Gary suggests we go on a date tonight. I ask what he has in mind.

"Why don't we eat dinner together and then look around the bookstore."

"Sure," I say. I'm enjoying our illicit romance.

That afternoon is our once-a-week "Community Meeting." I see Lester standing outside The Swamp as I'm leaving my room. He's shoveling popcorn into his mouth from a bowl. He really gives that jaw a workout.

The point of the community gathering is to air problems and settle grievances between residents. Two counselors, John and Bill, represent mediation and management. The counselors elect the granny and announcer.

The granny is expected to keep the peace amongst the fractious elements of the dorm, as well as delegate the work details. I've been carrying the ice this past week. Starting tomorrow I'll vacuum the lounge, sweep the patio, or set the tables at meals. Performing these menial duties is an important part of the process. It stimulates a sense of responsibility toward our peers as well as ourselves. I like it.

After the meeting commences, there is some grousing by the counselors about sloppily made beds. Every morning the counselors inspect the rooms. We're expected to make our beds, put dirty towels in the linen hampers, and generally keep things orderly. Clothes are either in drawers or hanging in the closet. Mess is not tolerated. A list of infractions and passing notices is posted on the bulletin board next to the office each morning. Untidy campers are identified by name and offense. I got busted yesterday for leaving a pair of slacks hanging on my chair. I felt embarrassed seeing my name on the board.

Paul, as outgoing granny, is asked to give the names of the new granny and announcer. Before every activity the announcer gets on the microphone outside the office and gives a five-minute warning. "Five minutes until circle for breakfast" is followed by "Time for circle." The announcer keeps us punctual.

John says, "First piece of business is to ask for a hand for Tom. He's been a dynamite announcer." We clap for Tom. He's very popular. Gary might be the new granny. He's well liked and respected. Our new announcer might be Richard, he has a great voice. I'd vote for him. Tom remains seated. His voice is loud and easy to understand. He enunciates well. He looks directly at me. My stomach sinks to the floor. "I'm pleased to name my successor. He's someone I'm sure will do a fine job." He focuses on several people, then makes direct eye contact with me.

"Daniel, you're McCallum's brand new announcer." I smile wanly as I try not look down at my feet. I feel very nervous. People clap. I feel a blush rising. This job means I'll be accountable to all these guys. I won't have a minute to isolate. I guess that's the point. I try to act gracious. I don't know whether to be flattered at being chosen or irritated. I'll try not to let my comrades down.

Morris is the new Granny. He's a popular choice. At the end of the meeting, he congratulates me. I congratulate him back. My legs feel much better today. The knots in the calves are looser and I have more energy.

Tom shows me how to use the microphone before dinner. We talk about his leaving next week. He's nervous about returning to his family, house, job, and life. He hopes he can stay sober. He's planning to attend an AA meeting every day the first month he's out. That's what AA and Betty Ford suggest graduates do. He says it'll get easier with time.

Gary and I eat with Tom and Parker. The meat loaf is delicious. It has little chunks of cheddar cheese in it. The zucchini is tender and buttery. I eat a slice of carrot cake and savor every bite.

I get up from the table, then exit, stopping for a drink at the water fountain before making my way to the little gift shop in the lobby. I browse through the recovery literature and check out the T-shirts hanging on the racks. Gary arrives. We smile at one another stupidly and make small talk.

The white-haired lady behind the counter is struggling to count a pile of coinage. I doubt if she's interested in spying on us. He kneels behind the rack of slacks and sweatshirts, then smooches my hand. I laugh and tell him he better behave or we'll get in tro uble. "No fraternization," I whisper.

It's strongly recommended that recovering patients stay away from new love relationships for the first year of sobriety. I can't imagine not having some sort of romance in my life. I didn't quit drugs to then sit home alone every night. That's unreasonable. I understand we're more vulnerable without the chemical crutches, but I can barely contain my lustful thoughts and I've only been here a week.

I get an erection that is so hard it hurts. I move away from Gary and grab a stuffed Mickey Mouse off the shelf. I ask if he'd like a souvenir. He says, "Sure." I look around. He shakes his head "No" at Mickey, then "No" to a box of Lorna Doones. The "One Step At A Time" T-shirt gets the thumbs-down sign, he says he already bought one.

I grab a bright blue book, the NA Bible. Betty Ford gave us each copies of the AA bible, but we have to buy our own NA book if we want one. Yes, this is perfect. We're both addicts more than alcoholics. We should have these. I hold the book above my head. He nods his head and says, "Yes. Will you sign mine?" I say, "Sure", then pay the lady for two books. It takes forever for the woman to total our purchases, but I don't care. Just standing close to Gary is thrill enough. The juices are flowing and it feels great.

Lester appears, a stain of red catsup on his blue Lacoste. We all exchange pleasantries, but I feel like he's intruded on a private moment. He yells to me from across the tiny store.

"Guess who was asking about you last night?" he says in a teasing voice. I hate these games.

"I give up. Who?"

"A certain movie star..."

"Let's see...who's in town this week? Mel, Michelle, Bianca, Babs.."

"You're awful," Gary whispers from the side of his mouth.

"Thank you", I murmur.

"Amanda Andrews was asking me about you."

"Really?" I say nonchalantly. If I pretend to be bored, he'll tell me everything. If I seem eager for his damn information, he'll dangle it over my head. I pretend to examine a box of salt water taffy.

"She asked me if you were as adorable as you seemed."

"What did you say?"

"I said you were precious."

"He is precious," Gary hisses. I hand my boyfriend his book and press a knee firmly against his hip. He puckers his lips. I say goodbye to Lester and walk to the water fountain, where I wait for Gary. He saunters up a few seconds later. We take turns drinking the cold water, then exit the building.

We smoke cigarettes and walk at a leisurely pace back to McCallum. I ask how family week is going. He's had to confront a lot of drug-related incidents with his ex-wife. He says it's gruelling, but cathartic. He says his wife is constantly complaining that he owes her money. She threatens to take him back to court if need be. He says he has the bucks, but feels she's blackmailing him. I listen, but offer no opinions or judgments.

We finish our cigarettes next to the lake. The ducks swim by. There are only three babies now. It's nearly dark. We walk to The Swamp. His cellmates are nowhere to be seen. He closes the drapes. We stand next to the bathroom and kiss for the first time. His mouth is big and his lips supple. He tastes of applesauce and tobacco. A sense of danger fans the flames.

We wrap our arms around one another and allow our tongues to meet and explore. He feels good. I like the way he kisses. As he nibbles on my right earlobe, I admire his backside in the bathroom mirror. His shoulders are wide, his legs strong and tan. His ass is big enough to grab hold of, but hardly fat. He looks quite a bit bigger than me.

The sound of talking out in the hall interrupts our triest. We separate. He whispers that I'm the first man he's ever kissed.

"What about the guy you had sex with?"

"We never kissed, Daniel."

"So what do you think? Do you like it?" I ask.

"You're very sexy. I like you, Daniel. I think we should continue this when we leave Betty Ford. What do you think?"

"Will we have a romance?"

"I'd like to give it a shot. How about you?"

"I think I'd like that."

I step into the bathroom and look at my long hair. I'm a little sick of it.

"Thanks for my book," he says as the door swings open.

Roberto blasts in and instantly begins to rant against Lester. Seems he's left wet towels in the bathroom again. I return to my room and lie on the bed. I forgot to sign his book. My head is incredibly clear. The kiss with Gary really stimulated me. Whenever I see an NA book again, I'll remember my first date night at Betty Ford.

Before sleep, I write the outline of my life story. When I finish around eleven-thirty, I'm pooped. Making a chronological list of my life and drugging is difficult. So much failure. I head to the big patio and share a cup of coffee with Alan, Tom, Morris, Tom, and Brian. I haven't seen much of Richie the last couple of days.

Alan and I discuss the status of Ron's going-away song. We've decided to each write half, then tomorrow night we'll assemble the entire piece. I have written two more paragraphs. He's done six. We agree to finish it tomorrow after dinner. He tells me I'll be a good announcer. "Damn right," I answer kiddingly. He tells me I'm a breath of fresh air in this place.

I hit the sack at twelve-thirty. Parker is hunched over his desk, writing another report. This one is on what a higher power means to him. He asks how the withdrawals are going. I assure him I'm improving, slowly but surely.

I set the alarm clock. Starting tomorrow morning, I have to be punctual or I'll let these guys down. It's important that I do a good job. I repeat the Serenity Prayer in my head. I've got it memorized now.

"God, grant me the serenity to accept the things I cannot change..the courage to accept the things I can change..and the wisdom to know the difference."

I effortlessly drift into sleep.

I spend all of Friday preoccupied with my new announcing duties. It's more entertaining than lugging buckets of ice back and forth from the cafeteria. I'm a little more relaxed with each broadcast.

The withdrawal discomfort is subsiding more and more. I feel depressed and anxious sometimes, but the sadness passes. They tell me it's normal to feel low during withdrawal. I've learned that anticipation of withdrawal discomfort is greater than the actual pain. This goes equally well for other fears. Fear begets fear. Reality is usually much kinder than my overactive imaginations.

My daily cravings for Percodan make me moody and nervous at times, but it passes. I'm learning a little patience. I try to examine what it is I'm feeling that triggers the overpowering need for chemical relief. The usual suspects are fear and raging insecurity.

In group we discuss these issues. It's really intense at times, but definitely therapeutic. I'm learning to process and explore problems, then move on. Burying the feelings only creates blind spots and bigger problems. I need to keep current with feelings. It's a new concept. I've been an anger and resentment packrat for years and years. Time for Daniel's clearance sale. Old merchandise must go.

After lunch, there's usually mail on a table in the lounge. I've received two cards from Howard this week. Today there's a typed letter from Sally and an envelope from my sister.

Sally sounds the same. She writes an entertaining letter. Her mother is visiting for a week and she's driving Sally insane. She includes a two page summary of the daytime soap opera we both watch. We started viewing it when we were in high shool together in Illinois. It's one of the few things we have in common besides drugs.

Richie offered to cut my hair tomorrow. Before he was a singer, he was a hairdresser. I'm not convinced of his abilities, but what the hell. It shows him I trust him. besides, how many people get to have a famous singer style their hair while in a drug rehab program? It's a kick.

The card from my sister is an illustration of a blooming garden. The caption on back says it's Monet's garden in Giverny, France. Inside, Linda has written a passage.

"This is the garden: colors come and go, frail azures fluttering from night's outer wing strong silent greens serenely lingering, absolute lights like baths of golden snow."

E. E. Cummings

She has written a brief paragraph. She received my letter and her thoughts and support are with me. She says to call anytime. She promises to write again soon, she misses me. I go back to my room and sit in the bathroom with the fan running, crying like I haven't cried in years. I miss her. I want my family to love me. I want everry thing to be all right. I shed tears for the lost years, the hurt feelings, the wasted emotions. I feel lucky that Linda is on my side. She loves me. That feels good.

During the afternoon, I have an appointment with Rita. I meet her in the exercise room. We talk, then she asks me to lie down, explaining that she's going to lead me on a relaxation exercise while the tape recorder runs. Then I can play back the tape to unwind anytime.

Her voice is mesmerizing. I stretch out across a mat on the floor. The lights are turned off. Everything's quiet except for Rita's voice. My arms are spread from my sides. Eyelids are heavy. She takes me on a journey of visualization. I go into a sort of auto-hypnosis. My mind's eye conjures images of sunny beaches and lush jungles.

The weight in my head and shoulders melts into the floor. After forty minutes, I feel high from the relaxation. I walk back to McCallum in a fog of pleasure, my special tape in hand. The colors of the sky and the grass seem more vivid. I swear my eyesight is improved. I feel more relaxed than I ever did on Percodan. It's amazing.

Roberto tells his life story during peer group. I was talking with him last night and he admitted to me he is gay. I suspected as much. He's married, but I get the feeling he's been secretly gay for years.

Today, he tells us about working for his drug dealer. He stole merchandise and wrote bad checks for drugs. When he gets out of Betty Ford, he faces a trial for fraud and several other charges. He'll probably serve time in prison.

He blames his mother for a lot of his angst. We remind him that he's created his own problems and he has to face them. He became a criminal to feed his drug habit. He had a lot of wild sex, too. He talks on through the entire ninety minutes. I'll have to wait and tell my life story on Monday. I'm glad for the reprieve.

I eat the last two cookies from Lester's mother before announcing circle for dinner. I told Molly today that she could invite my parents for family week. She asked me to sign a document allowing Betty Ford personnel to contact them.

Alan and I complete Ron's going away-song after dinner. He promised to have it photocopied before tomorrow night's double burning. I can't believe they'll both be gone by Sunday.

The Friday night AA meeting is excellent. Two recovering alcoholics tell their fascinating life stories. Then, they turn the floor over to patients. After listening to half a dozen fellow patients speak, I get up the nerve to participate. I stand up, walk to the front. I talk about how I'm trying to let go of resentments against my family. It feels good to share. Then the AAs pass out chips. Gary, Tom, Morris, and Parker get black chips that signify fifteen days of sobriety. Ron and Alan get white chips for thirty days of sobriety. I'm looking forward to getting my fifteen- day chip next week.

Alan and Ron's burnings the next night are special. The goodbye song Alan and I wrote is a big hit. Ron is very pleased. I feel sad to see them leave. After the burning, Ron and Alan sit in the lounge signing our AA books. I write a message in each of their books as well. Signing the books is a tradition. Both tell me to call if I needed to talk about anything. I'll miss my new friends.

I call home after the burnings. The machine answers. I begin to leave a message for Lance. He picks up. He sounds very cheerful. He asks how I'm doing. I give him a brief summary. I promise to write him a letter over the weekend. He says everything is fine. He's wateri ng the plants and bringing in mail. He asks if I can have visitors.

I hesitate, then suggest he come see me a week from Sunday. He says "Sure," I ask how classes are going.

"Fine, fine." I ask about his family.

"They're fine." He asks how I'm feeling. I explain the withdrawals a little and try to accentuate how positive and upbeat I'm feeling. He tells me I've got guts. I thank him for house-sitting and say I'll call again later in the week.

After hanging up, I sit on the big patio and gab with my peers. It's been nine days since I last took a Percodan. This drug-free period is the longest I've gone without drugs of any variety for over three years. I climb into bed at midnight feeling proud of my perserverance.

I'm awakened by loud voices at five after four. Parker turns on a light. I jump out of bed and head for the patio. Parker is close behind. We stand in the dark and listen to the shouts emanating from next door. Parker is wearing white bikini briefs. I have on a pair of loose boxers. The morning is cool. I realize I've got an erection and slowly turn away from Parker. I fill my mind's eye with images of blood and death, anything to kill the damn boner.

My cock deflates after a few seconds. Lester and Roberto come charging out of The Swamp, screaming obscenities and insults at one another. They shove and push. I see Gary inside, lighting a cigarette in the bathroom.

I shout, "Shut up, you guys. You're acting like jerks." My outburst diverts their attention. They step apart. I move between them and ask what's going on.

Roberto is in a total rage. He accuses Lester of fiddling with the
thermostat again. The room is unbearably hot, but Lester refuses to turn
the A/C up. I ask what Gary wants. He says, from the doorway, that he
wants peace and quiet and less cool air.

Lester says he's been outvoted, so he'll sleep on one of the couches
in the pit. He complains that Roberto threatened to "beat the shit out of
me." I suggest he discuss it with Morris tomorrow. As granny, he can deal
with this situation with more authority than I. Lester says he's reporting
Roberto's threats to the counselors. I say that's up to him. The group
disperses. Parker and I return to bed.

I spend most of Sunday morning writing a paper explaining how
drugs have interfered with my life. I enjoy the writing. I find it intellectually stimulating. It diverts my thoughts from Howard's impending visit.
I eat breakfast with Richie.

Howard is announced at one-fifteen. I walk to the main building. He
looks very handsome in his pale green shirt, jeans, and grey boots. He
stands about five-eleven, weighs about one-seventy-five, and is in good
shape. I haven't seen him in months. His moustache is thicker. He looks
a little tired and gaunt, but the same as I remembered him. Our eyes lock.
There's a twinkle in his hazel eyes. I realize I'm still attracted to him. We
hug. He kisses my cheek. I kiss his neck.

He hands me a shopping bag. We sit on one of the two couches and
I rifle through my booty. I ooh and aah about all of the thoughtful gifts.
There's a portable cassette player and a stack of new tapes. He tells me
there's a tape of his newest songs at the bottom of the bag. There is also
a carton of my cigarettes, a tin of fancy cashews, a tin of pistachios,
several magazines, and a box of chocolate chip cookies. I'm very touched
and tell him so. He says nothing gives him more pleasure than seeing me
happy.

We walk to McCallum and I excuse myself to stow the stuff in my
room, then lead him on a tour of the grounds. We talk about everything
under the sun. My anxiousness evaporates quickly. I feel comfortable
with Howard. I trust him. He doesn't want anything from me but my
friendship. I ask if he's seeing anyone right now. He's involved with a
young carpenter named Adam.

He says they're in a fairly serious dating mode. I feel disappointed,
but glad that he's happy. I tell him pointblank that I feel like an ass for
the way I broke off with him. I want to clear the air between us.

"Do you feel funny seeing me here?" I say.

"Not at all. I'm flattered you care enough about me to include me in
this."

"I'd like us to be friends again."

"Me too." I throw my arm around his waist and kiss him on the cheek.
"It's great to see you, Howard. It's funny, I think of you often."

"You look really cute with short hair. I don't think I've ever seen it like this. You look about fifteen."

"My friend Richie did the honors."

"Very nice." We stop at the pool and I smoke a cigarette. We hold hands and look into the deserted pool area.

"I expected an olympic sized pool for such a world-famous institution," he sighs.

"That's what I said at first. As you can see, it's nice here, but hardly posh."

"Where are all the celebrities? Besides you, of course."

"Of course. The really big names don't come out until dark."

We stroll toward the cafeteria. I'm starving. The sun feels hot today. I tell Howard that the worst of the withdrawal seems to be over. The muscle aches have improved dramatically the last couple of days. I'm feeling human again. Eleven days without a single pill.

We eat prime rib at a table by the window. Gary and Roberto eat nearby. Howard tells me that the bearded guy is staring at me. I wave them over and introduce them to one another. After they leave, Howard asks if there's something going on between Gary and me.

"Oh, a mild flirtation."

"He's hung up on you, Daniel."

"Really? How can you tell?"

"Oh come on. He couldn't keep his eyes off you."

"He's recently divorced."

"I don't care, he's got the hots for you."

"Do you think he's handsome?"

"Sure."

"I probably won't see him after he leaves next week."

"Let's get a dessert."

"Not yet...look over by the door, Howard. It's my least favorite person. Lester."

"He looks like a Lester."

"He's nice, really. It's just that he eats all the time."

"I can see that."

"Let's skip dessert. I'll get some of those cookies you brought. Lets go sit by the lake."

"Sure."

I introduce Howard to Lester, his mother, and sister. Howard is charming as usual. He has the best manners of anyone I know. We sit under the shade of a weeping willow on the other side of the lake. The mother duck and her brood of three paddle around the water's edge. We toss them bits of crumbled cookie. I ask Howard if he's ever seen a fish eat a duckling.

"No, I can't say that I have," he says.

Richie waves from across the lake. I yell for him to join us.

"Who's that?" Howard asks, his brown Ray-Bans shielding his eyes from the glare.

"I guess I better tell you before he gets here. That's Richard Montel, the singer. He's the one that cut my hair."

"I remember when he was arrested last year. It was for cocaine, I think. How's he doing?" Howard asks.

"Pretty good."

"Don't worry, I won't say anything."

Richie and Howard get on beautifully. They both have the music business in common. They discuss favorite vocalists, musicians, and so forth. I smoke cigarettes, listen, and enjoy the day. The smell of freshly cut grass wafts over from Eisenhower, where two Hispanic men push noisy lawn mowers. The scent reminds me of Genoa Falls.

I wonder if my parents have received the letter I sent. I can't imagine they'll be pleased. My addiction will probably be yet another disappointment on their already long list of grievances against me. I haven't seen them in over a year. I wonder if they'll come for family week. I remind myself that it's pointless to worry about it.

I return my attention to the present, to these two friends, to this sunny afternoon, to the fragrance of freshly sheared grass, to the pleasure of feeling clear-headed. I can't help feeling as if my life is just beginning again.

Chapter Ten

I spend the following Sunday morning tanning myself under the hot Palm Springs sun. Richie lies next to me. We listen to Howard's demo tape. They're the sort of lush romantic ballads that Richie sings so well. I thought maybe I could get them together for something. Richie says he really admires Howard's work. We both enjoy the demo. I'm in complete awe of their musical talents. The tape player Howard brought is a godsend, I listen to it whenever I'm in my room. He's a kind, generous man.

I turn onto my stomach. What a week it's been. On Monday I told the guys in peer group my life story. It was harrowing exposing my innermost self. I've discussed David's death with exactly three people before Betty Ford. They were Sally, Howard, and my sister.

The peer group was supportive. They asked questions and encouraged me to delve deeper into why I became an actor and why I later grew so disillusioned with it.

I probably became an actor to gain big doses of approval and acceptance. The acting, in and of itself, didn't satisfy any emotional needs, except for free expression, yet it extracted a high toll. It was hard to separate the manufactured emotional turbulence from authentic feelings.

When I started to grapple with my sexuality, it stirred feelings too personal to reveal. Acting started to feel traumatic. The last few months I worked on the show, I was throwing up at least once a day from the tension. I was unable to relax, except with chemical assistance.

On some deep level, I expected acting to make my life and problems work out. Acting would validate my existence somehow. When I started using Percodan to help me get through a work day, I realized I was an addict, yet felt helpless to change my course or actions. Perhaps drug addiction seemed safe compared to living in the public eye with exposed nerve endings.

On Wednesday the patch was removed. I stowed it in a desk drawer for my burning. With each passing day, I feel stronger in body, mind, and spirit. The muscle aches have diminished to an occasional cramp or headache. The worst of the withdrawal is over. Hallelujah!

108

The nurses told me to expect anxiety and recurring muscle discomfort for a year or so. An opiate addict's cells and tissue have ingrained memories of the dependency on painkillers. When I have a craving, I try to lie down and relax until the urge for Percodan passes, usually within ten or fifteen minutes.

I'm learning to function without drugs. It feels safe to feel again. Group therapy has taught me that confronting harsh truths won't destroy me. In fact, it only serves to strengthen my character. A little crumbling isn't going to break me.

I've avoided discussing David's death in group, in part because I'm still processing memories, impressions, feelings. I'm preparing to peel another layer away. This issue is obviously central to my recovery. I've stuffed the feelings for so long. It's time to get current. I've wasted enough time already.

Richie interrupts my thoughts with an offer to fetch refreshments from the lounge. I sit up, slick with perspiration on my face, chest, and back. The sun is intense. I request a can of apple juice. He asks how I'm doing. "Great, just great," I say. He puts on a shirt over his string bikini and disappears inside. I lie on my back, shut my eyes, and continue the review of my week.

Thursday was a big day. I was appointed the new granny. I felt and feel honored to be chosen. I'm McCallum's new leader. It's a definite boon to my ego. Why do I get the scary feeling the counselors see me as officer material?

For the most part, the men seemed pleased at my selection. Gary congratulated me, as did Parker and many of the other guys. There were a few undercurrents of jealousy, though. I can't worry about other people's hang- ups. Men are so damned competitive. I can be, too, although I've actively avoided my aggressive side for years, afraid to stroke the brutal side of my persona.

We made a new rule during the community meeting after I was installed as granny. The rule was my idea. There's a new guy, an addict named Mark. He's from New Jersey and talks a mile a minute. He was turning the place upside down with his flagrant violation of the phone rules. We aren't allowed to use the pay phone until the sixth day. Everybody follows the rule except Mark. He's totally outrageous. I realize it's tough here at first, I'm not unsympathetic to cold feet, but he has to follow the rules. He claims that pressing personal emergencies give him special rights to use the phone. He's been talking for half an hour to an hour every day. The guys, including me, were outraged. He needed discipline.

We took a vote and overwhelmingly passed a new rule. Anyone abusing the phone or consistently late for circle will lose phone privileges. Each violation will incur a loss of phone rights for one day.

The next evening, I caught Mark on the phone and informed him, as granny, that he couldn't use the phone until the sixth day of his unfortunate incarceration. He said I was coming down awfully hard on him. He said he might have to leave, this wasn't working out. I suggested he give things a chance.

I explained to him that the no-phone rule is protection from outside distractions. He's totally antagonistic. He says he doesn't like the rules. He wants to call his girlfriend in New Jersey, they're having difficulties. He's obsessed with her. I have an uneasy feeling about him. I don't trust him.

Friday night also featured Gary and Parker's burnings. As granny, I was responsible for starting them on time and making sure everything ran smoothly. They proceeded without a hitch. Later, around midnight, Gary asked me to keep him company while he did his laundry. The two washers and dryers spun and churned as we discussed his plans for the upcoming week. He invited me to visit him in Santa Barbara a few days after I'm sprung. We made out briefly, interrupted by a short visit with Roberto. He told us a hilarious story.

Roberto described an incident where he went shoplifting at Neiman-Marcus disguised as a woman. He wore a red dress printed with black roses, high heels, make-up, wig, the works. His large features would make him a rather masculine woman. He claims to have stolen three thousand dollars in women' s furnishings on this particular spree. He stuffed the scarves, jewelry, and assorted garments inside the girdle and a long black overcoat. The loot was supposedly intended as Christmas gifts for his wife, sister, and mother. He's a real character.

After breakfast the next morning, I walked Gary to his car. The rains left it pretty clean. I felt incredibly sad saying goodbye to him. As a result, I was in a funk most of yesterday.

Parker left at noon. A girlfriend picked him up. I asked what he'd be doing on his first day of freedom. He said he wanted sushi for lunch, then a movie, some sex, and a Cocaine Anonymous meeting in the evening.

We agreed to connect after I graduate, maybe go to a meeting together. He gave me a bear hug and kissed my cheek. For a straight guy he's very cool. I'm crazy about his inscription in my AA book: "Dear Daniel...Can we still be friends? I love you, Parker." All week we listened to a Todd Rundgren tape Howard gave me. "Can We Still Be Friends?" was our favorite cut.

Richie appears with the drinks. He has iced tea. At our feet is standard sun worshiping gear: tunes, cigarettes, lighter, ashtray, magazines, Oreo cookies, and several tubes of Richie's expensive suntan oils. I wear no sunscreen. I want as much color as possible, short of actually destroying my skin.

The Palm Springs radio station plays the song "Hotel California" by the Eagles. Howard and I once spent a Fourth of July weekend at a place in Laguna called The Hotel California. We were very happy together. I was taking small amounts of Percodan and smoking a little grass. I felt better than I had in years. What changed between that Fourth of July and the following Thanksgiving? Why did I break up with him? I got scared, but of what? I need to know.

My brain is constantly filled with thoughts and information that was never processed, only stored in the memory banks. Drugs helped me keep problems and unhappiness at bay. Chunk by chunk, I've been digesting past feelings and problems, trying to understand what I need to do to make myself happy.

I'm weighing my likes and dislikes, trying to craft the framework for a happy, sane life. Who and what will I be now that I'm not using drugs all the time? Do I want to work as an actor? Can I handle the stress of working? My head is crammed with questions.

One goal has been to forgive my parents. I know that David's death wasn't their fault. He was sick. I felt so helpless when he was ill and then, after he died, I had to hold someone accountable besides God.

I'm sick of feeling angry at myself. I've punished myself for years, with drugs, with repressed feelings, promiscuous sex, low self-esteem, and lots of anger.

I've grown about a thousand percent since I arrived eighteen days ago. It's been hard work. The reward is how good I feel. I'm not swinging from highs to lows. I'm learning to appreciate the middle. I'm slowing down and listening to the rhythms of life. I'm edging closer toward becoming the person I always wanted to be. It's damn scary, but I'm becoming a man.

The sun feels intensely hot. I hear the door open and clamp my eyes shut. It's Lester. Mr. Buttinsky. He sits on a patio chair in the shade of McCallum. Richie and I are spread on towels on the grass. The sprinklers water the lawn in a droning hiss.

Lester gabs about his family in a banal way. Listening to him drone on about his father's drinking makes me want to scream. Tomorrow the three of us begin family week. My parents are already in the desert, according to my sister. They're staying in a friend's condo and playing golf all weekend. Linda asked if they could come see me today, but I said no. We'll see each other later in the week, after they've been educated on addiction, co-dependency, and alcoholism.

I'm nervous about seeing them. I'd rather our interaction were monitored by the counselors. We're not even supposed to speak to our families until Thursday. That's fine with me.

Lester's kin will be here today, as will Richie's. His agent arrives tomorrow. We're all just a shade anxious. Richie told me his family hates the fact he's gay. They're very religious. His father died when he was a teenager, then his mother had a breakdown, so he was raised by his much older sister. He says she's a Holy Roller.

Lester is worried because his father is a big drinker and may not abstain from alcohol during the family week. He's afraid of his father. Am I afraid of mine? Why are my dad and I such strangers? What separates us? He was always off on business trips after David died, or at least it seemed that way, I felt very alone without a male presence in the house. My mother and sister were the dominant forces in our house. I went outdoors or to my room for privacy. I always liked women, but craved a male companionship that was sorely lacking in the years following David's death.

Throughout grade school and junior high, I had as many friends as I wanted, but I often preferred to be alone. It was a strain having to pretend I was straight every day. I dated girls and led a normal life for the most part, but secretly craved the freedom to be myself and love another man.

During my junior year of high school, I began my first love relationship with a man. Christopher was a year older, an average student who was Genoa Falls' premiere basketball star, number twenty-two. That fall, we were dating girls who were best friends, so we went on several double dates. We clicked instantly, there was a definite chemical reaction between us.

By Thanksgiving, we were sexually and emotionally involved. I fell in love with him. It was my first real love affair. We spent much of our free time together. We were best friends and boyfriends. I went to all his basketball games. We saw movies, went skiing, drove into Chicago for wild drinking sprees, took weekends in Wisconsin. We got very close, very fast.

Sometimes we'd check into a motel outside Genoa Falls to be alone and make love. The emotional and physical intimacy made me feel tremendously vital. Our sexual experimentation was thrilling and mind-expanding. We tried everything. At first, our double lives were exciting. The dishonesty eventually caught up with me. It hurt to keep my feelings for Chris secreted inside, far from the eyes of the world.

Our involvement ended the following summer, a few weeks before he left for college. I knew things were coming to a closing, but didn't know what to do. He had a full basketball scholarship. His life was headed elsewhere. I had another year of crummy high school before I graduated. I felt abandoned, even though I knew in my heart it wasn't meant to be a long-term partnership. I couldn't tell my heart to think rationally. I loved him.

We broke up on a muggy August night. We were parked next to a field of corn out on the old country road. We sat on the roof of his black Camaro and looked at the stars. The corn was over six feet tall. We were both dressed in shorts and T-shirts. Chris changed the tape in the car stereo. We shared a bag of grapes, drank a few beers, and listened to Roxy Music. Our favorite song, "Eight Miles High," came on. I never tired of its melody and clever lyrics.

Stretched across the hood of the car, he looked so relaxed and comfortable. His blond hair swept across a high forehead and covered his small ears. His lips were full, the upper one plumper than the lower. I loved his green eyes. I really enjoyed kissing him. I lit a cigarette and listened to Bryan Ferry's voice.

Eight Miles High
and when you touch down
you find you're
stranger than known
signs in the street
that say where you're going
are somewhere
just being their own
nowhere is there
warmth to be found
just those afraid
of losing their ground
rain grey town
known for its sound
in places
small faces abound
round the squares
huddled in storms
some laughing
some just shapeless forms
sidewalk scenes
and black limousines
some living
some standing
alone

Chris began to speak. He said he cared more for me than anyone else in his life. I inhaled on my cigarette and looked at the stars. I knew what was coming, I had sensed it for weeks and weeks. He said he treasured me, but couldn't continue our "special friendship" any longer. We needed to grow up. He had decided to marry his girlfriend the following spring. He said I should find a girl, too. We had fun together, but it was time to get serious and move on.

I already knew his limitations. He didn't have the courage to be different. He couldn't face being gay, so he chose something else. I couldn't do that. I wasn't interested in conforming for the sake of convention and appearances.

I told him I wouldn't marry a woman. That would be a lie. How could anything so good, like our feelings for one another and our lovemaking, be considered wrong? Who were we hurting? He said he wanted children, a family, respectability. I said that was up to him. I told him I really loved him. He ended the discussion by saying he didn't care to be a homosexual.

I reacted by removing the cassette from the stereo and shredding the tape in full view of Christopher. After a brief silence, I asked him to drive me home. I couldn't bear to look at his face any longer. I needed to be alone. After he dropped me off, I walked into my parents bathroom, dug around the medicine chest, and swallowed two Codeine tablets from a prescription bottle.

That's what pain killers are for, right? To deaden suffering. I wanted to kill the hurt inside my chest, to ease the panic before it ripped me in two. I needed to obliterate the shame of loving someone who couldn't really love me back. I was alone again.

I mourned the loss of Christopher for months. I walked around with a gaping hole in my chest. I felt disconnected and depressed. When my parents or friends asked what was wrong, I couldn't say. I had to lie. I kept the source of the misery a secret.

My senior year I started smoking pot and drinking more frequently. I turned to chemicals for answers. A thought that keeps coming into my head. Could Gary be hopelessly straight like Chris? And what about Lance? Gary is obviously very taken with me, but is he authentically gay? Maybe he's just mixed up. There's a sense of deja vu here.

I wish Lester would quit talking. He's reminding Richard it's nearly twelve-thirty. He asks if I have visitors coming. Richie says he doesn't know and promises to wake me up in a few minutes. Lester says he'll see us later. I hear the door creak as he returns indoors.

I do have visitors coming today. Lance is driving down this afternoon, as is Sally. She's in the desert for a weekend at a posh health farm. She calls it her weight-loss weekend. She phoned me on the McCallum pay phone last night to confirm her visit. I could tell she'd been drinking, health farm or not. Her words were definitely slurred. I asked whether she was feeling poorly. She swore she was giddy from starvation. Right.

Richie whispers to wake up. I tell him I'm already awake. He says it's time for him to get ready for his company. I'm covered with perspiration. The heat feels great. We compare tan lines, then I run through the sprinklers. Richie laughs as I allow myself to be drenched. It feels wonderful.

By the time I finish showering and dressing, it's a few minutes after one. I wear a blue T-shirt Gary gave me in the laundry room last night, navy trousers, red socks with little blue specks, and athletic shoes. I look in the mirror. I'm looking pretty good. The short hair looks a bit radical but nice. I smile at my reflection, then brush my teeth. A craggy man's voice comes over the PA system. Richie's guests are here, as are mine. I wonder who'll get here first, Sally or Lance? I'd bet on Sally. She's fascinated by aberrant behavior and the lifestyles of the rich and diseased. She'd get here on the time, she wouldn't want to miss a thing. She's a Geraldo, Sally Jessie, Phil, and Oprah addict. The more twisted and freakish the subject material, the happier she is. Maybe observing less fortunate people makes her feel less miserable. She's not a very happy person most of the time. Her husband's dullness is the current complaint.

When I arrive at the reception area in the big building, Lance is sitting on a couch reading a magazine. He lights up when I say his name. He's dressed in khaki shorts, cranberry-colored shirt, and thongs. He looks all-American. We hug. His cologne smells erotic. His hair is longer. He says he likes my haircut and points to a basket filled with spring flowers. Tulips, fragrant hyacinths, daffodils. It's a lovely arrangement. I'm touched. I have an urge to kiss him on the mouth, but stop myself. He also hands me a thin book called "The Tao Te Ching."

We walk to McCallum. I take the flowers and book to my room. We sit in the pit and talk. I hear my name on the intercom. Lance and I walk outside, stopping briefly around the corner of the building to smooch. He has a sensual mouth. I never tire of kissing him. Is it possible to love two different people simultaneously?

Sally is browsing in the gift shop. She's dressed to impress. A black tailored jacket is worn over a striking fuchsia-colored blouse, soft pink slacks, and black stiletto pumps.

Her purse is the size of a goose egg and covered with dazzling jewels. Her frosted auburn hair looks very pouffy. She's been fighting weight gain, but looks the best I've ever seen her. She buys two T-shirts that say "One Day at a Time" on them, as well as two coffee mugs.

I hug her. "So who's here?" she whispers in my ear. I tell her there are several guest stars, but I can't name names, that's against the rules. She has no patience and immediately begs me to spill the beans. She looks over at Lance. I introduce them. I told both the other would be here, but she seems surprised.

"Why are you buying coffee cups?" I say.

"Because, Daniel. I want something with the Betty Ford insignia on it."

"Why? To prove you were here?" We both laugh and she launches into wild stories about the people in her weight-loss weekend. I suggest we go eat before the dining hall fills up. Sally pays for her Betty Ford souvenirs and we three walk down the hall. She is ecstatic because she's lost four pounds in just two days. I ask how her husband is doing at home.

"Oh, he's such a nerd sometimes."

"She always says he's incompetent or a klutz, but her husband is really a bright guy," I explain to Lance. I don't want him to feel left out. Sally is addressing herself exclusively to me.

"I know that he's intelligent, for God's sake. What I mean is he doesn't have a grasp for everyday things. It's impossible to explain."

"Try," I say, looking over to Lance and grinning. He smiles and winks. I don't think he's ever winked at me before. He does it well.

"Well," Sally begins, speaking in a hushed tone for dramatic emphasis. She knows how to get her audience's attention. "Henry is probably a genius. The smartest person I know. But he called me last night and told me he had spent the entire day planting fruit trees in the garden."

"I didn't know he was a gardener."

"He's NOT ever planted more than a seed in his entire life."

"When did he decide to grow fruit trees?"

"Yesterday morning. It was his project. He went out and bought six trees, came home, and planted them." She speaks of him in a slightly sarcastic, disrespectful tone.

"I see."

"I think the job is burning him out. I really do. So I said to him, 'Henry, what sort of fruit trees did you plant, honey?' He says 'Oh, I got the Beverly Hills apples.' I said, 'What did you say?' and he tells me he's purchased half a dozen apple trees named after the city of Beverly Hills. He thought they'd grow well in Beverly Hills since they were called Beverly Hills apples. I've never heard of such a tree. How trendy. I don't want any Beverly Hills apples, thank you very much."

"You're discriminating against a harmless apple tree," I say.

"Absolutely. I'd rather have something else. I see the words Beverly Hills enough as it is. I'll have the gardener dig them up."

"You can't do that, it would hurt Henry's feelings."

"He'll never know. I'll have the gardener plant some decent fruit trees. He should have asked me before planting those stupid trees."

We step outside so Sally and I can have a cigarette. The three of us sit on a bench on the grass. I fill them in on some of the gossip. Sally says that being granny sounds like a terrible responsibility. She thinks I have enough to do as it is. I explain more of the program and the problems I've been sharing in group therapy. Sally is surprised that my assignments include writing reports and papers. I tell her I enjoy the work tremendously. Lance says I'd make a good writer. He tells Sally that a letter I wrote him a few days ago was very funny. She looks strained. I don't think she expected to share me with anyone, let alone a gorgeous gay college boy.

As they talk, I remember the time Sally had a nose surgery two years ago. We spent the week after her operation lolling around her fancy house, watching television, smoking cigarettes, and taking an endless supply of pharmaceuticals. I suggested she get Percodan from her doctor, which she did. We binged. She was in legitimate pain, I was in sympathetic pain. I fixed our meals the first two days and looked after her needs. Her husband was constantly working, so we didn't have to worry about him.

From morning to late night, we'd medicate ourselves and lie around, zonked, like a couple of junkies. We've done tons of cocaine and smoked grass together through the years, but that was the only time we took painkillers together. We're total co-dependents.

At lunch, we talk and eat. Sally dines on veggies only, as per her health program. I eat the beef, potatoes, and corn. Lance eats the turkey and veggies. They seem particularly interested in what takes place inside the AA and NA meetings. Sally is on her best behavior. She asks Lance questions and listens to his answers carefully. It's nice to see her making an effort.

She asks when my folks arrive. I tell her today. She asks whether I'm nervous. Her parents were always very generous and gave her the total run of their house and lives. My parents seem straight-laced and rigid to her. Her parents reminded me of grandparents, they were older and showered Sally with whatever she wanted. She was very spoiled. We've known one another since the sixth grade.

Between bites, I describe Lester's secret cache of snacks in The Swamp. She says he may be addicted to eating, then crunches an asparagus spear.

Richie enters the cafeteria with two older women. Sally sees him, then does a double take. "Yes," I whisper. "That's exactly who you think it is, minus the beard."

"Why didn't you tell me?"

"It's against the rules."

"Well, you could still tell ME, for God's sake."

"I knew you'd be surprised."

"He's a wonderful singer, Daniel. Are you friends?"

"Uh-huh."

"He's very handsome. What's he in for?"

"I can't say."

"I bet he drank and used coke. He's a coke addict, right?"

"I'm not going to say another word about him. He's very nice. I'll introduce you."

"Have you thought about going back to work when you get out?"

"As a matter of fact, I have."

"What have you decided?" she says between bites of broccoli. Lance is very quiet.

"I've decided to wait and see."

"How old is Richard, Daniel?"

"I don't know. Late thirties maybe."

"Wasn't he arrested last year?"

"Something like that."

"For drugs, right?"

"Quit fishing, Sally."

"All right, I give up. Lance, kick me if you see anyone else interesting. Are there some cute guys in your dorm?"

"Several."

"I'm dying for a cigarette."

"I'm done," Lance says.

We get up to leave. I wave to Richard. He looks tense. As we're walking from the building, I hear my name called. Amanda crosses from the cafeteria, a handsome young man on her arm. We introduce all of our company back and forth.

Amanda says she wanted me to meet her son. He's here for family week. I tell her I've got family week, too. Her son's about twenty years old. Sally acts very cool, but I can tells she's impressed that Amanda Andrews is tracking me down. We all make small talk for a few minutes, then they return to their brunch, we to a siesta lakeside.

Morris stops by to meet my friends. He leaves on Friday. He's been here for six weeks altogether. Sally takes an immediate shine to him. She really turns on the charm.

She excuses herself to find the bathroom and get a can of soda from the lounge. I see Lester and his family across the lake. Lance says his classes are going well. I like his positive attitude. He says my garden looks great.

I tell him I'm afraid of leaving Betty Ford. Why? Because my old friends might not like me sober. Or they might be uncomfortable because I remind them of bad habits or their own dependency problems. He assures me that drinking and drugs aren't important to him, but my friendship is.

"You're really thoughtful, Lance."

"I care about you."

"I care about you, too. When I get out of here, we should spend more time together. It might be fun getting acquainted without drugs," I say, flicking a ladybug off my arm.

"You've inspired me to take a break from drinking."

"Good for you. Don't do it for me, do it for yourself."

"I'm doing it for us both."

"I like that. So tell me, what do you think of Sally?"

"She's nice. Maybe a little intense."

"She is intense, isn't she?"

"I get nervous listening to her. She's so wound up," he says, looking across the lake.

"You're right."

"I don't dislike her, but she makes me uneasy."

"Interesting."

"How long have you known her?"

"Since I was in grade school. What else?"

"Will you get mad?" he asks.

"No, I won't."

"I don't trust her, Daniel. She acts like she's jealous of you. I can't explain. It's like she owns you. I got the feeling she was competing with you. It's weird."

"I sometimes wonder why we're still friends. We don't have much in common, except getting high. Every time we were together, we did drugs. Cocaine, grass, drinks, whatever was available. We even did LSD together once."

"What was that like?"

"Well, it was fun. I can see how it might be scary for some people. We laughed a lot and saw enhanced colors, weird shapes, but nothing frightening. It was fun, but intense."

"I don't really know her."

"What did she say to you?"

"Nothing."

"What did she say that has you upset?"

"It was her attitude. When you weren't around, she gossiped about you, you know? Said you were such a wonderful person, wasn't it sad you were in here? She said she hoped you and your parents worked things out. She didn't say much, but her tone was sort of bitchy. I can't explain it. I think she's trouble. That's all I can say. Be careful of her, Daniel."

"Thanks for telling me, Lance. I need other people's perspective on Sally, mine is distorted. It's funny you mention not trusting her. About two years ago, when I told my parents I was gay, she seemed very supportive, but I found out later she had been telling people I was gay for years. I felt totally betrayed, but kept my mouth shut. I didn't want to deal with the pain, so I stuffed it. I began to seriously question her morals and ethics and what sort of friend she really was. So that's why I want to hear your opinion, it may reflect my own."

She really controls her husband. Henry is her project in life. He jumps at her every whim, they're more like master and slave than partners. She hates it when anyone disagrees with her, particularly her husband. She's willful.

For years I've listened and watched her treat other people badly, always questioning why I was exempt from her wrath. I thought she was different with me, that perhaps she'd change if given the chance. Again and again she revealed her true self to me, but I ignored what I saw. I harbor great resentment of her for indiscreetly blabbing my personal secrets to impress her friends. That is totally disloyal. She always looks out for herself first.

We both escaped from Genoa Falls at different times for similar reasons. We were looking for happiness, warmer weather, and big success. We felt confined by our families and our pasts. We came to L.A., created new lives, and made our own rules. That's what separates us. I didn't lose my humanity when I turned away from reality through drugs and isolation. She gave up her career when she married Henry and became a wife and mother and companion. She strayed into a career controlling Henry as I was slipping into full-time addiction to Percodan.

My sense is that sobriety will bring an end to our alliance. I don't think I can deal with her or put up with her when I'm sober. Without drugs, she looks very unappetizing. It's sad, but true. Where does she get off criticizing her husband for planting a bunch of Beverly Hills apple trees? What does she care? What does she get out of being such a killjoy? She seems so angry at Henry all the time. That isn't healthy.

At three, Sally suddenly remembers she's due back for a stretch class in half an hour. Lance and I walk her to the reception area. We hug. She tells Lance how pleased she is to meet him, good luck with college, the usual pleasantries. She orders me to phone her this week.

"Daniel, I want a full report on your folks and that family thing...good luck, dear. Can you tell I've lost four pounds? Say goodbye to Richard. He's a fox."

With a theatrical laugh, she swings her plastic bag of souvenirs over the beaded purse and exits through the front doors. I realize at this moment that I'll probably never see her again. Something in me has changed irrevocably. I feel sad, but right. There's nothing good glueing us together anymore. Our relationship is spiritually bankrupted. I have a new and improved way of living.

I'll break things off gently, I don't want to hurt her. I care for her, but it's time to let go and move on. Sally and I had a long run together. The time is ripe to end things as friends instead of waiting until I hate her guts. We're going down separate forks in the road. We came from the same place, but our destinations are different. I feel a loss for the good times we shared, but I know an ending when I feel one.

Lance and I walk around the lake, stopping to neck behind a willow tree facing Eisenhower Hospital. He tastes so good. I pull away. If we're caught I'll get in trouble with counselors. I don't want to rock the boat. I suggest we head back. Visiting hours are almost over.

I tell Lance that I need to find someone from McCallum to tell their life story at tonight's patients-only AA meeting. Everyone I've asked has declined. As granny, I have the authority to choose someone, but that seems heavy-handed.

Lance suggests I tell my story. I had thought of it, but vetoed the idea. Spilling the intimate details of my addiction to a roomful of non-McCallum patients terrifies me. That's why I should do it, to prove to myself that the past, the wreckage, has no hold over me any longer. I'm not afraid of anything except drugs, lies, and dishonesty.

As granny, I would be setting a good example for sixteen fellow addicts, as well as the people from Amanda's hall. If I have the courage to reveal myself, I might inspire others to be brave. I tell Lance he's absolutely right, I should tell my story. We hug goodbye next to the water fountain. I thank him for the flowers and book. His magnanimous gifts, the visit, and house-sitting lead me to believe he really does care for me.

At the patients-only AA meeting, I give an encapsulated version of the life story I told peer group on Friday. Amanda's group and the McCallum boys are assembled in a big circle. It's a struggle to publicly admit tidbits like "I sometimes took upwards of eighteen Percodans a day," or "I tended toward promiscuity when I took drugs like Ecstasy." It's difficult, but I say a few words about David, forcing myself to look at faces, not the floor or walls.

After AA, we return to McCallum and supplement the usual Sunday night cold cuts with pizza. Tomorrow we return to our regular schedule. My parents will be on campus. That feels weird. I'm pleased they've come, but a little fearful of meeting them face to face.

I like my parents when they're people, not parents. Maybe we'll be able to revamp our relationship here. This place has a healing aura about it. I'm trying to keep an open mind about them. If they can begin treating me with respect, then we can start talking again. I feel very bad about our separation.

I sit in the pit and watch television with the guys. Lester calls me to the phone near ten.

"Daniel, telephone," he sings.

"Okay, thanks, Lester," I say, rising.

"Guess who's calling?" he asks.

"Who?"

"Gary."

"Good, thanks," I say, wondering why he felt the need to announce my caller to the entire room. I walk to the pay phone - "Hello!"

"Hi, Daniel. How's it going?"

"Good. I just told my life story in the patients-only meeting."

"Good for you. I'm proud."

"Thanks."

"So how was it?" He sounds tired.

"A little heart-wrenching, but good."

"I've missed you."

"That's really nice to hear. I miss you too, Gary. How are things at home?"

"Fine. Lonely. Did I tell you where I lived?"

"Sure. Santa Barbara."

"Right. My house isn't finished. It's in this ranch along the coast. We have an entire mountain top."

"Sounds fantastic."

"It will be when it's done."

"Are you working?'

"On the house, yes. I'm resigning from my real estate company tomorrow."

"Why?"

"I want to take six months off and build the rest of the property, plant some trees, putz around for a while. I've been wanting to do this for years."

"Good for you."

"Want to come up and help me hammer a few nails?"

"Sure."

"When?"

"In two weeks, like we discussed."

"So, are you going to meetings?"

"As a matter of fact I just returned from one in town." he said proudly.

"How was it?"

"Good. Very supportive. When you come to visit, we'll go toone, too."

"My folks will be here this week."

"Should be interesting."

"I guess so." My voice sounds smaller.

"Don't be afraid, Daniel. You're doing really well."

"Thanks. Have you been good out in the big, bad world?"

"I'm clean."

"You better stay clean or I'll find a new boyfriend."

"Noooo."

"Well, maybe I'll wait until after we fool around a few times, just to get my money's worth. How are your kids?"

"Great, I spent yesterday with them."

"I bet they were really excited to see you."

"They're good boys."

"What about your ex?"

"She just crabbed at me about the money."

"Why don't you pay her and get it over with?"

"Good point. Maybe I will. Have you been mistreating your McCallum boys?"

"Not yet, though I'm constantly tempted to throw my weight around with Lester, excuse the pun. I'm so rude. He's been getting on my nerves."

122

"Keep those apes in line. Long live McCallum Hall."
"Our alma mater. I better go. Thanks for calling."
"I can't wait to see the house."
"I can't wait to see you."
"I'll talk to you the next night or two."
"I'll be keeping tabs on you, buddy," he warned in a playful voice.
"Somebody should. I'm getting pretty horny. I hope I can control my urges."
"You're always horny. Behave yourself."
"I will."
"I love you," he says. I pause and take a deep breath.
"I think I love you, too."
"See ya."
"See ya."

Before going to sleep, I lie in bed and read the thought-provoking book Lance gave me. Parker's bed is bare, stripped down to the mattress. John said I'll have a new roommate in a few days. I reread a passage.

Fill your bowl to the brim
and it will spill.
Keep sharpening your knife
and it will blunt.
Chase after money and security
and your heart will never unclench.
Care about people's approval
and you will be their prisoner.
Do your work, then step back.
The only path to serenity.

The Tao Te Ching

I decide to read this every night as my last thought before sleeping. It compliments the serenity prayer quite nicely. I turn off the light and masturbate to mental images of sex Gary.

Chapter Eleven

During Monday morning group, Molly steers the discussion to death. Naturally, when it's my turn to share, I try to dodge the issue. The group won't let me. They already know a few details about David's death from hearing my life story on Friday. They suggest I feel guilty and responsible for his death.

"Of course I feel guilty, he was my brother. I was totally helpless to save him," I answer in a defensive voice. The memory of losing him is suddenly strong.

"Tell us what it feels like, Daniel. Describe your feelings," Molly quietly asks.

"I can picture him lying in his bed. He was pale. He was wearing flannel pajamas Grandma gave him for Christmas, the ones with elephants and lions on them. He looked shrunken. I felt sick to my stomach, like butterflies, only emptier. He was dead already, gone forever. I felt emotionally dead. I was afraid to feel too sad because it might suck me into a dark hole. I felt afraid."

"How were you responsible for his death?"

"For Christ's sake, he was my twin. I wanted to help. I was a kid. I didn't know what I felt, nobody told me anything. I knew him better than anyone, he knew me better than anyone. It was like losing a fucking piece of myself. I felt like I was being punished. I was terribly angry, but I didn't know why. I felt terribly alone."

I break into sobs.

Through the glaze of my emotional outpouring, I see surprised looks on my peers' faces. I'm usually so pulled together and friendly, now they get a glimpse of pain. I allow the anguish to gush forth, bending forward as if to spit the sadness out. After about a minute of this, I hiccup and slow down. More hiccups make me giggle. Morris puts an arm around my shoulder as support. What a drama. I feel as if I've lived through a scene from a Tennessee Williams play.

Molly says these feelings may hurt, but it's healthy to let them out, then I can let them go. I'm quiet the rest of the session. I don't feel embarrassed for revealing myself. I feel relieved.

At lunch, I spot my parents eating outside on the patio with the other

124

families. I catch my mother's eye. She smiles and continues chewing a bit of her salad. I ask Richie to save me a seat, I have something to do.

I step over to the patio and hug my mom's shoulders. She remains seated. She kisses my cheek. I can smell her Chanel. Dad is eating a salad, too. He rises. We shake hands, then I remove my sunglasses so they can see I'm fine. They're probably worried about me.

"Hi, Daniel", my father says.

"Hi, Dad. Thanks for coming."

"Hi, Mom."

"Hi, honey. You look good. I like your hair."

"How are you, son?" Dad says without a trace of anger or resentment. My fear had been that they'd hate my guts for avoiding them the last year. They're friendly.

"I'm really doing well, Dad. This place is great." I realize I'm breaking the "No fraternization with family members" rule, but fuck it. If this isn't a healing step, then nothing is.

"I better go, you guys. We're not supposed to talk until Thursday."

"Okay, honey. We understand," Mom says wistfully.

"Bye, Dad, bye, Mom. I'm glad you came."

I walk to the cafeteria. Richie says, "That was a good thing to do." I eat a hamburger and feel happy. My parents must really love me to be here.

After lunch, I find a letter from Howard on the mail table in the lounge. I walk to my room and lie across the bed, then rip open the envelope. He writes that he was very impressed with me during our visit. He wants to extend his support in any way possible. He says he thinks it's difficult, but he needs to share some unsavory news with me. If we're really going to move forward as friends, he writes, he needs to share something. He informs me that he's tested positive for the HIV virus. He doesn't think he has full-blown AIDS yet, but felt I should know the situation.

I'm not alarmed for myself, really. I was tested about six months ago, several months after we broke up. He says I'm probably fine. We always practiced safer sex. He says he found out he was HIV-positive when he was in the hospital getting treated for pneumonia about a month ago. He says I might want to be tested.

I feel stunned, but not completely surprised. Half the gay men I've ever known are dead or sick with AIDS. I've had three friends die of AIDS-related illnesses over the last eighteen months. I couldn't face attending any of their funeral services. Hell, I didn't even go to my brother's memorial service.

I feel very sad to think of permanently losing Howard from my life. I continue reading the hand-written letter. He writes that his present boyfriend is HIV-positive, too, so that's nice. He hopes to be around for a long, long time. He writes that I'm very talented and capable and deserve great happiness. He believes Betty Ford is a major step. He says he loves me and looks forward to seeing me again soon.

After finishing the letter, I sign up for the nine p.m. phone slot, then return to my room and write him a supportive letter. I need to connect with him now, as I'm feeling the implications of his news. I cry as I finish the letter. I really care for Howard.

Howard is all I think about the rest of the afternoon. I wonder how he feels. Is he depressed? What can I do to support him?

Before dinner, John asks me to walk to the Firestone Building and escort a new arrival, Tony, to McCallum, then take him to dinner. A granny's work is never done.

The man is sitting in the nurses' station, talking nonstop to whomever will listen. He's blitzed. His speech is slurred and he weaves when he tries to stand. He's in his fifties, stands about five-eight, Italian, nice-looking, but wild-eyed. He's wearing expensive, Italian-made clothes and smells of alcohol, gin maybe. My first thought is: I hope he isn't going to be in MY room. I introduce myself and ask how he's doing.

"Not too fucking well, bozo."

"Now, now, Tony, don't be abusive."

"You're right, I'm a real prick."

"Are you ready to go?"

"I just got here, man."

"No, I mean are you ready to walk to where you'll be living. It's called McCallum Hall," I say patiently.

"Will you be living there, too?"

"Sure. Do you have a suitcase?"

"Someone took it, maybe that stupid boy with the blue eyes."

"I don't know, Tony. I suggest you be nice to these people. They'll be here with you for the next month."

"Is that how long I'm supposed to stay?"

"Probably."

"I'll go crazy. Why do you look familiar?"

"I don't know."

"You're that actor from a show I used to like."

"Could be."

"I never forget a face. What's your name?"

"Daniel."

"What are you doing here? Aren't you a little young to be washed up?"

"You're charming."

"What are you hooked on, Daniel?"

"Painkillers. You?"

"Coke. God, I can't take narcotics. They make me sleepy. What were your favorites?"

"Percodan."

"Good stuff."

"What do you do out in the world besides use cocaine, Tony?"

"I produce movies."

"What's your last name?"

"Antollini."

"I've heard of you, Tony. You made some fine films. I really loved "Catch the Sun."

"I'm retired now."

"That's too bad. You look too young to be retired."

"Thank you, you're sweet."

"Are you high now?'

"You bet your ass I am. I dropped my tequila out on the front lawn. I threw my pipe out the limo window as we were coming up the road. It's probably in the gutter out front. Maybe I should go find it."

"I'm sure the gardeners will remove it. Let's walk to McCallum. Can you walk?" His face is sweaty and his red eyes appear unfocused. Maybe he should be in a hospital.

I assist him back to McCallum. Tony is out of shape and breathless. It takes us nearly ten minutes to complete a sixty-second walk. He looks like death warmed over. John takes Tony into the office, then asks me to return in fifteen minutes and take him to dinner.

Twenty minutes later, Tony stands next to me in circle. The rest of us repeat the Serenity Prayer, Tony mumbles and holds onto me and Tom. He's a mess. As we're walking to the cafeteria, I hear him asking Lester how much he weighs. I suppress the urge to laugh.

I escort him down the food line. He says, in a loud voice, that he can only eat the finest foods. He says everything looks terrible. It takes nearly ten minutes to load his tray.

We sit with Roberto and Mark. Tony tries to cut into his pork chop, then asks for some hot sauce. I fetch a bottle. He proceeds to splash his entire plate of chops, potatoes, and beans with the red liquid. He eats a few bites, then gulps down two glasses of water. I eat a sandwich quickly. He doesn't stop talking.

An hour later, he finishes the last bite of his chop. He's buzzed to the max. He hasn't stopped talking and ranting the entire meal. We're the last McCallum men to leave the cafeteria. I lead Tony back toward McCallum.

"So how old are you, gorgeous?" he asks, weaving to the right.

"Thirty."

"You look younger."

"Thanks."

"It wasn't a compliment, just an observation." Even smashed to the gills, Tony has a razor-sharp mind. I like him. He's completely fucked up, but interesting. I show him to the room he'll be sharing with another new patient, Radga, an eighteen-year-old speed freak from Singapore. He really doesn't want to be here. His family insisted he spend a month at Betty Ford or they wouldn't pay for his American college education. He looked young and scared when I met him outside the office earlier.

Tony gets into his room and immediately asks where his suitcase is. I tell him the counselors will be bringing it in a few minutes.

He flops down on the bed closest to the bathroom. Within a few seconds, he's nodding off.

"Tony, I'll let you rest," I say, tiptoeing toward the door.

"Did I ever tell you about the time I went to the Venice Film Festival with Julie Christie and Warren Beatty?'

"No, you didn't ,Tony."

"They were so beautiful. Took my breath away."

"How are you feeling?"

"Exhausted, Danny baby. How long have you been here?"

"Eighteen days."

"Good for you. Why do they call you granny?"

"Because, it's my job. The granny does things like meet new patients and show them around."

"Do I look terrible?"

"You look tired, Tony."

"Wake me if anything good happens."

"Okay. See you later. Welcome to Betty Ford."

I see Mark lurking nearby when I go to use the pay phone. Roberto told me Mark's been sneaking calls at weird times. If I catch him, there will be hell to pay. Howard answers on the third ring.

"Hi," I say.

"Hey, Daniel. What'cha doing?"

"Thinking about you."

"You got my letter?"

"Yes, I did. I'm really sorry, Howard."

"Don't be sad, Babe. I'm fine for now. I'll probably live for years."

"I hope you do."

"I hated telling you in a letter. Are you mad?"

"No, no. Listen, I was tested about six months ago and it came back negative, so don't worry about me on top of everything else. I'm fine."

"That's good news. You sound funny, Danny."

"I feel sad. I don't want you to be sick."

"Don't be sad. I need you happy. My health is fine right now. How's Betty Ford treating you?"

"Great, actually. I saw my parents today."

"How did that go?"

"I just went over and said, 'Hello. I'm glad you're here, Mom and Dad.' They were nice."

"Good for you, Daniel. This is definitely a good thing. I can see the world opening its arms to embrace the new you."

"Thanks. Howard?

"Yes?"

"I feel awkward. I don't want to intrude on your privacy. We can talk as much or as little as you want about your health situation, okay?"

"Okay. It can wait. I don't feel like you're intruding, not in the slightest."

"Are you feeling all right?"

"Sure."

"Does your friend treat you well?"

"Like a prince."

"I'm looking forward to spending more time with you after I get out."

"Me, too. We can go see some new movies."

"Great, I'd really like that. I' d better go."

"I love you, Daniel."

"I love you, too. Thanks for being my friend."

"Thanks for calling."

I make several surprise visits to the lounge, checking to see whether Mark is breaking the phone prohibition. He certainly acts suspiciously when I see him. He has shifty eyes.

I return to my room and work on a paper that addresses the feelings I had and have about the death of my brother. All the assignments have been pertinent to my personal program and issues. Molly has given me high marks on my homework assignments.

Sitting at the desk, I remember something about Tony. About fifteen years ago, his wife was murdered in their Beverly Hills mansion by a gang of cultists. The media gave his tragedy the full treatment. The trial of the murderers was big news. Tony was perceived as a broken man. Did he quit making movies then? Is that when he became a coke head?

Richard stops in to chat. We go to my patio and have a cigarette. He mentions that he saw Mark talking on the phone a little while ago. I throw my cigarette down. The blood is rushing into my face. I knew that guy was an asshole. Richard asks what's wrong. I explain the Mark situation. He thinks Mark is mentally and emotionally unstable.

"Stay away from him, Daniel. He's a twisted soul."

"No. It's the principle of the thing. He knows the rules and he's choosing to break them. I refuse to let him get away with it. If he fucks around everyone else will, too. Pardon me while I go tell him he's restricted from the phone for another day."

I knock on the door to The Swamp. A voice tells me to come in. Lester is sitting on the bed, eating crackers and reading a book on addiction. Roberto is hunched over his desk, writing a paper. Mark is sitting on his bed clipping his nails. I force myself to speak calmly.

"Mark? Have you been on the phone again?"

"I had to, babe. My girlfriend's freaking out without me there."

"I don't care if the Queen of England is waiting for you to give her a massage, you can't use the phone until after the fifth day. How many days have you been here?"

"Five days."

"You were told no phone until after the fifth day. You broke the rule, I reminded you of the rule, and still you gave yourself permission to do as you please.

"That's right. Sorry, guy."

"Well, you will stop using the phone until Thursday night. Not a minute before. Do you understand?"

"Why are you so hostile?"

"I'm hostile because you're fucking around with rules that govern all of us, Mark. You have a choice. Respect the rules and make the best of this program or be an asshole and make trouble. You can't fool me. I'll be telling the rest of the guys to notify me if they see you on the phone before Thursday. Your peers will see to it that you play fair or we'll let the counselors deal with you."

"You're just a patient here, like me." He pouts.

"That's right. And we all have jobs to do. You're carrying ice, right?"

"Right."

"I used to carry ice, and now the counselors have made me granny. I take the job seriously. Do you take your recovery seriously?"

"I don't know yet."

"Think about it. I know it's scary here at first, but breaking the rules isn't a good start. You're setting a bad example for the rest of the guys."

I turn and march out. My arms and legs are shaking with rage. That guy thinks because I'm nice and friendly that he can stomp all over me. I think I made it clear I wasn't a wimp. Keeping an eye on a forty-year-old man is really relaxing. What a day.

Chapter Twelve

At five minutes to nine on Thursday morning, I walk with Richie to the family building. As usual, Roberto and Lester were running late, so we left without them. We walk slowly. I smoke a cigarette and ponder what to expect from this day. My stomach is churning.

The week has been great, except for Mark's continuing abuse of the phone. Our counselor, John, asked him to look after Tony for a few days. He needs assistance with walking at times, and he can't write because his hands are too shaky.

In addition to cocaine, Tony was ingesting large amounts of a tranquilizer called Ativan. He's being given Valium to withdraw him from that. He told me he took the tranquilizer to come down from the coke. If he quit using it without proper medical supervision, he could have a stroke or heart attack and die. He's sixty-two, but looks considerably younger even in his present state of disrepair.

He's totally cognizant of what's going on. He refers to the Valium they're giving him as "goofballs." He's extremely bright and perceptive. I really like him. He got upset when a counselor suggested he might have to stay an extra two weeks since he'll be medicated the first two.

What amazes me is that this wreck of a human being had the will to get himself out of his million-dollar fortress home, into a limo, and here to Betty Ford. Even demolished on drugs, he knew he needed help and found it. That's pretty amazing.

He's in my peer group. Molly asked if I would help him write an outline for his life story. I said sure. He asked if I would write in his feelings journal, too. He doesn't really like Mark, he said. I told him I'd be glad to help.

So, the last few nights, I've sat with him in his room or patio and listened to wild stories about his life, friends, Hollywood, who fucked who, his wife's murder, his emotional and spiritual decline afterwards, retirement, more drugs, the hired female companions, the segue from snorting coke to freebasing, and more. He's got enough material for ten life stories.

Molly gave me the results from the test that gauges brain damage. She seemed surprised that my memory wasn't impaired. Both short-and-long term memory check out fine.

New arrival Mike is a case in point. He looks like a stroke victim. Years of pickling his brain with scotch has transformed a fifty-five-year-old man into what looks like an eighty-year-old wreck. He has great difficulty saying just a few words. He's not stupid, just slightly brain dead. It's upsetting to watch or listen to him speak. He's in my B group. He's a barely living testament to the horrors of alcoholism. I feel so lucky that I've jumped off the drug merry-go-round before ending up like him. He's the most desperate-looking individual I've seen here. A shell of a man.

I've learned to feel somewhat more relaxed with Lester. I'm forcing myself to be more patient and try to consider his human frailties and weaknesses. Like me, he's an imperfect creation, so he deserves my respect. I may not particularly dig his personality, but I can appreciate the good in him. He's so eager to please everyone. I'm impressed by his kindness. I'm sure he's been taken advantage of in the past. He still grates on my nerves with his incessant eating, but he's basically a decent person.

Tom and Morris leave manana. The last of the older crew, except for Lester. There are so many new faces around here. I'll really miss Tom's quiet, assured humor and Morris' hilarious stories about his ex-wives. They both really helped me feel welcome here.

Richie and I share a last cigarette before facing our families. I keep looking at my watch. He says I'm making him more nervous. At two minutes to nine, we ditch the smokes, embrace, and wish each other good luck. Bombs away.

There are quite a few people mingling in the foyer outside the doors to the modest-size lecture room. Inside are four rows of folding chairs. Half of them are taken. I see my parents sitting in the second row. Mom's purse occupies the chair between them.

I turn around and weave through the people gathered around decaf coffee, soft drinks, and plates of rolls and muffins. I fill out a name tag and affix it on my shirt, then grab a styrofoam cup of O.J. and a slice of banana bread. I'm getting a headache. I see Richie talking to two women, his sister and mother, I assume. He calls me over. There's nowhere to escape, so I walk over, a pleasant smile plastered on my face.

He introduces me to Felicia and Etta. Etta is his eightyish mother, Felicia his sixtyish sister. They are lovely to me, very warm and friendly. Someone reminds us it's time to gather in the conference room. Richie and I squeeze hands, then separate. I guzzle the last of the juice, ponder grabbing a quick smoke outside, but decide to be strong and face the music. Its time to join my folks.

A wide chalkboard and screen take up the front of the room. I wave to Roberto. He's sitting with his mother and sister. They're nice-looking people. His sister is about forty and much darker than he or the mother. Besides Richie and Roberto's families, the rest of the group is white. Most of the people appear middle class, with a smattering of the country club set, dressed in casual desert sports wear. My parents belong in the latter category.

Dad is wearing navy slacks, light blue Izod shirt, red socks, loafers. Mom looks really lovely in a camel skirt, pale pink blouse, and white cardigan sweater. She's had her hair frosted, too. She looks ill at ease. Her arms are wrapped around her waist.

She has a notebook perched in her lap.

"Hi Mom, hi Dad." I sit down between them.

Dad shakes my hand. He says he's very impressed with Betty Ford. Says he's learned a lot. His hair looks a little greyer, and his face a little more lined than I remember, but healthy. My guilt is assuaged somewhat. They managed to live and breathe and groom without me in their lives. My mother has a pained expression on her face.

"Is something wrong, Mom?"

"Your mother's a little upset, son."

"What's wrong?"

"I can speak for myself, thank you. Nothing's wrong, Daniel. The counselor just informed us that you and your father will be participating in this group therapy thing later, but I won't."

"That's absurd. I don't understand." My mother's indignation transfers to me as if by osmosis. Like a true co-dependent, I take on her worry and make it my own. The other people have taken their seats. A woman I've seen around campus starts writing on the board.

"Listen, Mom. I'll take care of this," I say, sure I can control the situation somehow. Why do I always find myself appeasing my parents? They can take care of themselves. This is absurd. I feel like I'm in the middle of one of their arguments when I was a kid.

"Don't rock the boat, honey," she says, looking straight ahead. Why can't I just let this go?

"I'll tell them I want you both there. This just isn't fair." I'm surprised they picked Dad for the group therapy session, not Mom. I wonder why they chose him?

"These people know what they're doing," she says, looking defeated. She feels left out. I understand her pain. My blood starts to boil. How dare they not allow both my parents into the group therapy?

The woman writing on the board asks if there are questions. My hand shoots up, then I stand. I feel very hostile.

"Yes, Daniel?"

"I was wondering why both my parents can't be in the actual therapy session with me?" I'm looking for a fight.

"Well, Daniel. The staff chooses just one significant other for each patient. We only have enough time to deal with certain issues. This program is the beginning of healing, a step toward greater communication and honesty. We can't do all the work here. There simply isn't enough time."

"This is family day, so I want them both there." I sound like a spoiled brat.

"If you want to discuss this further, please come talk to me or one of the staff during the break."

"Fine," I say. "This place is about as flexible as a steel door."

I sit down and immediately realize how immature I've been. All for the sake of pleasing both my parents. How absurd. It's not their fault I'm such a co-dependent. I've just acted out an unpleasant example of my dysfunctional behavior in front of a roomful of strangers. I hope they enjoyed the show. What's a drug treatment program without a few nutty outbursts?

After the lecture on co-dependency, the room breaks into smaller units for the group therapy segment of the day. Richie, Roberto, Lester, and I are in a conference room with our chosen significant others.

Richie and his sister go first. The group is facilitated by Molly and a counselor I've never met before, Don. We sit in a circle. Patients sit across from significant others. They try to steer the dialogue to the most pressing points.

Richie and his sister take turns speaking their minds.

She talks of his drug-crazed behavior and perversions. He in turn asks why she can't accept him for what he is. He wonders aloud how a supposedly Christian person can be so condemning and hateful while preaching love and understanding. He calls her a hypocrite.

They speak back and forth for about twenty minutes. Molly and Don interject with questions or comments. Richie and his sister both get teary by the end of their dialogue. They hug briefly, then sit down again.

My Dad offers to go next. My stomach drops to my toes. I'm supposed to launch into a summary of my grievances. It's almost too painful to begin, but I do.

"Please speak directly to your father, Daniel. " Molly says. I nod. I feel fearful of appearing disloyal to my family. Airing the family's dirty laundry won't win me points with Mom and Dad.

"Well, I guess my biggest problem in spending time with you and Mom is that you won't support me. In anything."

"That's not true. Your Mother and I are very proud of your acting work."

"You fought me tooth and nail until I got the series, remember? Then, when I told you I was gay, you both tried to dissuade me from a life of homosexuality just like you discouraged me from becoming an actor. You've never supported me."

"We don't see it that way."

"Speak for yourself, Dad. Mom's not here."

"You've always been given the best of everything."

"Please skip that speech. Lets get to the heart of this whole thing. When David died, you abandoned me. Sure, I know, you had to travel on business, blah, blah, blah. I lost David and my parents in one fell swoop. Admit it."

"That's not true, Daniel. You were a difficult child."

"Right. It's always my fucking fault. I won't have you in my life if you can't support me. I want a friend, not a parent."

"You shut me out, son." I wish he'd quit calling me son. It makes me feel bad.

"Why shouldn't I? You weren't available to me except on rare occasions. You were too busy working. Oh, and your important social calendar. I didn't fit into your schedule, right?"

"Don't be absurd. We were always there for you."

"Sure, if I needed a ride or money. Where were you when I was dying inside? When David died, something was smothered in me, but nobody could see it or help me. You didn't even try. That's how I feel. I'm sorry."

"I suppose we're strangers in many ways, Daniel. I never said I was perfect, but you never talked to me. You got angry or became withdrawn. You stuck to your room, your pets, the woods. We couldn't get through to you, so..."

"So you gave up."

"On a certain level, maybe. You were impossible to handle."

"So were you and Mom."

"What does that mean?"

"It means that I won't be spending time with my family if it means watching all my relatives getting drunk. That's been a thorn in my side for years. I can't deal with it."

"You're blowing this drinking thing way out of proportion, Daniel, and you know it."

"Remember Christmas a year ago, Dad? You were angry at me because I told you and Mom I was gay. You really alienated me with your hostility. The week I spent with you and Mom was an ordeal. You made me feel like a total outsider. Mom was horrible too. I was taking over a dozen pills a day while I was at your house.

"When we had Christmas dinner with Linda and her in-laws, you and Mom were totally unfriendly to me. I was your gay son, and you didn't like it. You were afraid other people might see it. So you made me miserable."

"I'm sorry if we hurt your feelings. I don't mind that you're gay, Daniel."

"Then what's the problem?"

"Well, it wasn't as easy for your mother."

"Exactly. As usual, she and everyone else comes before me. To be a part of her team, you blow me off. That really sucks, Dad."

"She was legitimately concerned about your welfare."

"Let's call a spade a spade. You've always taken her side against me. She has you wrapped around her little finger. I lost respect for you. You treated me like I was second best." Molly interrupts.

"What do you want from your father, Daniel?"

"I want to be loved. I want to know my father and mother care about me but don't have to control me to care. I can't change who I am to please you anymore. That's why I stopped seeing you. I couldn't pretend I didn't feel the tension level rise every time I walked in the room. You treated me differently after David died. I want you to love me as much as you loved him. I know I'm a disappointment. I wish I could make you happy, but I can't. Why can't you be proud of the fact I'm different? Can't you honor my choices? I want you and Mom to be my friends, not my keepers. That's what I need. I want to be treated with respect."

Tears pour down my cheeks and burn my eyes. A choked cry erupts from my throat. I drop my head to hide the eruption of emotion and pain. I don't want these people to see my face. I allow the years of hurt feeling and rejection to flow forth. All eyes are on me, but I can't stop.

"I don't hate you and Mom, Dad. I stopped seeing you because I felt so bad about myself I couldn't handle your criticism. I don't want to be mad anymore."

"I love you, son. I always have. I'm sorry that you perceive otherwise. I never loved David more than you, not for a minute. That's the truth. We felt very lost when he died, we also tried to give you breathing space because you were in such sorrow and pushed us away. You wouldn't let us help you then or ever, really. I accept you for what you are, and I'll try to show it more often. I'm very proud of you. I'm proud of you for coming here. We're glad to be here."

I continue to cry, really let it all out. The room is silent. When I'm done, Molly tells us we've made a solid step forward.

Lester and his mother discuss his abusive behavior while using. They both acknowledge that they share a food addiction. This is quite a breakthrough for Lester. I'm glad for him. They make a commitment to continue family counseling after Betty Ford. I'm drained from the confrontation with Dad. At noon we break for lunch. Molly and Don encourage us to eat together in family groups, to keep the process going.

We three take our sandwiches and soft drinks and sit on the grass under a shady tree. I feel exhausted, but empowered by the session with Dad. I can start with a clean slate now. I can let go of the past.

I summarize the session for Mom, who is very interested in everything. We eat turkey sandwiches and drink diet soda. I give my parents an outline of my drug addiction over the last few years. They listen. I apologize for cutting them out of my life. I explain that I didn't feel I had any other options, the pain was too great. I tell them whatever problems we had should have been worked out, but it wasn't possible. I try to act forgiving.

I try to explain how bad I felt about myself until I came here. I talk about the lingering loneliness since David died. They seem supportive and understanding. I start to cry again from the sheer emotional release. My mother rubs my back.

Before the afternoon session, I chat with Amanda and her cute son for a few minutes. Then I introduce Richie and Lester to my parents.

The rest of the afternoon is spent in communications exercises and a lecture. I feel like a massive block of cement has been dropped from my feet. What a relief. When Mom asks whether I'll be coming to see them sometime soon, I say, "Sure. Thanks for asking, Mom." We say goodbye outside the family pavilion at four-thirty. I want to get back to McCallum in time to see Tom and Morris get their graduation medallions. I tell my folks I'll call them when I get out. They say they love me and wish me luck. I run back to McCallum, feeling a distinct sense of accomplishment at the day's events.

I get back to McCallum in time for the medallion ceremonies. We join hands in a circle and say the Serenity Prayer, then pass around a medallion for Morris, then Tom. I stand next to Tom. He's very handsome.

Each of us offers a thought or sentence to commemorate the graduates' accomplishment. The three counselors are part of the circle. It's a very special time. Tomorrow, these men will be out in the world, faced with freedom and temptation. Everyone has nice words for both men. At tonight's burnings, we can say more.

My successor as granny was named while I was in the family meeting. His name is Roger. He arrived a week ago. He's a painkiller addict like me. He's in his early forties. We've spent a lot of time talking. His withdrawal has been bad. His leg cramping seems worse than mine. We share withdrawal stories. I try to be especially supportive of him, since I can relate to his particular suffering. We've become fast friends. He'll be a great granny. He stands over six feet tall and has a large frame. When he's nearby, I feel like as if I have a bodyguard.

I congratulate him and make a date to work on the new chore schedule after dinner. He wants to pick my brain on the ins and outs of being granny. He tells me to choose which job I'd like to do this week.

Mark is missing from the medallion circles. He shows up as we're entering the cafeteria. I could slough off dealing with Mark, but that wouldn't be fair to Roger. I'm granny until tomorrow. I call Mark over and ask him where he's been. He claims to have been walking around the lake, thinking. What a bullshitter. I tell him to inform his granny next time. We aren't supposed to wander around at will.

Roger tells me, as we're pushing our trays down the food line, that Mark was seen standing in the parking lot in front of Betty Ford and talking on the phone at least twice this afternoon. I thank him for the info, set my tray on a table, and walk directly over to Mark.

"Mark?"

"Yes, Daniel?"

"I understand you were out in the parking lot. What were you doing?"

"I can explain."

"You're one hell of a liar, Mark. You told me you were walking around the lake."

"I was. Then I went to the parking lot. I'm still thinking about leaving and a friend was going to stop by."

"Visitors are allowed only on Sundays, Mark. You know that. This is ridiculous. You're the least co-operative person I've ever met here. Shape up."

"Don't get so hyper, Daniel. Chill out."

"You Chill out Mark, I'm sick of your lame excuses."

"Don't be mad."

"I heard you were on the phone."

"This is true. I might leave, so..."

"I don't care what you're doing. You are not supposed to use the phone until tomorrow."

I return to my food, but I'm too angry to eat. I leave the cafeteria and return to my room. I lie on the bed for a rest.

A knock. I must have fallen asleep. Before the door opens, I'm sure it's him. I'm right. He comes inside the room. I get up and prepare to walk past him. He throws his arm up, blocking my passage. What an asshole.

"What do you want, Mark?"

"I don't like taking orders from a kid."

"I'm not a kid, Mark. I'm thirty years old."

"Quit making my life difficult, man."

"Quit breaking the rules, man."

"Just ease up on me."

I try to maneuver past him, but he stops me. He grabs my arm. My skin crawls. We're standing face to face. Physically, he's much bigger than I. He wears a hateful scowl on his face. His eyes are narrowed.

"What's your problem, Danny?"

"Daniel, not Danny."

"Don't you like me, Daniel?" He's a certifiable creep.

"Like or dislike has nothing to do with this and you know it. I don't appreciate your attitude, Mark. It's a bad influence on the rest of us. You're getting special privileges because you're a bully and take what you want. I won't stand for it. We're here to get well. You seem to be here to use the phone. I'm sick of reminding you of the rules, then having you flaunt them in my face."

"What's your beef with me? Maybe you're not seeing my good side."

"I guess not. Please let go of my arm." He doesn't.

"I'm a sophisticated man, Danny. I can't be locked up in a dump like this without contact with the outside world. Be nice to me and I'll be nice to you."

"Either you let go of my fucking arm or I'll scream bloody murder." He drops my arm and steps back.

"Hey, just kidding around, Danny."

"My name is Daniel. Please step out of my way."

"Get off my back, kid," he snarls, poking a long, grotesque finger into my chest. The anger I feel is immense.

"If you ever touch me again, you'll wish you hadn't, you asshole. Now get out of my way."

I push past Mark and storm to the office, where I lodge a complaint with John. I tell him Mark is sticking his nose up at the rules, treating the program like shit, and threatening me. The next time he lays a finger on me, I say, I'll call the cops and see his ass in jail. I'm livid. I feel violated by Mark's threatening tone and physicality. John says he'll speak to him, that I should try to calm down, let go of the anger. I say I'll try.

I walk around the lake. The sun is dropping. There are still three ducklings left, and they're growing feathers. I see a shadow of what appears to be a large fish in the shallows near Eisenhower.

The burnings later in the evening are my last as granny. Tom and Morris are such sensitive, caring men. I feel lucky to have known them, let alone officiate at their goodbye burnings. After tomorrow, I may never see them again. Neither wanted a special song written, so after they both have fed their papers and personal effects to the flames, we gather in the lounge and serenade them with a rousing rendition of Jimmy Buffett's "Margaritaville."

By midnight I finish another paper I've been writing for Molly, this one on cross addiction. Then I go to the pay phone and call Lance at my house. The machine picks up. I tell Lance hello and a few details of the day. I say I miss his cheery disposition and killer tan, then hang up.

Roger is pacing the halls again. We sit outside and talk for nearly an hour. He tells me more about his life story. I warn him about Mark's rebellious attitude. We write up the list of new chores and post it on the bulletin board. I choose to sweep the big patio every morning.

At midnight I say goodnight and hit the sack. I'm exhausted. The day has been exciting and enervating all at once. I feel as though I've crossed an important barrier into a new chapter of my life. I'm replacing the worn-out components with newer, more flexible parts. I'm nearly ready to return home. A week from tomorrow, that's exactly what I'll do.

Chapter Thirteen

Before my eyes open, I think: "I'm free." Today I leave Betty Ford for home. It's scary. I climb out of bed and shower. I feel totally hyper. My roommate, a twenty-year-old student from Ohio, is still asleep. He arrived last weekend. He's an "intervention" patient. His parents gave him a choice: either confront his addiction and seek treatment, or lose their financial support. He chose a month in rehab over life as a homeless bum. He's still in denial about his problem.

Even after telling me stories of outrageous activities involving drugs and drug behavior, he refuses to accept that he abuses drugs. Maybe he's too young for rehab, maybe he hasn't sunk low enough yet.

The past week has been a whirl of activity and change. Roberto and Lester left for home. Mark finally buckled down and started applying himself to the program. I've talked to Gary on the phone almost every night. Usually he calls me. Our friendship and romance is heating up. We have a date for me to drive up to Santa Barbara in just two days.

I feel excited that both Lance and Gary are potential romances for this next stage of my life. Howard and I have spoken again on the phone; he's been fighting a cough. He sounded terrible on Monday night when we last talked. I think he's sicker than he admitted. I'll know more when I see him for dinner Friday night. He's having me over for a BBQ at his house.

On Wednesday I completed the fourth and fifth steps of AA. Our treatment program includes completing the first five steps of the twelve-step program while in Betty Ford. Out in the world it may take a recovering person years to get through the first five steps, but they accelerate it here for obvious reasons. We need to feel committed to sobriety. Successfully completing the first five steps is a good foundation for recovery out in the world.

The fourth and fifth steps felt very healing. The fourth step asks us to make a "fearless moral inventory." The fifth step requires the addict/alcoholic to share these pains, guilts, feelings, or whatever with another AA or a religious person. I spent a week making my list. Just writing down years and years of resentments, angers, and hurt feelings was spiritually cleansing.

On Wednesday morning, I had a ten-thirty appointment to meet a man of the cloth for the fifth step. We had our session in a small room at the other end of the campus. Jared was a fiftyish Protestant minister. He was friendly and immediately put me at ease. I never removed my written list from my pocket. I just opened my mouth and the words came out. I shared my hurts and pains and hopes and disappointments. For ninety minutes we talked and discussed feelings, regret, religion, guilt, enlightenment, sobriety, love, David's death, my loneliness as a child, my sexuality, parents, work, responsibility.

There was no judgment on his part, only interest, support, and a few observations. He said I was doing very well and had a good head on my shoulders. Instead of listening to myself, I turned to drugs and shallow friends. He said I obviously wasn't a bad person. He said there needn't be shame about the fact I'm gay, God loves us all, no matter what. He made me feel there was more love for me in the world than I could possibly imagine. He said it was okay for me to let go of the past, yet retain the good memories of my brother. To heal, I needed to let go of the guilt and sense of responsibility for his death.

At the end of our talk, he said the reconciliation with my folks was a really fine step and that he would be proud to have a son like me, gay or not. I forced myself to remain composed while saying goodbye, but I became tearful.

The counselors suggest that patients who have just finished their fifth steps take a long walk or sit in the meditation room for a while. The emotions can be overwhelming. They're right. I smoked a cigarette as I walked to the main building.

Near the front of the lobby are a set of doors. Inside is a two-level room covered with soft carpeting. One entire wall is a massive window overlooking a lush garden, waterfall, and glistening pool of water. The lovely garden is planted with grasses, tropical flowers, passels of bromeliads, pink and magenta bougainvillea spilling across the walls. It is idyllic. I hadn't ever been in there before.

I took off my shoes, grabbed a big throw pillow, and sat next to the glass. As I gazed into the water, I realized this leg of the journey was over. In two days I would be going home. I had come a long, long way.

Tears started to stream down my cheeks, I couldn't stop them. I realized I didn't have to stop myself. It's okay to feel. I knew at that moment I would make it. I realized I was a good person, that all the nice compliments I had received from Jared, the minister, were true. Like a mystical ball of fire, it set my brain and heart afire. The tears couldn't drown the burning awareness inside my mind and spirit that I really was a good person. I didn't feel bad anymore. The guilt was consumed by orange flames, leaving only an imprint of the former pain in memory. I'd never forget who I was or where I came from.

I didn't try to control anything, I just went with the moment, felt what I felt. An overpowering wave of love and acceptance for myself and the world suddenly swept over me, quelling the fires, restoring me to emotional balance. I felt changed. I felt cleansed. There was no going back to the person I was a month ago.

I had confidence, hope, possibility, and love flowing inside my veins, enriching me immeasurably. Here in this place, I've learned to have faith in myself again. I've begun to trust my inner voice. I've learned to bond with men again in a non-sexual fashion. It's miraculous. I've rediscovered a joy in life. I've found my way through the initial sequence of the recovery maze. I felt reborn.

That same amazing, magical night, I received a thirty-day sobriety chip at my last Betty Ford AA meeting. I feel very proud of what I've accomplished during this month. It's been years since I went a whole month without some sort of mood-altering chemicals.

Yesterday afternoon I received my Betty Ford graduation medallion. Richie and I shared a medallion ceremony. We each received a half-dollar-sized coin inscribed with the serenity prayer.

During the ceremony, Molly said I certainly deserved the medallion. She said I really worked the program and then some. She said I showed enormous amounts of courage, dug in deep, took chances, and was a model patient. She said she'd miss me. I felt totally choked up during the brief ceremony, but remained composed, though my lip quivered a little. The medallion is very precious to me.

Last night was the burning for Richie and me. Everybody said wonderful things about us both. It was flavored with good will and hopeful wishes. I felt more popular than I ever did when I was appearing on T.V. every week. It felt like a million dollars to watch most of my rehab paperwork burn, as well as the anti-withdrawal patch I wore for two weeks. It felt exciting to watch them burn atop the same hot coals as the McCallum men that came before me. I felt part of a greater whole, a piece of a strong, resilient quilt. Don and Allan burned their papers here. Morris, Tom, and Paul too. Roberto and Parker. Lester and Richie. The men of McCallum have a united spirit that resides inside all of us. In a few weeks Tony will be feeding his papers to the fire, as will my roommate and Roger and all the rest. Addiction brought us together here at Camp Betty. A commitment to restoring ourselves brought us together. Recovery pulls us apart. I was filled with love and kinship for them all.

Roger has been an excellent granny. The guys respect him and groove to his Texas-style humor. His Codeine withdrawal is finally tapering off. He'll remove his withdrawal patch in a few days. He gave me a T-shirt last night. It says "Don't Mess With Texas" in big red letters.

I think Richie and I scandalized a few of the men when we hugged and kissed on the lips during the tape-recorded portion of the ceremony. It felt very natural to express ourselves physically, so why not?

I'm riding back to L.A. with Amanda. We're scheduled to meet in front of the main building at eight. At seven-fifteen I walk to Richie's room. He's throwing his toiletry case into a suitcase. He has a beautiful wardrobe. I'd like to go shopping with him sometime. We'd have a blast. He's flying to New York this morning. He decided to finish his record, then come home. Amanda had suggested the three of us drive to Los Angeles together, sharing the weirdness of rejoining the real world as a group, but he declined. I'm glad to have a Betty Ford friend for the first free hours. I feel pretty awkward about leaving. I want to go home, but I'm afraid of old temptations.

He looks very dapper in black trousers, grey cotton sweater, and a white panama hat. We've already exchanged phone numbers and addresses, writing them along with messages in our NA books. He's ordered a cab for seven-fifteen. We carry his luggage and bags out to the parking lot in front of Camp Betty.

A cab is already waiting. We embrace and wish each other luck. He waves to the taxi driver, then says he'll be back in L.A in six weeks and we should hang out. I tell him he'd better stay sober. He says he's hopeful. His tone contradicts his words. I have a feeling he's not going to remain sober for long. Maybe he hasn't hit a low enough point. I don't know.

I carry my duffels and tape recorder to the front entrance at eight. Amanda is already piling her luggage and considerable belongings into the trunk of the cab. The driver is leaning against the hood, watching her arrange her things.

We kiss cheeks and wish each other a good morning.

"I thought we were going to rent a car," I say.

"We are. We need to get all my gear to the airport, then we can pick up the car."

"Oh, right."

"Don't worry, Daniel, we'll make it. I feel rather bizarre today. What about you?"

"It feels like the first day of school," I mumble.

"I know. I'm so glad we're driving to L.A. together. We'll have a real adventure."

"Sure, it'll be fun. We never got to talk much in here."

"I know. We'll have plenty of time to get acquainted."

"Do you live in Los Angeles?" I say, squinting to avoid the bright morning sun.

"New York. I've been here working. Let's get going, okay?"

"Whenever you're ready." The trunk is overflowing with her stuff. She hands me a box.

"Whats this?" I ask.

"My Betty Ford coffee mugs. I got a dozen to give to my friends for Christmas. Maybe a few of them will take the hint and check in here themselves."

"What a great gift."

"Thank you, pal. Oh, no. Where will we put your duffelbag?"

"I can sit on it to the airport."

"We'll put it in front with the driver."

"Fine."

"Let's fly."

"Let's."

She's dressed in a lavender suede skirt, black blouse, tan leather jacket, and flat sandals. Her dark hair is pulled off the face. Her light blue eyes twinkle and glimmer. She wears the graduation medallion on a chain around her neck. I'm glad to hear she's working again, she's an excellent actress.

As we coast down the driveway, we leave the grounds of Betty Ford and Eisenhower Hospital behind. Turning onto a wider road, I feel a wave of dizziness. I lean back and close my eyes.

"Are you all right, Daniel?"

"A little dizzy."

"I'm having double vision. I think we're like prisoners who get sprung after ten years in a five-by-five jail cell. Sensory overload. It'll get easier," she promises.

"I hope so. This is absurd."

I open my eyes and look around. We're driving by wild desert, homes, stores, but it feels like a place I've never been before. I've been to Palm Springs dozens of times, but it all looks alien.

We arrive at the airport. I remember this place. Amanda pays the driver, refusing to accept my money. We pile our stuff on the curb. She darts inside to get the car. She already reserved a convertible.

I smoke a cigarette and point my face into the sun while I wait. The morning is heating up fast. This weather is bizarre. It was in the nineties again yesterday.

She pulls up behind the wheel of a candy-apple-red Mustang. I clap. She gets out and takes a bow. We load our gear into the tiny trunk and back seat. We drive to the exit. Amanda stops, then asks me which way to turn.

"I don't have a clue. I don't have a sense of direction even in the best of times," I say.

"They gave me a map."

"Thank God, we'll obviously need all the help we can get."

"Yes. Let's see. I think we go to the right. Yes. We'll stop for gas, too. Are you hungry?"

"Starved. I didn't eat breakfast. I was too excited."

"Me too."

"I'll eat anything that you like, except for Mexican. Too early for that."

"Let's go to a market and see what looks good."

She locates a food store and parks. We're nearly inside the store when I happen to look back and see that the convertible top is down. All our goods will be stolen since most of them are in the back seat of the car. I point-out this hilarious faux pas to Amanda, then we walk back and raise the top.

Wandering around the huge supermarket is like being inserted into a strange new world the size of an airplane hangar. My brain crackles and pops with all the stimulus. We were protected from these kinds of activities and environments in Camp Betty. Shopping for food sober is different from doing it high. The drugs ran interference with the stresses and the zillions of choices.

We decide to drink orange juice, we both like that. There are too many brands for me to choose from. I close my eyes and grab one. I feel drunk as I stagger down the aisles, my feet loaded with cement. It's all too much. Freedom is a shock to my system. I follow Amanda to the meat counter. She's breathing heavily. We discuss the situation and agree to get out of the store as rapidly as possible. She suggests shrimp as a main course. I endorse the idea and shuffle off to locate a bottle of cocktail sauce.

By the time we reach the car, I feel like a week has passed. The fresh air and openess quickly regenerates my energy. Nothing looks familiar, except for the lifelike replicas of dinosaurs near the freeway.

Somehow, Amanda manages to get us on the freeway headed toward Los Angeles. I peel shrimp and pass them to her as we zip along. The radio provides a melodic backdrop to our constant conversation. It's weird because we don't really know each other, yet it feels so comfortable together. We've been through similar experiences and speak like languages.

The film and television business forces actors and technicians to form quick, close relationships during the duration of a shoot, anywhere from a few days to many months. Working on my television show, I saw and acted with a constantly changing roster of players. Intimacy develops unnaturally fast. I've had several affairs with people I was working with. Once the show is completed, things usually die as rapidly as they begin. Out of sight, out of mind.

Amanda and I both know we only have a limited time together before our lives draw us into separate orbits. So we delve right in. There's no point in being shy or awkward together.

We share pieces of our pasts, future plans, Betty Ford gossip, and compare notes on some of the other patients. She's very quick. Our conversational rhythms jive. She tells me about the media flack she received after she did a series of commercials touting a cruise line. She says the bottom line was money. She hadn't worked in years and was really desperate for the cash. She reports a steady stream of job offers since then.

She asks why I'm not working. I explain the circumstances leading up to leaving the show. She watched the show and thinks I'm very talented. I'm flattered, but non-committal about working. I don't know what I want to do yet.

The jumbo shrimp are delicious. The moist meat melts in my mouth. The tangy horseradish and tomato flavors really taste zingy. We guzzle O.J between courses. She smokes constantly and drives effortlessly. Her hand to eye coordination is superb.

Several cars slow next to us. Amanda has a very recognizable face. Naturally, people want to say hello when they recognize her. She's friendly in an old-fashioned, movie-star manner. She graciously offers a wave, smile, or a "Hello." I keep my sunglasses plastered to my face.

We miss two exits and turn-offs, then stop to use a bathroom and buy more cigarettes. Finally, we reach the outskirts of Los Angeles. Amanda asks whether I would mind spending a few minutes shopping in Beverly Hills. She wants to buy a watch at Tiffany's. She wants to treat herself today. I say I'll go. What else have I got to do today? Cruising down Wilshire into Beverly Hills, we rehash our first day in Betty Ford. She says I look a hell of a lot better today. I tell her she looks thinner and her eyes are significantly clearer.

We walk into Tiffany at noon, three-and-a-half hours after leaving Palm Springs. Usually, the drive takes less than two hours, but we're still adjusting to the real world.

Tiffany's is the epitome of a shop that caters to the filthy rich. Shelves are crammed with silver, crystal, jewelry, gifts, china, all of it extremely expensive. I feel underdressed, but quickly get over it. The shop is mostly deserted, except the two of us and a flock of salespeople.

Amanda and I browse. She asks my opinion on a few watches she's chosen. They're all lovely. I prefer the narrow one with the little rubies inlaid in the white gold face. It's simple and classic. The others are nice, but somewhat garish in comparison. I give my opinion, and leave her to make her decision. I purchase a small porcelain box for Lance. It's in the shape of an elephant.

Driving up the hill to my house, I fall silent. Amanda suggests we attend an AA meeting tonight at eight. She's wearing the diamond watch I liked. It looks very slick and elegant. When we get to my house, I suggest she come in. She has to get home, she says. She's beat. We sign each other's NA books on the hood of the red Mustang. We decide to meet at the church where the AA meeting will be held and maybe get a bite to eat afterwards. I remove my duffel and tape recorder from the back seat. We hug and say goodbye. As she's driving past me down the hill, she honks and blows me a kiss.

Before lugging my duffel up the stairs into the house, I open the book and read what she wrote.

"Dear Daniel-
Hello, my new old friend. I'll always remember our first
day in and our last day out (especially the grocery store.)
Anytime at all...
Love, Amanda"

When I get inside the front door, the phone is ringing. I decide to be brave and start answering the phone in person. I've relied on the answering machine to screen calls for too long. The caller is my drug dealer.
"Hi," I say.
"So, where have you been Daniel? I've left several messages."
"Actually, I went into rehab. I just got home."
"No kidding? How was it?" He sounds amused.
"Great. I've been clean and sober for a month."
"What a drag, man. So you're outta the Percodan grind?"
"I hope so."
"No drugs?"
"No drugs."
"What a bummer, man. That's like flying with one wing."
"Call me a cripple, but that's what I'm doing," I say with conviction.
"Well, good luck man. Call me if you have a change of flight plans."
"I will. See ya."
I sift through my mail. Bills, bills, bills. There's a welcome-home card from Gary. He signs it "Love, Gary." I'll call him later. In two days we'll be together.
Lance is due here at five. We're scheduled to have an early dinner. I invited him to say thanks for house-sitting. He took excellent care of everything. The plants are well watered, the tables have been dusted, the carpet is vacuumed.
He arrives on time. We hug, then we sit on the couch and neck. I've been thinking about my relationship with Lance. Is this a serious thing for him or a fling? I don't have a clue. So, I decide to test the relationship waters. I ask how things are going with the girl from UCLA. He says they see one another a couple of times a week and she wants to have sex constantly. I feel jealousy and anger rise, but remind myself I don't own this person. He can do as he pleases.
So, I childishly resort to emotional revenge. I tell him about Gary. Lance doesn't bat an eye. He acts totally unfazed. He says "That's cool." He doesn't seem jealous. I guess I hoped he'd show more feeling. He's the latest in a long line of sexually ambivalent men I've been involved with, starting with my first boyfriend. Chris is now married with three

children, a house, and a dog.

I tell myself to let go and not project my needs onto Lance. We have no commitments. I sit down next to him. He looks really cute in his tight jeans and red shirt. The animal attraction I feel is stronger than before. My entire body tingles with renewed sensitivity.

Every touch sends electric impulses charging my brain. I rub his crotch as we kiss. I'm definitely in the mood for love. He seems willing.

We roll on the floor and strip our clothes off. We explore one another's bodies. He's a great kisser. Just rubbing our warm bodies together brings me to the edge of orgasm. The touch of his skin feels amazing. Sex never felt this good on drugs, not even ripped on Ecstasy.

After we both come, we lie on the carpet, side to side. I remember the Tiffany elephant. I walk to the bedroom and retrieve the white box. I place it before him on the carpet. He smiles and unties the red ribbons.

He opens the elephant box very carefully. He breathes through his nose and looks genuinely happy as he examines the delicate box. He thanks. We hold one another close and watch the city lights come up. In the distance, the Hollywood Freeway snakes past the downtown skyline. The strip of cars resembles a diamond encrusted bracelet, sparkling and glittering in the encroaching darkness. I'm home!

Chapter Fourteen

At nine on Saturday morning, I'm cruising north on the slippery freeway. Gary's house is located about twenty miles up the coast from Santa Barbara. The drive from L.A. should take about two-and-a-half hours. In the back seat are a three foot-high-potted macadamia nut tree and my overnight bag.

It's drizzling. Traffic is light. The hills and mountains are rapidly greening from the winter storms. Much of the scenery is enveloped by a shroud of fog. The visibility is so poor that I reduce my speed to forty-five. I'm listening to an awful tape Howard gave me last night. He said he heard this group was hot. Not. The two cuts I force myself to listen to are terribly over-produced. Too much electronic drums, too many background vocals, too much echoing, too much everything. It's nerve-wracking. Thumbs-down.

Howard's barbeque last night was fun. The pneumocystis, a lung infection similar to pneumonia that preys on people with the HIV infection, is under control again. He showed me how he sprays a drug called Pentantamine into his lungs with an inhalar.

He looked a little thin and tired, but his mood was upbeat. His boyfriend Adam is sweet. He's twenty-two.

As Howard was uncorking a bottle of Chardonnay, he told Adam he was first attracted to me because I looked like Peter Pan. Then he asked if I wanted a glass of wine. I said no. He said he wasn't trying to push me, but didn't want to be rude either. I made it clear they could carry on as they normally might.

While Adam was outside grilling the meats, Howard told me they met in a support group for HIV-positive men. He said it was nice to be in a relationship with someone who could understand HIV-related stress, fears, and health problems. He compared it to me needing to spend time with other addicts.

He said it was difficult for him to have sex with someone who was not HIV positive. Instead of enjoying the sex, he'd spend every moment worrying about infecting the person and feeling guilty.

Then, he turned to me and asked whether I'd take care of his cat Trixie in the event he died.

Was he planning to die soon? I told him Trixie would be treated like royalty if and when she needed lodgings elsewhere. Howard laughed and kissed me on the cheek. I told him I was glad he had Adam, but to know I was available if he needed anything. He said "Thanks" very quietly and looked unbearably lost. I stepped close, put my arms around his waist and pressed my lips to his.

His eyes widened in surprise, then he realized this wasn't risky sexual behavior and relaxed, closing his eyes. It was a very warm moment. I wanted to convey my feelings for him but not come on in a blatantly sexual manner. I didn't move my lips, they just touched his. I hoped to communicate my feelings for him. I wanted to let him know he was loved.

Hearing Adam come through the creaky back door, I pulled away. Howard smiled and went back to pouring their wine.

The steaks and chicken had a sweet plum flavor. Adam said the secret was in the barbeque sauce. We ate at Howard's massive oak dining table and listened to music from the stereo. They wanted to hear more about my month in rehab. I tried to be open and informative. I told them about Gary. Howard remembered him from the day he visited. He said Gary was very handsome.

Trixie the cat begged for scraps under the table. I sneaked her tidbits of chicken. She rubbed against my legs and purred wildly. We're old friends. She's huge, the size of a bobcat. I've never seen a larger domesticated feline. Trix is a Maine coon cat, a species known for its immense size. She must weigh over thirty pounds. Some housecats have a dowdy, frumpy look, like they're lazy. Trixie has powerful legs and a sleek, orange-and-grey body. She has wide, gold eyes. I'm crazy about her.

The Spanish-style house is situated in a canyon about a half a mile from my house. When we were dating, I'd sometimes walk back and forth. The interior uses much wood and stone and masculine colors. Everything is tastefully furnished.

I remember when I'd sleep over, we'd make love, then sleep on Howard's huge brass bed. Trixie would sometimes wake me by snuggling close and singing her purr into my ear. Other mornings, the din of birdsong would wake me before the sun rose. I'd lie there naked, startled by my good fortune at having such a special person beside me. I'd touch his skin just to be sure he wasn't a mirage or dream.

His bedroom is on the uppermost floor. The shuttered windows open into tops of the eucalyptus forest that grows behind the house. It felt like we were perched at the top of the world. I loved him. His home felt like my home. For a while, it felt like paradise.

Nearing the outskirts of Santa Barbara, I put an old favorite in the tape deck, the soundtrack for "Last Tango in Paris." Gato Barbieri's wailing sax complements the beat of the rain on the windshield. I manage to stay in my lane most of the time, but it's a battle.

There are roadside vegetable and fruit stands, but they're all boarded-up. Acres and acres of strawberries and lettuce cover much of the valley. Everything looks exceptionally green.

I spot a stand that is open for business. I stop and buy three baskets of strawberries. I eat one as soon as I return to the car. It tastes delicious, warm, and sweet.

The highway snakes along the coast, hugging the mountains on the right, the ocean on the left. The misty vistas are dramatic. Huge waves crash against the stony embankment separating the slender beach from the highway. Only the lower foothills are readily visible. Dark rain clouds thickly line the sky. The steady downfall continues unabated.

A lone banana farm is wedged into a sliver of land between the ocean and a mountain. The wide banana leaves flap in the intense wind, lashed and sliced by sheets of rain. I light a cigarette and turn the music off. I need to concentrate on getting myself to Gary's in one piece.

The turn-off finally comes into view after a public beach. A graveled road leads to a guard station. I give my name and Gary's to the guard. He checks them on his clipboard, then gives me a guest identification tag and directions to the house. I'll drive eight-and-half miles, to mailbox number fifty-seven.

The road is rife with treacherous hairpin turns, but it's beautiful. The ranch covers thousands of acres and is undeveloped except for an occasional house. There are herds of black-and-white cattle, as well as the odd horse roaming the many grassy paddocks.

The distant mountains provide a dramatic backdrop to the softer, rounder hills that flatten as they inch toward the Pacific. The perimeter of the beach is bordered by a steep, red cliff that bridges land with the Pacific. The houses are few and far between and manage to generally blend into the environment.

The wind gets stronger, the rain slows to a trickle. The sides of my convertible top rustle violently. The irritating squeak of the windshield wipers is giving me a headache. I have a craving for drugs. I'm nervous about seeing Gary. What if this was a terrible idea? We'll see each other here and wonder what the hell we're doing. Or maybe he's decided that sex with another man is morally reprehensible and back out. Maybe he and his wife have reunited.

I watch a herd of cattle trot single-file along a swollen creek bed. They seem to be enjoying the rain. I smile and drive on.

The road bends and curves more and more as I go on. I drive very cautiously. Signs warn motorists of a twenty-mile-an-hour speed limit and to beware of cows and deer. Scrubby grasses and weeds grow in profusion along the road, creating a carpet of mossy green on the slopes and prairies.

When the odometer reads eight miles, I start looking for numbers on

152

the mailboxes, but some don't have anything written on them. Big help. There's a black pickup parked next to a curve up ahead. A man wearing a yellow parka is riding a skateboard past the truck. I'll stop and ask him for directions. A reddish-brown Doberman runs alongside him. Why is he skateboarding in the rain?

The moustached man nods. I wave back. He looks vaguely familiar. I pull over and turn off the ignition. As I climb out of my Jeep, he jumps off the board. It's Gary. He cut off his beard. My pulse quickens. I can hear my heart beat inside my eardrums.

"Gary! Hi."

"Hello there, Daniel." He sounds enthusiastic in a low key way.

"I didn't recognize you without the beard."

"Do I look different?"

"Sure. You look very handsome. Come here." Gary shoves the skateboard under an arm and moves closer.

"The guard called to let me know you were here," he says. "We came down to meet you. You look really great." The dog sniffs at my legs and crotch.

"I didn't know you had a dog."

"Meet Chance."

"Hi, Chance. You're a handsome boy. He's beautiful, Gary." I lean down and allow the dog to sniff my hands.

"Thanks. Why don't you follow me up?"

"Sure."

"How about a hug first?"

"Good idea."

We hold tight. I immediately feel aroused. He kisses my neck. I turn my head and meet his lips with mine. My mouth feels dry. He doesn't resist. The softly falling rain dampens my hands, forehead, and cheeks. Chance breaks things up with several barks. Gary smiles and says he's delighted I'm here.

We caravan up a dirt road that is rapidly turning to mud. On the right is the raging creek. On the left is a hillside with scattered groups of sedate cattle. Gary slows and points to the right. A mother deer and two spotted fawns rest in a patch of grass under a gnarled old oak. We continue on, slowly climbing around the treacherous mountainside, carefully avoiding the numerous potholes and washouts.

Sitting at the apex is a small, one-story, grey-and-white house. It faces the Pacific and boasts views up and down the coast. The storm obscures the full scope of the vistas, but it's obvious this land is totally undeveloped for miles and miles. The ocean is less than a mile away, as the crow flies. No aesthetically unappealing strip centers or fast food joints here. This ranch, this house, are totally isolated from the outside world, like Shangrai-La.

The parking area is located a level below the house. I park behind Gary. Chance comes sniffing when I step out. I kneel down and pet him. The rain is dumping on us again. Gary opens the passenger door and removes my bag. I explain that the macadamia nut tree is a housewarming gift. He thanks me and leads the way up a flight of stone steps. I set the tree outside the front door and follow him inside.

The living room is warm and rustic. Everything is natural wood. Two grey leather couches form an L in the center of the room, facing the fireplace in the corner and a wall of picture windows overlooking the overcast Pacific.

The view on a clear day must be amazing. The beamed ceilings are vaulted. A stereo is set up on a couple of crates in the corner. To the right is an unfinished kitchen. There is a sink, fridge, and a gas stove, but the cabinets haven't been installed yet. Big gaping holes remain. I follow Gary beyond the kitchen, into a hall connecting with the three bedrooms.

On the left is a room with carpeting and a small single bed. Gary says when the wind blows, the floor in here heaves up and down. Next to it is a simple bathroom, then another room with a cement floor, no furniture and no walls. Visible through the non-existent wall on the right is the master bedroom.

The room is elevated from the rest of the house. We take the three steps up. It has a view of the coastline, a T.V., dresser, its own bathroom, and a large bed. Gary is still holding my duffel.

"So, where will I sleep?" I say. I don't feel like beating around any bushes.

"That's up to you, Daniel."

"No, it's not up to me. This is your house. Where should I sleep?"

"Wherever you want."

"I'd like to sleep with you."

"I'd like that too." A flash of lightning lights the sky. The rain falls harder. I lie on his bed and check the mattress for firmness.

"Yes, I could sleep on this," I say. Gary sets my bag on the dresser, then drops next to me. I can't stand having him near and not touching him, so I turn to face him. His eyes are shut. I rub his neck.

"Do you have drugs in your fingertips, Daniel? That feels so good."

"Your skin feels soft."

"Do you think this place has possibilities?"

"It's great. I can understand why you love it. How big is the ranch and how much property do you actually own?"

"The thirty-five acres surrounding the house. The entire ranch is over fifty thousand acres. We have seven miles of private beach."

"Can I nude sunbathe if I want?"

"Sure."

"Are any of the cows I saw yours?" I ask.

154

"Sort of. Each owner pays community fees to cover operating expenses. We have a man who farms the cattle for us. We split the profits or earmark the funds for improvements or new cows or whatever. Do you like it up here?"

"Yes, I do. It's going to be hard to go back to over- populated L.A. after a few days here. This is idyllic, Gary."

"You might decide to stay longer."

"I might. You never can tell."

"No, you never can tell," he says very slowly. I stop massaging his shoulders, fall into a pillow, and shut my eyes. He inserts his hand under my sweater and shirt and investigates my belly. His touch really excites me. I'm eager to make love with him. His skin feels great. The rain taps out a steady beat on the roof. The house smells like a wood-burning fireplace. I open my eyes. Chance is sitting in the doorway, watching me with a quizzical expression on his face.

I pull off my sweater and turn on my side facing Gary. He has a shy, unsure look. I smile and unbutton his shirt. He just looks at me. He instigates a deeper kiss. We explore mouths. I feel no artifice or shame, only desire. We need to have that intimacy now, get it out of the way, let off some steam.

Within a few minutes, we're completely naked on the bed. He's a sensitive, giving lover. He asks if it feels good for him to run his tongue down my chest. We arouse one another again and again, lasciviously investigating the pleasure zones. I get the lubricant and condoms from my bag and set them on the bedside crate.

We roll around for quite some time. We discussed safer sex and exactly what it entailed back at Betty Ford. Lying on top of him, I look down into his eyes. He's in love with me, I can see it, feel it, sense it. I knew it before he left rehab, but now, stripped of everything, it is even more obvious. He doesn't have to tell me he loves me, I can see it for myself.

We lock mouths. His tongue brushes my teeth. Our hard dicks are pressed between us, and barely touching. The hair on his upper chest is golden brown. His lips are thick and supple. I want to eat him up. The rain falls harder. The dog lies on the floor and snores lightly. Gary reaches for the lubricant. We gently stroke one another's cocks. His mouth finds mine and he slowly slips his tongue back into my mouth. I don't try to do anything but what feels natural. He whispers what a great kisser I am. The time passes quietly, slowly. Each moment is fraught with feeling. We take all the time we want. There's no reason to hurry, we have nothing else planned. I listen to the faint roar of the ocean and realize there's no place I'd rather be than here with this man. The intimacy is startling. The rest of the day and evening is lost in lovemaking. The next morning, it's still raining.

We decide to shower and drive into town for lunch and a movie. We won't be planting any macadamia trees in this weather.

As we're driving into town in his truck, he suggests we fly or drive up to see his kids on my next visit. He owns a small plane and has a pilot's license. Would I consider flying with him?

I'm hesitant because I've never flown in anything but a commercial airliner. I say I'll think about it. He says it's great fun. He tells me he's been flying for eight years and never had a single mishap. He's very enthusiastic. I don't want to say,"I don't know you well enough to trust you with my life," but that is what I'm thinking. I say I'll go if the weather clears up. If it's raining or cloudy, count me out. Hopefully this storm system will hang around for another day or two. The truth is I'm terrified of flying in a small plane. Television news is always reporting stories of private planes crashing into mountains and freeways.

We get along well. We both like to eat at casual, unpretentious restaurants and generally have a laid-back good time. He's a little moody, but not in an intrusive way. If he's quiet and contemplative, that's his mood, not mine.

I think he's a little shaken by his full-fledged sprint into gay lovemaking. Maybe he's realizing it might be hard to go back to the way he was.

We both like to have a lot of sex, which works out nicely. It's hard not to be physical with him. When we're in public together, at the movies, or getting a coffee afterwards, I'm very aware of strangers watching us. There is a current, a connection between Gary and me that is obvious. He trusts me a great deal and often asks my opinion. We have a great time together and tremendous chemistry. There's magic. Could it be love?

The third day is sunny and clear. I agree to fly with him at sunset. Why not? I trust him. It's hard to separate trust issues from actual fear. Late in the morning, we head for the beach. He drives the pickup right onto the sand.

There isn't a soul in sight. We lay out a blanket to sun and listen to the waves. It's still too cool to swim, but I get my feet wet. The water is icy. Chance wants to play, so I run him for a quarter-mile or so. Big wads of gooey seaweed have washed ashore during the storm. I find several small shells, which I throw back into the surf. The mountains loom behind us, protection from the prying eyes of the outside world.

At four-thirty, we climb aboard his red-and-white, twin-propellor plane. The airfield is exactly that: a field with a paved slice of landing strip in a sea of waist-high weeds and flowering mustard. There are maybe six or seven planes parked to the side of the shack that occasionally serves as a combination snack shop/airport. Gary turns on the ignition, then radios our flight plans to an airport inland. My stomach is a jumble. I have a sudden urge to take some drugs, but remind myself to calm down and not whip myself into a panic. I tell myself to relax and trust Gary.

He certainly seems to know how to use all the instruments. He tells me to buckle up. I'm sitting behind him. He says I can sit up front in the co-pilot's seat, but I'm not ready for that. It feels safer back here. He guns the engine. I take a deep breath and cross my fingers. Gary laughs and squeezes my knee.

Within a few minutes, we're soaring above the ranch, headed north along the coast. The sensation of being suspended thousands of feet above the earth in this tiny craft is far more thrilling and immediate than flying in a big jet. I can feel the changes in altitude and updrafts instantly in this plane. We bump around a little, buffeted by the wind currents. I love it.

We gain altititude, the sun reflecting into my eyes. I don ever-ready sunglasses. My knotted stomach relaxes. I enjoy the beautiful view of the ocean, beaches, and coastline. I release the fear, let it go.

We buzz far above herds of cattle and verdant fields of grass and scrub. The mountains appear even larger from the sky. Wisps of ivory clouds frame the sun and ocean. Gary smells like cigarettes and aftershave. I lean forward and pinch his waist. He asks me to sit beside him. I unstrap my belt and carefully lurch into the co-pilot's seat. The view is incredible. The central coast is rugged and unspoiled. There's a tremendous sense of awe and freedom witnessing such pristine country.

We hold hands. He shows me how to steer the plane for a few minutes. We cross inland, overflying the rapidly flowing Santa Ynez River. Everything below us is green. Years of drought followed by the heavy rains has brought dramatic reversals in the parched earth. Masses of yellow mustard flowers cover the hillsides and fields. The native vegetation has grown knee-high.

He executes a turn and we return to the coastal route. Morro Bay comes into view, dominated by a massive island of rock. We circle the Morro rock and head back down the coast. A halo of warm golden light surrounds the sun as it dips into the Pacific.

Gary explains how a few of the gauges and meters operate. Nightfall slowly overwhelms us. The plane has a tiny headlight. The moon is just a shade past being full, but is bright all the same. The night sky is crystal clear. There are no bright city lights to interfere with star gazing here. Gary identifies Venus, the Dippers, and other constellations. He points out his house as we near the landing strip.

I tell him I feel comfortable and safe with him. He says he feels the same with me. He says he never felt this way for anyone else, not even his ex-wife. He says he thinks he's falling in love with me. I tell him I fell in love with him back in Betty Ford. He leans close and we lock mouths for several beats. The thrill of necking with Gary mid-air is better than Percodan. He breaks the moment, reminding me to buckle up, we're ready to land.

Chapter Fifteen

I
t's a Tuesday afternoon the following week. Eleven days have passed since I left Betty Ford. I'm kneeling on my roof, wearing red shorts as I sink gladiola bulbs in two wooden planter boxes. The sun is blazing overhead. I feel good. I've been to two AA meetings over the weekend and everything, sobriety-wise, seems to be fine. I joined a gym last week and have started taking aerobics classes. Every day I feel a little better about myself. Even my long-inactive acting career has picked up steam.

Driving home last week after my weekend with Gary, I made several decisions. First, I made a commitment to hire an agent and try to get acting work. If I enjoy it, I'll continue. If not, I'll find something else to occupy my interest and time.

Secondly, I decided to join a gym and start taking better care of my body. I've taken my health for granted for too long. Regular exercise will increase my respect for my body and mind.

Thirdly, I've given myself permission to fall in love if it feels right. I remember that they told us in rehab to stay away from new love relationships for a year. Well, I don't think that's possible for me. I feel too alive to ignore or minimize my need for love. I've spent years hiding from intimacy. Without the subterfuge of drugs, I'm vulnerable to romance like anyone else. I'm human.

I paid a surprise call on my old agent last week to discuss resuming the acting career. She greeted me with genuine enthusiasm. Sitting together on a navy couch opposite her desk, I decided to be honest. She didn't seem fazed when I told her about my stint in drug rehab. She said it never occurred to her that my erratic behavior was connected to drugs. She agreed to represent me without any discernible hesitation.

Yesterday, I went on auditions for two television shows. One went very well, the other was average. The casting people all seemed to remember me and were very friendly. My agent said she'll call as soon as she gets word. Both shows shoot next week.

The phone inside rings. I drop the bulbs and run inside. My first thought is it might be my agent. I pick up. The caller identifies himself as Adam. I don't recognize the voice. I wrack my brain to remember. I ask if it's the Adam I met at Howard's. He says yes. I ask how he's doing. I wonder why he's calling.

I've left two messages for Howard since Friday. He still hasn't gotten back to me. The last time I spoke to him was on Wednesday, after I got home from Gary's. We caught up a little, but he wasn't feeling well and couldn't talk for long. He was hacking and complained of shortness of breath. He worried that the pneumocystitis had returned. He was taking a new antibiotic. He said he'd call me in a few days. Adam is painfully silent. Something's up. I get the urge to grab a cigarette, but stand still.

"Is Howard all right?" I say, suddenly aware that something might be terribly wrong.

"Howard died early this morning, Daniel. You're the first person I've called. I'm sorry."

"What?" A chill zaps my spine and brain. I feel a tremendous need for some Percodan. There is pain and hurt swelling inside me. I must keep cool.

"He couldn't fight the infection in his lungs," Adam says.

"When I spoke to him last week he said he was sick."

"He had an opportunistic virus that lodged in his lungs. Something different from the pneumocystis. His lungs filled with fluid. They tried to fight it with antibiotics, but the infection overpowered him."

"I'm going to...how could this happen? Who's his doctor?"

"Don't be angry, Daniel. They did everything they could, really. He just couldn't beat it. He had low T-cells, too. Look, I've seen enough of my friends waste away for years and years, slowing losing their sanity and health. At least Howard didn't have to wither away before he died. I don't mean to sound callous, but I'm glad he died with dignity."

"You're right, Adam, I wouldn't want to see him suffer. It's just hard to accept, that's all. I'm stunned. But when did he die?"

"This morning. It was fairly peaceful. He lost consciousness and never woke up. He wasn't in any pain, Daniel."

The idea of Howard lying in a hospital bed, his lungs filling with liquid, drowning, strikes at my core. Adam details the last hours of his life. I can't bear it, but listen anyway. My insides feel frozen. Why can't I cry? A black hole opens inside my stomach.

I tell myself to let go, but I can't. Not yet. I need to think. I listen as Tim details what medications and procedures they used to treat Howard before he expired. My vision blurs and I feel light-headed. I stoop down on the living room floor.

A whoosh of emotion swirls inside. Adam is talking about having a service for Howard in four days. Howard's brother arrived yesterday and suggested a memorial on Saturday. I kneel and lean against the couch. I need a cigarette, I need something quick. I can't take this, I really can't.

I tell Adam I'd be willing to help in any way possible. He says thanks, but all it entails is contacting Howard's friends. I hear myself offering to call some of them. Adam says sure and gives me half a dozen names, several of which I remember from when I dated Howard. I can't believe I'm going to do this. I've never told a person that someone they know has died. I feel I must do something to help Adam. He must feel very alone right now.

We discuss a time for the service and tentatively agree on noon. That way we can give his friends the bad news and a time for the service without making multiple calls.

I ask Adam how he's holding up. He says he's wrung out. He's been at the hospital since Saturday night. I say he can call me anytime if he needs to talk.

He asks about Trixie. When do I want to take the cat home? I say I'll pick her up tomorrow. He says he lives nearby, in West Hollywood, and can meet me at Howard's house anytime. I ask if he'd like to come over, meet for a meal, or take a walk or something?

He says he' s going home to sleep, but asks for a raincheck. "Anytime," I say. I ask what time Howard died. Seven-fifteen this morning. He gives me his phone number. Then after what seems like either a brief flash or eternity, we end the call.

I pick the phone back up and dial my dealer's number. I need some medicine, I can't make it through this alone. I need to kill this pain, this rage, this guilt. I need to escape the terror I'm feeling. He answers. I hang up.

I remind myself this is when the going gets rough. When things go haywire, I used to use drugs as crutches. I won't do that anymore, dammit. I didn't spend the last forty days sober just to blow it when the first pain arises.

I must use all that I learned in rehab to get through this. If I need support, I can call my friends or go to an AA meeting or something. I must not call my drug dealer. I must not.

I ask myself what it is that frightens me so. I try to relax and allow the truth to come. I feel sad because Howard has died. I feel sad for his untimely death. I feel sorry for myself because now we'll never be together. I feel guilty. I feel like I did when David died. I feel desolate because of a familiar old fear: being left alone.

I light a cigarette and move into the garden. I sit on a chaise and stare at the city below. I realize I'm afraid to feel because it might hurt. I feel so fragile. David and Howard are the only people I've loved that died. I've had friends who died AIDS-related deaths and I felt really bad, but I didn't love them like I did Howard. We were like brothers and lovers.

That's what scared me, that he knew me too well. While we were seeing each other, I worried that eventually he'd discover my dirty addiction and dump me, because I was so badly flawed. I couldn't trust others, I couldn't trust myself. So, I ran for the hills. I wasn't able to tell him I was an addict until Betty Ford. I was glad we reestablished contact, but now he's gone. We won't be friends anymore. He's dead.

I throw the cigarette into the water and let the sadness and despair pour out. The tears and sadness feel terrible. I allow it to escape from my body. Howard wouldn't want me to torment myself by bottling it up. He'd want me to take care of myself. He'd be disappointed if his death drove me back to drugs.

I try to finish planting the bulbs, but can't concentrate. I keep thinking about Howard. I must call the names on my list now. I sit at my desk, light a cigarette, and dial the first number on the list.

Afterwards, I feel totally drained. I knew three of the people from the era when Howard and I dated. They instantly remembered me after I identified myself. They seemed surprised to hear my voice. I gave them the unfortunate news and said Adam and Howard's brother were planning a service for Saturday. All were very kind and very sad. He always had a lot of great friends.

I light a cigarette and call Gary. He doesn't answer. I call Amanda and get a maid. I call Sally and remember I probably better not reestablish contact. I haven't spoken to her since I left Betty Ford. She'd want to commiserate by getting loaded. I need to avoid that now. My emotions and defenses feel beleaguered as it is.

I call my sister. She's home. I tell her about Howard. She met him once and really liked him. She knows all about our relationship, its ending and that he visited me in Betty Ford. She asks if he died of AIDS. I tell her "Yes." She says "Oh, no" several times and sounds authentically sad. I cry a little. She asks what she can do to help. I tell her she's helping just listening. I tell her I'm going to Howard's service on Saturday. She says that's nice of me, then asks how I'm doing without the pills. I tell her it's not easy, but I'm doing pretty well.

I tell her about my romance with Gary. She says he sounds like a hunk, then asks what happened to the young man that was house-sitting while I was in Betty Ford. I tell her Lance is a college student. I don't tell her I've decided not to get involved any deeper with him until he decides whether he's gay or straight or whatever. I tell her I love her and will call in a few days.

I turn the answering machine on, close the bedroom drapes, strip off my clothes, and climb into bed. I feel like I've been trampled by a herd of angry elephants.

The phone rings several times, but I don't get up to answer. I lie in bed and think, cry, and sleep. I can't stop the sadness over Howard's death from bubbling to the surface. I didn't realize I loved him so much.

When we were together, I usually felt good about myself. When I quit seeing him, it hurt. By pushing him away, I rejected the healthier side of me, the side that grooved to such a fantastic man and didn't want to be taking pain-killers all day long. I sequestered my love for Howard in a pocket deep inside me. I feel guilty about that, but I had to do it at the time to survive.

I spent the year before rehab feeling worse and worse about myself. I escaped into drugs, but felt lonelier than ever. That's what got me to go to Betty Ford, the loneliness. Over New Year's, in London, I finally realized that the drugs weren't helping make me happy, they were pummeling my spirit into the ground. I was a slave. I finally mustered enough sanity to get help. I get freedom from drugs, Howard gets death.

I burrow under the covers. Like a child, I hide. My mind's eye recreates a picture of my dead brother. He was lying on top of the covers like he was sleeping. I remember creeping very close. I reached over and touched his cheek. He looked pale and his skin felt brittle and cold. My parents had him cremated the next day. They took him out of our room on a stretcher, like he was sick instead of dead.

My parents were devastated. Mom was sedated some of the time and they started fighting a good deal. They were tormented by guilt. I reacted by developing terrible stomach pains. Our doctor gave me a prescription for pills to calm me down. So, at age eight I started taking tranquilizers. The pills helped get rid of the pain and anger I felt trapped in my core.

I remember the first time I saw Howard. We met standing in line for a movie at the Beverly Center. We were both alone and ended up sitting together through a very bad film. I was instantly attracted to him and ended up having dinner at his house afterward. We had steaks, baked potatoes, and green beans. He opened a bottle of chardonnay. I was wildly smitten with his looks and wry humor.

We made love that same night. It was the best sex I'd ever had. We spoke or saw each other afterwards on a daily basis for the next year.

Howard was a casualty of my addiction. After I said I couldn't see him anymore, we didn't talk for nearly six months. I wrote him a letter that explained my situation, leaving out the part about me being a drug addict. I had to break with him, I had to be by myself. I ran from him, I ran from everything.

He tried to stop by my house to see me, but I pretended not to be home. I didn't answer his phone messages. He wrote me a letter after he got mine.

He wrote that he still had high hopes and nothing but good wishes for me. If I ever wanted to talk to a friend, his door was always open. He said he treasured and loved me.

He didn't know exactly what was going on with me, but suggested I might be at a crossroads. He had noticed that the closeness of our relationship was sometimes difficult for me. He sensed a great unhappiness and despair under my sunny exterior, but felt helpless to help.

He realized the break with my parents had been hurtful. He wrote that he understood I wasn't angry at him, but he still felt sad about losing my friendship. He said I deserved good things and was too hard on myself. He said I had brought great joy into his life. He wrote that he loved me. I feel an irrevocable loss. I know it's not my fault he died, but I wish we could have had more time together. I wish I had handled things differently.

Now, I can't run and hide. I don't take drugs anymore. I'm vulnerable to pain, open to suffering. At six, I get out of bed and take a pee. I open the shades. The city sparkles through the darkness. I light a cigarette and put on my pants. The answering machine has three messages. I hit play.

One message is from Adam. He asks me to call. The second is from Sally, asking how I am and what's up. The third is from my agent. She says I got one of the jobs. Come Monday, I'll be portraying a date rapist for a television program. The show is popular crime drama series. I'll get the standard union-scale pay plus ten percent. The billing will be fine. She congratulates me, says I'm on my way back into the mainstream, then hangs up.

I hit the erase button and realize I'm smiling. Even though I feel like shit, I'm damn proud of myself. I did it. I got the job, for Christ's sake. I really did it. They want me. Me, an addict, a fuck-up. I did it. This pulls me right out of my funk. I jump around for a few seconds, then light a cigarette.

Tomorrow I'll have a new roommate, Trixie the cat. I'll never forget Howard as long as she's around. I haven't had a pet since I left home at age eighteen. I never felt settled enough out here to have a real pet. I love animals, so it should be fun.

I finish the cigarette and make a mental list of what Trixie will need. I'll bring her usual feeding dishes and litter box from Howard's. The change of residences will be traumatic. We'll look out for each other now.

The rest of the week is busy. I manage to hold myself without drugs or heaps of self-pity. I think about getting and taking Percodan about fifty times, but don't.

I'm constantly reminding myself that growth is a slow process. Gary has been very supportive, calling me twice a day to talk. He offered to accompany me to Howard's service, but I said I needed to do it alone. I dread going, but feel I should.

I've gone for two costume fittings for the T.V. show since Tuesday. I got my script, too. I've been studying it and memorizing a few scenes. The dialogue is well written. It's fun playing a bad guy for a change. My first job in over three years.

Saturday arrives. I'm due at Howard's house in forty minutes. Adam and Howard's brother have taken care of everything. They'll be serving a few refreshments before and after the memorial service. Adam told me on the phone yesterday that the brother has already put the house on the market. He said Howard left the bulk of his money to an AIDS charity and a few bequests for friends. He said Howard's brother is the executor of the estate. The brother has an envelope for me. I asked what was in it, but he didn't know. My stomach tightens at the thought of this memorial service. I can't take any more drama. What could be in the envelope?

I sent an arrangement of white and blue lilacs yesterday. I wanted to do something to help. Adam asked if I would like to say a few words at the service. I said I'd rather not. I'm doing the best I can just showing up.

I'm dressed in a green shirt, tan trousers, and brown herringbone sport coat. I want to look good for Howard. Trixie startles me, wrapping her considerable body around my ankle as I comb my hair. She's been all over me since moving in Wednesday. We've become very chummy. She sleeps next to me in bed, purring and licking my arm or face. We're very comfortable together, kind of like Howard and me.

While spraying cologne, I repeat the serenity prayer out loud. The words give me strength to be brave. I can do this. I can go over to Howard's.

I put on sunglasses, grab house keys, sprinkle a handful of liver cat treats on the hall floor for Trix, and leave. I've decided to walk the half-mile to Howard's.

I smoke cigarettes as I walk along the narrow streets that bisect the hillsides. The morning couldn't be more pleasant. It's about seventy degrees and sunny. A great day for a California-style funeral. The singer Sylvester's version of the song "Band of Gold" keeps playing inside my head. I hum the melody. I remember listening to it on Howard's car stereo as we drove down the coast two summers ago. We were headed for a Fourth of July weekend in Laguna. We were happy. I can't get the damn song out of my head, so I softly sing the words as I walk.

Baby, why did you leave me?
Why did you leave me? Leave me this way?
You know, there's something, baby, that I want to say,
Tell you, now that you're gone
All that's left is a band of gold
All that's left are the dreams I hold
and this band of gold
And the memories of what love could be
If you were here with me.
Hide away, in the shelter of my lonely room
Feel the sadness, feel the gloom
Hoping soon that you'll walk through that door

Love me, like you did before, baby.
Now that you're gone
All that's left is a band of gold
All that's left are some dreams I hold
and this band of gold.
And the memories of what love could be
If you were still here with me

I feel totally drained. I sit on the curb and cry. I keep seeing Howard's face. I can't believe he's gone forever. I miss him so much. I feel so alone. This past week has been as much a trial as my first week at Betty Ford. They never said sobriety was going to be easy, but this is absurd. They also taught us that our higher power never gives us more to deal with than we can handle. I suppose that's true.

I did it with hard work. I've chosen to apply the principles I learned in rehab to real life. For the most part it seems to be working. When emotions get heated, I try to acknowledge the problem and work it out. Honesty is key.

However sad I feel at this exact moment, I know damn well that it's less painful with time. Just yesterday, I caught myself singing with the stereo as I did calisthentics. Reading my script in bed last night, Trix waltzed in, then stretched all thirty-three pounds of feline flesh across one of the pillows. I laughed and asked if she thought she was queen of Egypt.

The air smells sweet and clean. I get to my feet and slowly but steadily head toward Howard's. It's hard enough to cope with his death on my own, let alone deal with his other friends, I'm nervous. Maybe sharing the loss of Howard with people who loved him will be comforting. Rehab was immeasurably enhanced by the support of my fellow addicts. I'm trying to keep an open mind. My old self never would have showed up today. It would have been too painful. I would have run for cover.

I reach his house and smoke another cigarette as I walk around the property, looking in the windows. I hear voices over the terrace and garden wall. I'm sweaty from the walk. There are quite a few cars parked along the street. I walk around to the front door, ring the bell, and let myself in.

Everyone is outside, sipping refreshments on the brick terrace. The bougainvillea hedge along the back of the property are covered with masses of fuschia-colored blossoms. It's just beautiful. A slice of the city is visible through sides of the canyon beyond the flowers.

There are black folding chairs set up in three rows on the grassy lawn below the terrace. I remember playing badminton here two summers ago. Two enormous pots of blooming rose bushes flank a podium set on the grass. A table has been set up with bottles of wine, water, and a few soft drinks. I think about having a sip of wine, but decide not to. There are with my lilacs. Clusters of soft lavender and white blooms spill down. I can't help smiling and leaning in for a whiff. They smell like Illinois, like my parent's yard, like David and fresh-cut grass, like-childhood innocence.

Adam comes over. We hug. He looks teary. I leave my shades on. We've spent quite a bit of time talking on the phone this week. I feel like we're friends now, instead of Howard's rival boyfriends.

When I picked up Trix on Wednesday, he showed me a beautiful wooden credenza he built for Howard a few months ago. It was in the bedroom. The piece was exquisite. Tim is obviously a very talented craftsman.

It felt eery standing a few feet from the brass bed where Howard and I used to sleep. It felt familiar, as did the dense forest of eucalyptus trees outside. I shifted the louvered shutters up and down for the last time. I knew then that Howard would always live here, at least in my imagination and memory.

I'm glad there's no music playing. My head couldn't handle any more stimulus. Howard's house is so beautiful, so peaceful. Birds sing in the trees. I tell Adam everything looks really nice. He asks how I'm doing. I tell him I'm okay. He introduces me to Howard's look-alike brother, Doug. Doug asks me to come with him to the dining room. I feel awkward. He opens a briefcase on one of the chairs and hands me an envelope.

My name is handwritten across the front. Doug relaxes for a moment. He says Howard spoke very highly of me and wanted me to have this. I tell him I loved Howard very much and how much I'll miss him. He suggests we talk again after the service and leaves the room.

I sit at the long-dining room table and carefully open the envelope. Inside is a handwritten note dated the day before he died.

Dear Daniel—

I want you to be happy and continue what you've been doing at Betty Ford. You're growing up! You're a fine man. I love you very deeply. I'm really happy we've spent some time together these last few weeks. We didn't have time to discuss all that we might have. I want you to know one thing. I hold no ill will about our separation, so kiss that damn guilt goodbye. Do it for yourself, do it for me. I love you. Don't be sad. We'll be together again, I know that. The enclosed is some mad money for my best friend. I have faith in you. I love you.

Howard

P.S. You're the only person who will love Trixie like I did.

A check for fifteen thousand dollars falls onto the polished table. A band of gold. Tears pour down my cheeks. I hope nobody comes in. I can't stop the tears. My glasses steam, so I remove them and blot the moisture with my sleeve. I feel so sad and yet so happy. I feel released. Howard really did understand that I loved him. I can't believe he took time to write this while he was sick. He obviously knew he was close to death.

I know now that my brother never deserted me, he was just misplaced by me. I couldn't find him because I didn't know which road to take. Howard's death will help me heal and find more truth. I will never really be alone. I may be lonely at times, but I'll never be alone. I'll always have Howard and David and anyone else I loved inside me. I'll have them in my heart. Maybe the end of one thing is really the beginning of another. I feel Howard's presence, his essence, in a place I haven't visited very often in recent years: my soul.

The tears dry. I stand, folding the wet sunglasses into my trousers pocket. I carefully place the letter and check inside the jacket pocket next to my heart. Adam enters, saying he'd like to sit with me for the service. I smile and swallow. I tell him there's nobody I'd rather be with right now. He asks for a hug. We hug. Then, arm in arm, we step towards the terrace and sunshine, brothers.

Author's Biography

Robert Reese was born in Geneva, Illinois. He was educated at the University of Arizona and the ULA Writer's Program. His second novel, "African Dreams", will be published next year. Mr. Reese lives in Los Angeles, California.